Praise for *Two Little Girls*

"The fantastic writing kept me hooked from the very first page."
—*The Guardian*

"Tense, twisty, and compelling, *Two Little Girls* asks the questions no mother wants to answer."
—Lisa Hall, bestselling author

"Laura Jarratt is a fabulous new voice on the crime fiction scene. More like this, please."
—Lesley Thomson, author of *The Detective's Daughter*

"Ambitious and articulate."
—*Daily Mail*

Two Little Girls

Two Little Girls

A NOVEL

Laura Jarratt

sourcebooks
landmark

Published by Sourcebooks Landmark, an imprint of Sourcebooks
P.O. Box 4410, Naperville, Illinois 60567-4410
(630) 961-3900
sourcebooks.com

Originally published as *Mother* in 2020 in Great Britain by Trapeze, an imprint of The
Orion Publishing Group Ltd. This edition issued based on the paperback edition published
in 2020 in Great Britain by Trapeze, an imprint of The Orion Publishing Group Ltd.

Library of Congress Cataloging-in-Publication Data

Names: Jarratt, Laura, author.
Title: Two little girls : a novel / Laura Jarratt.
Other titles: Mother
Description: Naperville, Illinois : Sourcebooks Landmark, 2022.
Identifiers: LCCN 2021037053 (print) | LCCN 2021037054 (ebook) | (trade paperback) | (epub)
Subjects: LCGFT: Thrillers (Fiction)
Classification: LCC PR6110.A755 M68 2022 (print) | LCC PR6110.A755
   (ebook) | DDC 823/.92--dc23/eng/20211006
LC record available at https://lccn.loc.gov/2021037053
LC ebook record available at https://lccn.loc.gov/2021037054

Printed and bound in the United States of America.
VP 10 9 8 7 6 5 4 3 2 1

For Paul

1

EVERYTHING I DO IS FOR my daughters. Everything. That's what mother-hood is to me.

That's why we'd come up here to this remote spot in the Scottish Borders at the end of October, to get a week away together somewhere beautiful with fresh air and lots of walks. Somewhere completely different from our busy life in the bustling, city-like town of Reading. Some time together, just for us.

Dan hadn't been able to come, and the girls were disappointed at having to leave their dad behind. But he had a big case and couldn't get away. This murder case he's been defending has dragged on and on. Sometimes his work just can't stop for us.

I lock the cottage up, put the key in the little safe by the door, and join the girls in the car. It's been a lovely week, but it's time to go back now. Back to reality and a five-hour drive home.

I stop at a small farm shop on the edge of the village adjacent to where we've been staying. We've been driving past it all week, and I've kept mean-ing to go in. I hear Portia huff as I pull into the car park. Yes, it's another delay. She knows it, and I know it.

But when we enter, I fall rather in love with the little place, and I can see from the way her eyes soften that she isn't as averse as she pretends. We're the only customers in the shop, and the silence is welcome, not oppressive. An old woman behind the wooden counter is making up gift bags of sweets, and she smiles and nods at us as we pass.

I drink in the sight of the raw stone walls, the sound of the rough, boarded floor beneath my feet, the smell of the fresh bread in the woven baskets. I brush my fingers along the sides of the ripples of wicker. Becca follows me, copying, until she comes to a basket of buns and stops expectantly. I smile and put one in a bag for her.

I fill the shopping basket up with the kinds of little delicacies that will remind me of our time here: jars of local jam and honey, a farm-made cake, that sort of thing. I buy far too much. If Dan were here, he would roll his eyes at me and whisper, "Lizzie, *really*?" And I would ignore him, because of course I need a jar of rowan jelly in my life. And some bramble jam.

I heave the basket onto the counter, being careful not to let a pot of heather honey roll onto the floor. The old lady at the register smiles fondly at Becca, who is by my side.

"Well, isn't she the spitting image of you!"

As a reflex, my hand strokes Becca's long blonde hair, and I smile back at the elderly woman. "I know."

"Can I get this for the trip, please?" Portia puts a granola bar on the counter by my elbow.

"Of course." I add it to my basket.

I see the shopkeeper glance at Portia, but there is no comment about us looking alike. My oldest daughter, with her heavy black eyeliner and dark clothes, hugs her shabby coat closer round her thin frame as she skulks off around the shop again, her artfully tatty and customized trainers soft on the floorboards. Her dark brown hair is knotted back against her neck but, as usual, is trying to escape and half falling messily from the band.

I sigh as the old lady packs up our items, remembering that little girl who used to run toward me with the same messy hair but a big, beaming smile. What happened to her?

"Are you on holiday?" the shopkeeper asks as I pay.

"We were, but we're on our way home now. I'd love to come back here. It's such a beautiful part of the world."

Becca nestles against my side, leaning her head against me. I stroke her hair again, the silk of it smooth under my fingers. My second child—so, so wanted and waited for for oh, so long.

I leave the shop regretfully. Those rows of pickles and home-baked cakes, the ease and simplicity of it all, make me unaccountably happy in a way our city life no longer seems to. In a way that reminds me of my childhood in

Trelauchan, that little Cornish village where everything was slower and less complicated. I don't think of that village often, but the memory floods back now, sudden and sweet, carrying me in the crest of its wave.

Becca shivers against my side in the sharp wind, the fragility of her seven years catching at my heart in the constant joy-sorrow of motherhood. They grow up, our babies, and that is such a bittersweet spike in a mother's heart.

Portia scuffs her sneakers along the ground, kicking at the gravel, and gets into the car without a word. She sits back in the seat behind me in silence and jams in her earphones. She rarely sits in the front with me, despite her age. I think that's a measure of how much more connected she is with Becca than with me.

I start the car up and pull away. It has been a little slice of heaven out here. Granted, it would be more heavenly if Portia weren't resuming her usual adolescent sulkiness now that we're heading back, but as I tell myself every day, it's just a phase. And at least we've had a break from it over the last week. I recoil at the thought that Becca will be like that, too, one day. Portia never speaks to her father that way, which fills me with a simmering resentment. The little girl who once put me at the center of her world now looks at me as the more annoying of the two she has to tolerate parenting her—that's how it feels some days, at least. It's part of the breaking of the close maternal bond, of her becoming a young woman, or that's what I've read on the subject. That's why the hostility is directed at the mother.

It doesn't make it hurt any less, however.

I dread when it's Becca's time to cut ties. She's our sunbeam, smoothing out Portia's moods, Dan's tendency to retreat inside himself, and of course, my desperate need to be a mother again.

Will she push me away as Portia does now? Perhaps not; perhaps I'll be lucky. Portia's so much her father's daughter—moods like the tides, curling away from me into a shell where I can't reach her. Teenage hormones merely ramp that up to an extreme.

I'm still turning those thoughts round and round in my head an hour into the journey. I can't have the music on loud enough to distract me, as the girls are sleeping. Becca shifts when we hit a bump in the road and turns drowsily to rest her head on the other side. Portia doesn't move. I can barely see their outlines in the back of the car. It's so dark out here, miles from anywhere. But I can hear their soft, slow breathing. It reminds me of when I held them in my arms as babies, those long, sleep-deprived nights, which were so hard back then and are so treasured now through the filter of time.

Just before she fell asleep, Becca said to me, "Ooh, we get to see Daddy soon. I missed him."

And I had agreed with her, even though I felt Portia glaring her frustration at my lie, like lasers into the back of my head.

I've set off too late for that, and that was deliberate. Dan will be in bed by the time we get home. I will struggle in alone with the cases, then wake the sleepy girls to stagger up the stairs to their bedrooms. I will pull the duvet over a fully dressed Becca and tuck her in. I will try to do the same with Portia, but she won't let me. And I will deal with the fallout in the morning.

2

ANOTHER HALF HOUR INTO THE drive, and I wish I'd left earlier. The girls are still asleep. The rain batters down on the car and bounces on the tarmac ahead. My wipers are going at maximum speed. It's tiring to drive like this, and my knuckles are tighter than normal on the steering wheel.

The prospect of struggling into a silent house with the cases seems less attractive now. I could call Dan, plead stupidity, and ask him to wait up for us, but he's got to leave early in the morning. He's in court tomorrow in Exeter, and it's a long commute.

It'll be another forty-five minutes of this annoying, windy road before I reach the haven of a highway. I remember driving this route on our way up here last week and admiring the forest rearing up on either side of me. I can't see much of it at night. Trees reach up into a black sky, tall and still, dark sentries as I pass them by. It's impossible to know exactly where you are out here. Each twist and turn looks the same as the last.

I wish one of the girls would wake so I had someone to talk to. The more time I spend in my own company on this desolate road, and the closer I get to home, the more the sense of dissatisfaction grows.

It's been so beautiful, this last week, and I don't want... I really don't want to go back. It's not just end-of-holiday blues. It's so much more. Perhaps I blame Dan unfairly for how wrong things have become. If he'd been here and we could have been together, being the people we used to be, maybe I would feel differently now. It's not Dan—it's our lifestyle. It has sucked us up in its empty rush. Always trying to keep up, never actually getting there, and so we fall further and further behind all the time. Falling between the cracks. We are casualties to a life we cannot keep pace with, one that pulls us apart from each other.

I will arrive home to a house that hasn't been cleaned thoroughly for far too long. To clutter I don't know what to do with. And I have no motivation to make it right. Just quickly flicking over everything while trying to keep up with my job is exhausting enough.

I am forty-five years old. I am a family-law barrister at the peak of my career, and I am tired.

There, I've said it. I am tired, often physically and usually mentally, but always emotionally. I hardly know who I am anymore, and there is certainly no time for me to find out. I'm not sure I know who Dan is now either. We could get a cleaner to deal with the house and the mess that only kids can create, but part of me balks at that, at the waste of money. I wasn't brought up to let someone do my cleaning for me, and we could have an extra holiday with what we'd spend on it.

Besides, what I really want is to be away from all of it. Away from the frenetic, ceaseless pace of how we live. I want to step away to somewhere like the village we've left behind, like the one I grew up in. I want to breathe fresh air and live in a place where people stop to let each other pass and smile and say hello. Not one where they mow you down on the pavement in their rush to get to wherever they must be now, now, now.

I thought I loved our city life. I loved my work and how where we lived gave me the best chance to grow my career.

But when I glance back at the silhouettes of my sleeping girls in the rearview mirror, I question that. Now I think I put up with all of it for them. It's lost its luster for me. Dan and I have convinced ourselves that the life we have is what they need, that it gives them everything they want. But does it? Does it really? It's such a sweet ache to watch your daughters sleep. I could watch them forever and never get bored. I don't think I need this crazy pace in my life any longer. Maybe I never needed it. I don't know, but it's taking its toll now. He doesn't seem to feel the same, though, or if he does, he's not sharing that with me. Whenever I try to talk about it, he finds something urgent to do—at least that's how it seems.

The wipers swoosh on, marking time like metronomes. On and on, like the beats of my life. That's what I do: just go on. I rub my eyes to banish weariness.

Swoosh, swoosh, swoosh.

If I could move everyone out here, would it really be different? In my head, Portia loses her sullenness and Dan relaxes back into that driven but fundamentally family man he used to be. There's no guarantee that will happen, though. The disappointment descends on me as a blanket of fatigue.

Maybe there's no way back and no way forward either.

A sudden flash of light ahead catches my attention. A flash in the distance, through the trees, but then it's gone. I strain my eyes into the darkness, but there's nothing beyond the beam of my own headlights.

Odd. There doesn't seem to be another car coming, yet I had the distinct impression that the light came from the trees. Of course, it's hard to say for sure on a road this winding.

I think I see a shadow moving on the road ahead, and I peer out beyond the light coming from my own car headlights.

There is something; I really think there is.

Yes, there, just there. I can see something moving.

Something's definitely moving.

The shadow comes at me fast, and I pull my foot off the accelerator.

Lights in my eyes, sudden, bright-white, blinding. I can't see…

It's coming at me. I can hear it. I wrestle the steering wheel to the side. I can't hit it. It will kill us.

I swerve the car to the other side of the road, but I can't get out of the way. I'm swinging the wheel, and I can't see. Those lights, they white out everything.

I jerk the wheel again.

We hurtle off the road, and something crashes into the windshield. Glass showers me, and I brush the shards from my face with one hand as I desperately hang on to the wheel with the other.

A low branch hit us, I think. At least it didn't take out the headlights.

The road is gone, and the car is careening down a bank, jolting and shaking so badly that I can't keep the little control I have.

I'm braking furiously, but we're not slowing.

We're going to crash… The trees… I can't keep avoiding them.

I pump the brake frantically, but the car keeps going. We hit something, and the steering wheel is pulled from my grasp.

Are we in the air?

Or skidding?

"Mum, what the…?"

I hear Portia's frantic voice behind me as we hit something again and the car nearly flips.

No…no…it does flip. We are flying.

Nothing above us or below.

I am flung toward the roof as the car spins silently in the air, and then I smash down into the seat again.

I realize, as I hear Portia's scream, that we aren't going to come out of this. That my daughter's scream will be the last thing I hear.

3

WE IMPACT.

I brace myself for pain, a killing pain. But instead, a gush of ice-cold engulfs me.

Water. We have hit water. It rushes in, choking me. So cold.

I don't know where—what? I can't think; the cold numbs everything.

We're sinking. The car is sinking. No windshield. Water flooding in. I don't know if this is a river or a lake, but I do know I have to get out.

The car fills with water, and I feel the pressure build and suck us down. There's no time to lose. The air will be gone soon, and the girls will drown.

I wrestle with the seat belt buckle. My fingers are so cold I can't feel the button, and there's a shot of pain as I break a nail in the buckle. I hammer at it with my thumb, and the buckle shoots loose.

This can't be a river—it's too deep, surely. My girls. I have to get them.

The car sinks faster and faster. The pressure of the water as we drop builds around me, pushing into my ears, up my nose—the gushing cold. I'm choking.

The *girls* are choking.

I pull back the seat belt strap and reach through the icy water while I twist in the seat. The steering wheel traps me for a moment, but I pull on the back of the seat and wrench free.

Every second is precious.

The car headlights are mercifully still working, and in the gloom of the reflected light through the water, I can see the shapes of the girls flopped lifelessly in their seats.

Still we sink further. Where are we? Is there no bottom to this place?

I half pull, half swim through to the back of the car, where I fight to unbuckle my girls. Becca groans while Portia merely twitches. Both are unconscious.

I wave my arms about in the water frantically to stay near them and not be pulled back to the front of the car. The water is over their heads, entering their lungs. I am out of time. We need to get out of here this second.

I fight with the doors in the rear of the car, but I can't open either of them. The pressure of the water is just too great. I'm going to need to get them out through the front, through that broken windshield.

And now, now I know.

I know, with the most horrible and sickening certainty, that I cannot get both my girls out of this car. If I drag one unconscious daughter from here, she will sink and die while I fetch the other.

One girl, one chance.

I have to get her out…one of them. I have to get her out now.

4

IS THERE A MOMENT IN the life of every mother with more than one child when she fears she will be in this predicament? When she has to save one child and not the other? Even if that only crosses her mind for a second as a fleeting and awful possibility, I believe we all have that thought at one time or another.

It is obscene.

From the moment they are born, you know it will be their life over yours. Their life over your husband's, and that is just the way of things.

But to have to choose one over the other?

The vilest of choices. The one we pray we will never have to make.

There is no time for analysis down here; there is only instinct and a time span like a camera shutter. I reach back between the seats and grab a handful of cloth. I haul my daughter through the seats. She gets stuck, but I twist and tug until she is through, and then I pull, pull, pull until she is out of the car.

My lungs are bursting, and I kick upward, towing her precious weight behind me. I've swum in the sea often; I used to surf when I was younger. I use every particle of that muscle memory to kick up, up, up toward the surface. To save my baby.

When I think I have no more breath and my mouth will have to open and suck in water and drown us both, I break the surface.

The moonlight above shines down on a still, calm lake that stretches for miles through the forest. I pull my daughter's head onto my shoulder and kick for shore.

It isn't far, but I have to find a bank shallow enough to haul her onto. Scrabbling around by the edge of the lake, nails tearing on the soil and stones, I manage to find a submerged rock to lever against. Muscles straining in the icy water, I heave the inert body in my arms upward, and she slops onto the bank. I use the last of my strength to drag myself out after her.

She isn't breathing. Was this all in vain?

No…think…think… She's swallowed water. She needs resuscitation. I can do this.

Years ago, when I surfed, I'd done this in a first-aid course. They say when you need a skill like that, you don't forget it. I only hope that's right.

My heart thumps as I place my shaking palms on her chest and slam them down onto her rib cage.

One…

No answering spurt of water…

Two… Come on, come on, please… Three…

Still nothing. I shiver madly, not just from the cold but from the fear that it is too late, that I can't do it. I can hardly make my frozen fingers meet to pinch her nose shut. I remember at the last minute to tilt her head and open her airway. And then I blow two sharp breaths into her mouth.

Still nothing.

Don't panic. Keep calm.

I slam my hands back onto her chest…

One… Two… Three…

And transfer quickly back to her mouth to blow—

But then—oh, thank you, thank you, thank you—she coughs as my mouth covers hers. She coughs the lake back into my mouth, and as I sit back on my heels, she coughs and breathes and moans.

"It's OK. I'm here," I bend and whisper into her sodden hair. "Mummy's here."

There is a faint answering nod of acknowledgment.

For *her*, I am here.

Out across the water, the car lies by now at the bottom of the lake.

I can't call it a decision, getting back in the water. It's a reflex. I don't even know I'm doing it until I'm half-in and the chill shakes my body again. I strike out across the lake, back to where I think I surfaced, where I hope the car lies.

My bones are ice, and my heart feels as if it will freeze too. I am struggling to breathe.

I swim on, maddeningly slowly, but it is as fast as I can move.

There is no relief when I reach the spot. I'm not even sure it's the right place. I scan the water for clues and curse myself for not getting a better visual anchor of the area before I swam to shore. It'll be dark down there, too dark to see if I'm in the wrong place, unless, by some miracle, the headlights are still on.

I take a great gulp of air and dive. As I plunge down, reaching and reaching for the waters below, the cold strikes me harder—a more intense chill with each foot I descend.

It eats up the breath in my lungs faster than I can believe, and suddenly I am fighting my way back to the surface, gasping and gulping at the air as my head breaks out of the water. Teeth gritted, I struggle to tread water, my limbs obeying the cold rather than my commands.

I'm going down there again. I have to.

I take another gulp of air and dive again. Kick, kick, as fast as I can. The lake water stings my eyes as I peer into the darkness, looking for a trace of light from below.

But it's worse this time. I don't get as far before the icy water knocks the air out of me, and I have to go back up.

I scream in frustration as I surface and slam my fist into the water. The cold, the cursed cold, and my body's traitorous reaction not to let me drown. Rationally, I know that if I stay out here much longer, I won't make it. But I have to try once more, because, if I can see those lights, if I can find that car, the adrenaline will kick in and carry me through.

I plunge down a third time, and I know it's our last chance. My head is dizzy, and I am so numb. I try—I kick so hard, and I imagine the water is warm and that the car is just past my fingertips. That helps for a few moments. Until my mouth opens and lake water sucks in.

I don't know which way round I am, and I don't know if I'm swimming up or down. I don't know if the light I can see is the car headlights after all, and I reach out trembling fingers.

But no, it's the moon. My head surfaces, and I cough out the water I swallowed.

I have nothing left. My fading senses and spinning head tell me that. And if I die out here, who will take care of my child, lying helpless and unconscious on the bank?

So I swim for shore. And again, it is a reflex. While I still have a beating heart and some breath, while the cold has not stopped them, I swim unsteadily back to the shore. Everything inside me screams like a banshee, because I'm leaving her again. But my body has taken over from my mind, and I swim on.

I am too weak. Maybe I could still have saved her. But my body has failed me.

I couldn't get her. I couldn't.

I haul myself out of the lake onto the bank again. The girl I scoop into my shaking arms is still breathing but even less aware of anything than she was when I left her. Even if I could get back in that water and try again, I know now that will be impossible. She needs me here. She needs my help to survive. I push her into the side of the bank and cover her with as much of my body as I can.

As I lie here with her, hoping someone will find us because I haven't got the strength to go and look for help, my thoughts are pulled back to the car. To what happened down there in the depths of the lake. To my choice.

My deadly and dreadful choice.

I cannot weep for my other girl. I do not have the strength. I can only do all I can now to keep this one alive, so I lie and wait with my arms locked round her and my face pressed against hers.

My core temperature is dropping. I know this because the cold no longer hurts. My hands and feet don't throb anymore. I can't feel the scratches on my face where the windshield cut me when it broke. Worst of all, I have stopped shivering. I am so tired. I just want to sleep now.

Someone must find us, please—somehow. It can't all have been in vain. Not now.

5

NOW
February, three months later

THE ARRESTING OFFICER'S WORDS RING in my ears. "Elizabeth Fulton, I am arresting you on suspicion of dangerous driving leading to the death of a child."

He is standing in my sitting room, in my home, in what should be a safe place for me. I cannot process what he says for some time, and I stare at him. He returns my stare with indifference.

"She's not *a* child," I reply in a flat voice. "She was *my* child."

His face is impassive. Of course it is—that's his job. "Could you accompany us to the station, please?"

I come quietly. I'm alone in the house, so there's no one to help. I nod my acquiescence. Both officers watch me carefully for signs I'm going to do something amiss, but they allow me to get my coat from the hall and follow them to the car.

I don't ask to make any phone calls. You might call it shock. Or perhaps you'd say it's guilt.

The traffic is bad on the way to the police station, and I have plenty of time to think. Will I call a lawyer? Or will I call Dan and let him deal with it all?

Or will I actually not call anyone?

It's an interesting conundrum, and I allow my lawyer's brain to deliberate over the possibilities.

We arrive at our destination, and I'm distracted from my train of thought by how hideous the building is. I've never been here before—my branch of law is family work, not crime. The police station we enter is a typical utilitarian structure of 1960s brutalist design. I detest 1960s architecture. One of the courts where I frequently appear has a similar design, and I still shudder at the ugliness every time I enter it.

"It's not a very pleasant building," I say to the police officer as he herds me in. He gives me an odd look in return.

I'm taken to the charge desk, where my possessions are removed and I am read my rights. "Thank you. I know them," I reply when they ask me if I understand. I decline the chance to call anyone but ask them to let my husband know where I am. He'll worry, after all.

"Do you think she's OK?" I hear the desk sergeant quietly ask the man who arrested me.

"I don't know," he answers. "Maybe not. She seems a bit too detached?"

"Yeah, I think so. I'm going to put her on frequent observation. Let's do a last check to make sure she hasn't got anything she could hurt herself with."

I appreciate the thought, but I'm fine. As fine as a woman who is responsible for her daughter's death can be, anyway. I can hear them talking, but I feel like I'm not really here, as if I'm floating. The sounds are echoey, almost like they're speaking through water. My head feels odd, lighter than the rest of me.

It's not fear. I'm not afraid. I'm simply nothing at all; I *feel* nothing.

I am shown to a cell. It's very polite of them, because they do show me rather than take me. But it's also more than a little weird, like some sick version of being ushered to my hotel room. Again, I appreciate the thought, and I'm sure they don't treat everyone in the custody suite this way.

There's a blue mattress on a metal bench, and I sit on that, my legs crossed up in front of me and my arms around them.

The walls are white. White. The color chokes me.

I am alone. From somewhere down the corridor, I can hear a door slam and catch some faint, muffled shouting.

My heart beats faster, and a cold slick of sweat forms over my skin. I concentrate on my breathing, in and out, in and out, slowly. Trying to calm the panic, trying to keep the memories away.

But they won't be held back. Not here. Not in the silence. Not within the white walls.

6

I WOKE FROM A DREAMLESS sleep. A sleep like the dead. I didn't know where I was at first. It was that drugged state I remember waking from after the emergency C-section I needed to give birth to Portia.

I was in a white room. It wasn't mine. And the bed wasn't mine either. It took me a hazy while to recognize the metal frame for what it was—a hospital bed. I was in hospital, and there was a line in my arm.

Is she alive?

That was my first thought. But there was no one to tell me.

I lay there for a while, too out of it to move or take much in. Eventually, I realized there was a call button by my hand, and I pressed a weak finger against it. I had such little strength.

A nurse came in.

"Is she alive?" My voice sounded unnatural—so weak and raspy it was barely a voice at all.

"Who?" she asked.

I couldn't manage any more. I was slipping back already. I couldn't focus on her face. I was losing her. I let unconsciousness take me back under to safety. Away from choices and dead daughters.

I don't know how long I slept for after that—hours or days—but when I came to, there was a different nurse in the room. She was standing at the bottom of the bed, filling in a chart.

"Oh, hello. You're back with us," she said with a smile.

"My daughter?"

"Your husband is with her. Would you like me to get him for you?"

Dan was there.

"How is she?"

She sat on the bed next to me. "She's still very poorly, but she's stable at the moment. She's been on cardio-pulmonary bypass, which means a machine is doing the work of her heart and lungs while we bring her body temperature up to normal. The good news is, she's had a CT scan, and there is no sign of brain swelling."

"She's not breathing?" I couldn't quite comprehend this. My brain wasn't working properly. It was sluggish and foggy. "She's on life support?"

She patted my arm. "That's normal right now. You and your daughter came in with severe hypothermia. We had to treat both of you aggressively to get you back with us. I'll tell you more when you're feeling better. I'm going to find your husband and tell him you're awake. He'll want to see you."

Will he?

She saw the change in my expression and looked away. So she knew.

I let her go without responding to her, feeling as weak as a newborn as I lay there on the bed.

The time dragged endlessly when she had gone, and I stared at the ceiling and waited. I had always loved the color white—before this hospital, that is. I didn't think I would ever love it again. I used to think of it as fresh, reminiscent of Scandi-style boathouses, the color of new beginnings and new life. Of purity, of perfection, of peace.

Now, it was not about beginnings to me anymore; it was about endings.

After the clock hand moved on half an hour, after staring at the clinically pristine ceiling, white scared me. The white of rooms with monitors that pumped blood throughout the body of your baby, that breathed for her. That waited for her to die?

If she died now, I had lost everything.

A white that could take her from me forever. Cruel, sterile, without a soul.

White—the most merciless color. The color of ghosts.

If I had to lie here much longer waiting for Dan, I would have to face what I had done. And worst of all, I would have to face why.

7

NOW

THE CELL DOOR OPENS, AND I sit up uncomfortably, my legs cramping from being in the same position for so long.

"Your lawyer is here to see you," a woman officer says, beckoning to me.

I get up and follow her, hobbling somewhat. "I haven't asked for a lawyer."

"Your husband sent him." She shows me into a room. "Do you want to refuse legal advice?"

"I really don't think she does," a familiar voice says. The man turns and smiles. "Hi, Lizzie."

"Hi, Aidan." I cast a glance at the policewoman. "It's OK. I want to speak to him."

She nods and closes the door behind her.

Aidan's smile turns to a grin. "Lizzie, haven't seen you for ages! And I was hoping it'd be over some tapas and a bottle of wine, not like this." He has a few more lines round his eyes and several more grays peppering his shock of dark hair than when I last saw him, but the beaming grin and the generous hug he envelops me in are unchanged. Aidan and Dan have been friends since university, both cycling freaks who think there's no better way to spend a Sunday afternoon than tearing up and down hills for fun. Me, I used to borrow Aidan's large and stupidly enthusiastic dog and go for a gentler stroll and meet them at the pub later. Before I had the girls, of course.

It was inevitable that, faced with this, Dan would draft Aidan in. And that he would know Aidan would get a hold of me if I proved difficult.

I sink into a chair opposite him. I haven't got the energy to be difficult.

"We don't have long before they question you," he says, more soberly. "Dan's gone into orbit with them over this. Says you're not in a fit state. Threatened them if they dared to speak to you without me present. I had to tell him to knock it off in the end, as it wasn't helping. They're already hostile because of who he is—he's come across them too many times in court. Now, how are you feeling? Dan says the doctors have only just given the all-clear that you're to try to return to normal activity."

Yes, it's been a long road to this point.

"I'm OK, I suppose."

He taps a finger on his chin. "I'm going to be honest with you here, Lizzie. You don't look OK. You don't look yourself at all. We've got fifteen minutes before they speak to you. I had to fight for more than five, so hit me with it. What's going on?"

"You know about the accident?" My voice is stiff. I don't intend it to be that way, but it happens anyway.

"I know what happened with the girls, of course," he says gently. "You don't need to go over that part, unless you want to. But what led up to the accident? That's what we need to talk about now."

OK, I might just be able to manage that.

I take a deep breath. "It was half term, and I'd taken a week off to spend with the girls. I decided to take them away. We rented a cottage up in Scotland, a really pretty little spot."

"What about Dan?"

"He was working. He had a big case and couldn't get away, so I took them on my own. I had it blocked out in my diary for months, so we could have a break."

Aidan grimaces. He's had many girlfriends, but Anna, the only one I ever thought he was truly serious about, left him because he couldn't deal with how much time she spent working. And, he'd said, even when she wasn't working, she never switched off from it; her mind was always on her job. She ran her own business and that's just how it was, she told him. In the end, the pressure of his continual expectation that there would be more from her was too great, she said, and she finished it between them.

"Were you OK with that?"

Aidan has known us for a long time, even if he and I haven't caught up for a while. There are more than two decades shared between him and Dan.

"I have to be."

He snorts. "So you're not. Come on, Lizzie. You know I need to know to defend your position properly."

I sigh. I really don't want to do this. What I want is to lie down in a corner and let everything just happen. I don't care anymore. I can't summon up the effort to care what they do to me. Whatever it is, I'll deserve it.

I suppose too much of this must show in my face, because he rubs his forehead with his palm and lets out a huff of frustration. "Lizzie, I understand you're not yourself now. Hell, how could you be after what's happened? But you have to let me fight for you here. One, that's my job, and two, Dan is frantic out there."

I am numb. I think some part of me has been numb ever since I plunged into that icy water. A part of me that never got thawed out. I wonder if that cold will spread through the rest of me in time, freezing me completely.

Aidan reaches across the table and grabs my hand. He gives it a gentle squeeze. "Come on, Lizzie. Dan needs you. And that daughter of yours needs her mother. If you won't do it for yourself, do it for her."

8

DAN PUSHED OPEN THE DOOR of my hospital room. "Can you leave us, please?" he said to the nurse behind him.

"OK. For a few minutes," I heard her say, "but I need to keep checking on her."

He came in, his skin gray with fatigue and his dark hair ruffled and scruffy. The faint lines that had arrived round his eyes and mouth in the last few years were etched deeper.

"Lizzie," he said, and after twenty years of marriage, he didn't really need to say more. He sat on the bed and put his arms round me gingerly.

I breathed into his shoulder. Everything in here smelled foreign and frightening; he smelled of home. "Tell me what they won't, Dan. How bad is she?"

He sat back. "She's alive, Lizzie."

"Tell me, Dan." And again, after twenty years of marriage, I didn't need to say more.

He rubbed his eyes. "She's in a stable condition, but she's not come 'round yet. She has a head injury from the car accident, and she has severe hypothermia. You had that, too, but she's far worse off because she had water in her lungs. The doctor said you must have resuscitated her and that saved her life."

I nodded. Even that hurt.

"Well, that got the water out so she could breathe again, but they said that's not the end of it. After someone has nearly drowned, a process happens inside that damages the lungs and restricts the oxygen around the body, so they won't know for a little longer whether she will be OK."

"What are they worried about?" I could feel panic rising.

He looked down at his hand wrapped round mine, his fingers carefully avoiding the IV line.

"Dan?"

He looked back up at me. "Brain damage. That's what they mostly seem concerned about. But also pneumonia or her heart stopping."

I wanted to sit up and tried to struggle, but Dan put his arms around me and held me back. "No, Lizzie. It's not going to help her if you make yourself worse. You've been ill, too, and they weren't sure you were going to make it until yesterday."

I stopped struggling against him and lay back, exhausted. "She's brain-damaged?"

"No! No—listen, Lizzie, she could be fine. She could make a complete recovery."

"But she might not."

He slumped back, his hands over his face. "No, she might not." He sat motionless for a moment, the struggle to stay in control evident in how his knuckles whitened where he clutched at his hair. He was trying to keep it together for me. I could feel his battle. Then he swallowed hard and looked up at me, his mouth tight with the effort of holding so much back.

"Dan, I need to understand this. You have to explain it to me."

He stared at me. He had great violet smudges of exhaustion under his eyes, and I realized that he was probably so tired he couldn't think straight. "I need to get some coffee," he said. "There's a machine right down the corridor. I'll be straight back."

And true to his word, he did come back a couple of minutes later with a cup of black coffee. He sat back down and sipped it.

"Wish I could have some," I muttered.

"You're nil by mouth—nothing to drink," he replied, "or I would have gotten you one."

"Yes, I know." I all but lived on caffeine at home some days. "Tell me from the beginning—everything."

He took a mouthful of coffee. "The police came to tell me about the accident and said that the two of you were seriously ill in hospital, in a specialist unit for hypothermia cases—you were airlifted here. That was two days ago, and I came haring up here immediately."

"Did you see her straight away?"

"Yes, because they were doing a procedure on you, and she'd just come out of a CT scan. As she had a head injury, they were checking for swelling, but that was clear. They put her on this bypass machine and then started trying to get her body temperature up. They said that's the tricky bit, because they have to do it carefully or the body goes into shock. That's why it's taking so long."

"And the brain damage?"

"They won't know until she wakes up properly. They said brain damage normally starts after five minutes in the water, and nobody knew how long she was down there, but they also said that the coldness of the water could have protected her brain. I asked them if there was a chance she could make a full recovery, and they said that there is still a long way to go, but yes, she could. We have to hope, Lizzie. We have to!"

The door opened, and the nurse returned. "I know you're not going to want to leave now, but she must get some rest," she said to Dan, "and so must you, or we'll have three patients on our hands. They've got a relative's bed for you near your daughter's room. If she wakes, they'll come and get you, but they're not expecting it. They're going to try bringing her round in the morning, so you really should get some sleep now—she's going to need you tomorrow."

Dan looked at me. "Go on," I said, though I didn't want him to leave. I could see how much he needed to rest. "I'll try to sleep too."

He hesitated. "Just five more minutes," he said to the nurse.

"All right, but really only five more," she warned. "And then I'll come and chase you out."

She left the room, and he linked his fingers through mine. "How do you feel?" he asked. "Awful?"

"Pretty bad, yes. Like I've been run over by a truck, and then it reversed and ran over me again."

He smiled at my attempt to deflect his concern. "The doctor said that's normal. Although he wasn't quite as descriptive when he told me what to expect." His face sobered. "Thank you for getting her out. I don't know how you managed it, but thank you."

It was the moment I'd been dreading. Tears sprang into my eyes and he took a sharp intake of breath.

"I'm sorry, Lizzie. I shouldn't have said that. You're not ready to talk about this, and the doctor warned me not to try, but…I'm just so grateful that you did get her out, that we still have one of the girls, and that's because of you." He stroked my cheek to brush away the tears.

"I couldn't get back to the car, Dan. I tried, but I couldn't. And the car was full of water…We were drowning…and I went back and I couldn't—"

"Shush—don't talk about it now. You're not well. I made a mistake bringing it up. You can tell me when you're better. The police told me how fast the car would have gone down. It's a miracle you got one of them out, Lizzie." He wiped my cheeks again. "Please don't get upset. You're going to exhaust yourself. Are you OK?"

It was best that he went now. I couldn't cope with this. Even though I felt abandoned by the prospect of him leaving, it was impossible for me to deal with his sympathy. "I'm all right. I need to rest, Dan. Maybe you should go now. I'm just going to go to sleep. I can't stay awake any longer. I'm so tired."

He looked at me uncertainly, but I must have looked exhausted, as he bent and kissed my head. "I'm sorry. I should have realized. Try to get some sleep, then, and I'll see you in the morning," he said.

It was only when he left that I realized he hadn't asked me how the accident happened, and then I also realized that I couldn't recall all of it. I remembered leaving the shop with the girls. I remembered the rain. But then it was hazy. I had a few flashes of possible memory, or perhaps nothing. No, nothing until the water began to choke me. Nothing until I had to make my choice.

Despite what I'd told Dan to get him to leave, I lay awake for a long time that night, trying to pull back some of what happened, but it remained lost to me.

9

"YOU CAN'T REMEMBER?" AIDAN REPEATS.

"No. The doctor said my memory might come back, but also that it might not. That it could have been from injury or shock. They weren't sure. It didn't seem to matter at the time, so I'm not sure I took it all in. Other things were more important. It's been three months now since the accident, and I still can't remember any more than I could straight after it happened."

"Don't worry about it," he says soothingly. "I'll deal with all of this. The police have been told you weren't well enough to be questioned about this before now, and that's made them hostile. So has Dan kicking off, but I suspect the arrest is to try to rattle you into confessing because they think you're faking. Let's focus on getting you out of here and home. Tell them exactly what you've just told me, and let me do the rest."

He goes to tell them we're ready. My heart is pounding so hard it hurts.

Soon I am ushered down a corridor to an interview room, where two of them are waiting for us. I am cautioned.

"You do not have to say anything, but it may harm your defense if you do not mention when questioned something which you later rely on in court. Anything you do say may be given in evidence." It is strange to be on the receiving end of those words.

How am I here in this capacity now? It's not right. I haven't done criminal work in years, but I should be in Aidan's chair if I'm here at all. This doesn't happen to women like me, normal women who haven't done anything wrong. I don't know what to say. And I have the oddest feeling, as if I am floating above all this, looking down on it.

I want it all to just go away.

I look from one police officer to the other. The first is a woman somewhere in her thirties. She looks tired, and she stops to blow her nose. Her eyes are watery. "Sorry," she says. "Runny nose. Bear with me."

Her companion is a younger woman, who wriggles a little in her chair at the nose-blowing, as if afraid she might catch it too.

Aidan smiles politely, and the woman looks relieved but also somewhat disconcerted. I wonder if she knows how expensive he is and whether that bothers her. He's not your typical custody-suite, on-call type, generally dealing more with high-level fraud than the routine burglaries and assaults that make up the day-to-day business that will be seen here.

"So, can you explain to us in your own words how the car accident occurred?"

I glance at Aidan, and he nods. "We were driving home from a family holiday. The weather was bad. The car went off the road. I don't know how. I can't remember."

The two women exchange a glance.

"Come on, Mrs. Fulton. I'm sure you can do better than that."

Aidan cuts in. "My client has told you what she remembers. She has told you accurately, because that's all she does recall. Have you spoken to the doctors who treated her about her memory loss?"

"I'm aware she had some memory loss after the accident. We were unable to question her for some time," she replies frostily.

"But have *you* spoken to her doctors?"

"I will. Now, I'd like to ask Mrs. Fulton some specifics. Mrs. Fulton, what is the last thing you remember before the accident?"

Aidan nods at me to answer.

"We stopped at a shop just before we left the area. I've got a good memory of that part. Then we were driving, and the girls fell asleep. I thought about calling my husband on the hands-free but changed my mind, as he had to get up early the next day. And that's all I remember until the car went into the lake. I really don't recall anything else properly."

"Properly? So you do have some other memories?"

"I don't know. Sometimes I think I have a flash of something. Like when you try to dredge up something at the back of your mind, but you can't quite get it—do you know what I mean?"

"I can't say I do," she replies.

"Oh, come on!" Aidan says with a professionally judged laugh. "My client is suffering from amnesia. She has no recollection of the event. She's described the form her amnesia takes. Do you have any evidence here on which to base this arrest?"

"The car was on a clear stretch of road. A child lost her life. Weather conditions were poor due to the rain, but after investigation of the tire pattern shown on the road, it's clear that no braking took place before the car left the roadway and plunged down the hill. The most likely explanation for this, Mr. O'Toole, is that your client fell asleep at the wheel. Perhaps that's why she can't remember the accident?"

I don't know why, because it certainly sounds like a logical and entirely rational explanation, but as soon as she says it, I am convinced she is wrong. "No, that's not what happened."

"But you can't remember," she counters smoothly.

To reply, "No, but I know that didn't happen," might be true, but it won't exactly help my cause. I need to use my brain here. The trouble is, it's not working anymore. "I wasn't that tired. There was no danger of me falling asleep at the wheel."

"It was late, it was dark, and the road was quiet. These things can creep up on you."

I remember briefly and suddenly my regret at leaving it so late to travel home, and the rain—the hypnotic sweep of the wipers.

"Is this your evidence?" Aidan interrupts. "This is pure conjecture. Have you recovered the car and examined it?"

"Not yet. That's proving difficult due to the depth of the lake."

"Proving difficult? You've arrested my client on the faintest of evidence, and you've not completed your investigation of the crime scene. You've had three months to do it, and you still haven't managed it. You know as well as I do that you can't do this, and you need to release her."

Ten minutes later, I am sitting in Aidan's car being driven home, the police officer's parting words still ringing in my ears. "When we do recover that car, Mrs. Fulton, we will be back in touch." But they have released me without charge.

"Ridiculous," Aidan rages as he drives. "As I said at the start, what they thought was that they'd pressure you into confessing you probably had dropped off at the wheel."

"I think they really believe I did."

"Maybe, but they can't work on beliefs. They need evidence."

"I didn't, Aidan. I don't know what did happen, but—and I know this sounds crazy from a woman who can't remember—I'm sure that I didn't fall asleep. I just know it."

"Why haven't they gotten the car yet?"

"The part of the lake we went into is incredibly deep. They told Dan at the time that it would be a specialist recovery operation to get the car out. It was hard enough for them to get divers down there to…"

To recover her body.

He glances over at me but doesn't press me to finish. "They've probably run out of budget for the recovery operation, then. It seems to be happening all the time now—mismanaged investigations, because they're short on finance. Anyway, it's bought us some time. I'm going to get hold of your doctors up there and find out their view on this."

"OK."

"You just hang in there with this. We'll sort it." And he pulls up outside my house.

Before I've even gotten out of the car, Dan has opened the front door and rushes down the steps. "Lizzie, why didn't you call me when they let you go?" He grabs Aidan by the shoulder. "Mate, I owe you so much for this."

Aidan hugs him. "You owe me nothing." He looks up to a figure standing on the steps by the front door. "Hi there! How are you? Look, I brought your mum back."

My daughter walks down to me, her eyes red-rimmed and her face still damp from tears. "I thought they weren't going to let you out."

I put my arms around her thin frame, and for once, she lets me. "Oh, Portia, I'm so, so sorry."

10

THEN

IT WAS 3 A.M., ACCORDING to the clock in my hospital room. The time for poets and the depressed to be awake. And mothers who have lost their child.

The hospital was not still and quiet. Hospitals are never still and quiet. In the distance, beyond the door of my room, I could hear buzzers sounding and then pacing feet, muffled voices calling out. Beyond my door, battles were being fought. Some were won. And some were lost.

Inside my room, however, nothing stirred. Since the last check on my vital signs an hour ago, I had been undisturbed. I lay perfectly still in the bed, facing upward into the dark. Like a corpse.

I could not remember what happened before the accident, but I remembered the events when we crashed into the water all too well.

Of course I did. I let Becca die, and in the worst possible way. I made a choice, and I chose for her to lose.

Traces of light from the corridor penetrated through the crack around the door, and I closed my eyes to block them out. I deserved this punishment. I deserved to remember and to remember every waking moment of my life from here on in. Because Becca would never remember anything again.

My littlest one. My sunbeam.

And I left her down there in the cold and the dark.

I chewed my lip as I worked through the flashes of memory that were clear to me. My lips were dry and cracked, and I quickly tasted the ferrous tang of blood.

The pressure of the water forcing me back as I unbuckled the girls from the back seats. Fighting to get to them again.

And then time stopped.

Time stopped as I remembered, as it did not stop in the original incident. Time slowed to a crawl and hung frozen while my conscious mind processed the thoughts of my subconscious, of my instinct.

I could only get one girl out. Any longer down here, and I would not have been able to fight the pressure of the water. That would have been the end of us all. We would have all died down here.

One girl, one chance.

Somewhere further down the hospital corridor, I could hear shouting and running feet. I barely registered it, motionless in horror as I remembered those last moments.

I reached back into the car. I reached back, pure instinct. And I remembered what drove me, what guided my instinct.

There it was in my mind, surging forward from subconscious into conscious: my first sight of her, staring in the nearsightedness of the newborn, and my sudden complete and overwhelming adoration. The birth of a baby—the birth of a mother. Her mouth at my nipple and the rush of oxytocin binding us forever. Those days and months of holding her and watching her eyelashes grow, drinking in every inch of her skin, worshipping my tiny person.

The irrevocable and invincible mother-daughter bond.

When it came down to it, there was no choice. It was already made. It was Portia. It would always be Portia.

Poor little Becca didn't stand a chance.

Because she wasn't my real daughter.

That's the truth of it.

11

WE SIT TOGETHER, SHELL-SHOCKED. AIDAN left ten minutes ago after filling Dan in on the events at the police station.

Portia, still too thin and pale after the accident, sits on the old velvet sofa with her knees tucked in and her arms wrapped around her legs while I sit on the other end. Dan rests his head back in the armchair, his eyes closed as he thinks.

"They didn't believe I don't remember what happened before the crash," I tell them both. "They're accusing me of falling asleep."

"But you didn't, did you?" Portia asks me, and I think her dark eyes look mistrustful.

"No, I'm sure I didn't." But her eyes make me doubt myself.

Dan looks up. "Portia, do you not remember anything? I know we've been through this, but think again—is there anything at all that could help your mother or jog her memory?"

Portia shakes her head. "I was asleep. When I nodded off, she was definitely awake. I remember Becca asking how long it would be before we got home, and then I dozed off because it was going to be hours. The next thing I knew, I was being thrown around in the car, and there was glass everywhere. Then we were in the water."

"You screamed," I reply slowly, as I hear the sound in my head. "I think you screamed."

Portia nods. "Yes. Yes, I did."

"Anything else?" Dan sits forward, his eyes sharp with hope.

But there's nothing. Nothing else—no remembered sight, just the sound of Portia's shriek of horror. The memory chills my blood. "No, I'm sorry," and I turn away so I don't have to see their disappointment.

I feel disembodied, as if I might float off like smoke at any moment. As if I'm not truly here.

I want to touch Portia to ground myself, but I'm afraid she won't let me. She wears an invisible skin of prickles, this daughter of mine, designed to repel her mother's touch. Just as Dan can shut me out by seeming to go somewhere else in his head, so Portia has inherited that talent.

I wonder what we have done to deserve this hell we find ourselves in. Dan and I have tried so hard to provide for our girls. We have been such a unit. We have had to be, after all. You don't survive fertility issues and come out the other side without fighting for each other. We may have drifted recently as a couple, but until the accident, we were an invulnerable fortress of family, the four of us. I would have never left Dan, no matter how we might have lost our way with each other. He is the man I chose to be with for life. It's the world that's gotten in our way and pulled us apart from each other.

We started trying for another baby about two years after Portia was born. I didn't expect any problems: Portia had been conceived quickly and easily. Her birth was a different matter, but I was assured there would be no lasting complications from that. After two more years of trying to get pregnant naturally, however, I wasn't so sure. It was then we discovered what secondary infertility was. It came as a surprise to me that some women can struggle to get pregnant again after their first baby. I'd always thought of infertility as something where a woman never got pregnant at all. It was a shock to find out that there's a kind you can get after you've already had a child. There are so many possible reasons for it but also many cases in which the reasons for the infertility are inexplicable. It seemed I fell into that latter category. Dan and I had all the tests, but a reason was never found. We tried IVF—eight punishing and expensive cycles of it that all ended in failure. So, in the end, we made the decision to adopt, and after three years, a baby came to us.

She was ten months old with fluffy, white-blonde hair and blue eyes. On the drive home from that first meeting with her, Dan said to me, "This might sound crazy, but I really do think she looks a bit like you." The introductory meetings went well, and very soon, Becca arrived in her new home—an explosion of new life who brought us back together again after that stressed, fractured time of infertility and longing. She completed us. And it was true that she did look a little like me—the same coloring, the same face shape. But what people saw as she grew were my expressions, my mannerisms playing out—we spent so much time together, she and I, that my smile was her smile, my eyebrow raise of surprise became hers, my habit of sticking the tip of my tongue out when I was concentrating I would see on her too.

"Little Mini-Me," Dan would say with a laugh.

Gone.

All gone.

How quickly life changes. One day, you have a beautiful, loving, vigorous daughter. The next, she's lost.

A huge, howling sob tears through me—an animalistic thing. I am aware that tears are flowing down my face, and I cover my eyes, for I can't bear to see Dan and Portia staring motionlessly at me, not knowing what to do.

The first time I broke down like this, Dan tried hugging me, but it didn't help, and as it goes on week after week, month after month, he still doesn't know what to do with me.

I don't know what to do with me either.

Sometimes I can hardly look at Portia because of the guilt.

Sometimes I can't breathe from it.

12

BACK THERE IN THAT HOSPITAL room, I had to face the truth. I had to look at what I'd done and acknowledge it. Anything less was an insult to Becca.

It was an unspeakable thing. I took that little girl as my own when she was under a year old. I loved her. She gave me her whole heart and I thought she had mine, but in the end, I couldn't let my biological daughter die to save her.

I would have never believed this before, but there was no arguing with the facts now. I did not love my adopted daughter enough to give her a chance. I was no better than her real mother. No, I was worse—at least she'd had the sense to give up Becca for adoption when she'd been taken into care. She might have been a rotten mother, but she'd given her little girl a life by letting her go, and it was me who then took that life from her.

Darling little Becca, who never caused us to shed a tear. Whose smile brightened all our days. Who loved us unconditionally.

And I let the lake take her.

Vomit rose in my throat, and I half fell off the bed and scrambled to the bathroom on the other side of the room. I didn't even make it to the toilet but hung over the basin, retching into it. There was nothing in my stomach but the fluids I'd been encouraged to drink.

When the retching stopped, I slumped to the floor, my face against the rough linoleum.

In those deciding seconds in the car, I'd thought of my first sight of baby Portia, of her moments in the early days. But I'd had special moments with Becca too. I watched her first steps as she toddled toward me with a beaming grin at her own cleverness. Her first word was "Mama." She sat on the lawn as a toddler with chubby bare legs and picked daisies that she handed to me. "Wub you," she said to me when I tucked her in at night.

I never knew biology mattered so much. I appalled myself.

Of course, of course I was not sorry Portia survived. But it's the way in which I made the decision that made me feel dirtier than I had ever known it was possible to feel. A terrible, terrible sin against that little girl, from which there was no returning. No forgiveness.

We were finished as a family. There would be no coming back from this.

13

DAN CROUCHES IN FRONT OF me, trying to force a tissue into my hand. Portia is gone.

"Lizzie, please stop. It isn't going to bring her back."

I take the tissue from him to placate him. I don't think I even know what to do with it, where to start clearing up the wreckage. I glance at the end of the sofa where my daughter had been sitting. I didn't even hear her leave.

"She can't stand seeing you like this," Dan says softly. "You're her mother. She doesn't know how to deal with it." He doesn't add that he doesn't, either, but it's written all over him.

I scrub at my face ineffectually with the tissue. I haven't told him about my choice yet. I don't know how to begin to. He tries not to talk about what happened that night—he waits for me to be ready, but I never am.

"Lizzie, is this because you think you did fall asleep at the wheel?"

His voice is the gentlest thing imaginable.

"If you did, I can imagine how you feel. And I will help you. You are not going to get prosecuted for this—I will see to it."

I take the tissue box from him and clean myself up. It takes a while.

I take a few deep breaths to ground myself again. "The thing is, Dan, I didn't do it. I did not fall asleep. And I know it sounds utterly ludicrous when I can't remember what did happen, but I just know that me falling asleep isn't why we ended up in the lake. I don't expect you to believe me—why would you when it sounds mad?"

There's a long moment where he tries to read my face, but he finds me writ in a foreign language now. I've been to a place he hasn't and seen things I never want him to know.

"I don't know how to help you anymore, Lizzie. And I think you need some help. It's been three months since Becca died, and while none of us are 'over' it or ever will be, you seem to be spiraling down and down. Or that's how it appears to me."

He wants me to contradict him, to say that I'm OK. But the thing is, I'm not. My surviving daughter runs out of rooms because she can't deal with me. My husband doesn't recognize me. Dan is right: this is getting worse, not better, and I don't know how to turn it around.

"Maybe you're right. Maybe I should see someone. Maybe that will help my memory come back, too, and God knows we could all do with that happening right now."

He heaves a sigh of relief and sits back on his heels. "OK, OK. That's good. I'll see if I can find someone who's recommended to deal with…this kind of thing."

What, Dan? With daughters who are dead because of their mothers?

I'm too tired to deal with this anymore, too tired and heartsick, so I nod so we can all go to bed and pretend this conversation has helped. I don't sleep when I get there, though. I lie with my eyes closed, remembering the day we came back to Reading after the accident and just what I put Portia through then.

Dan opened the door and I went into the hall, Portia following me. The house was cold, the cold of a place uninhabited for days. Dan dragged a suitcase in behind us as we shivered in the hallway.

"Damn," he said. "I should have gotten my mother to come 'round and turn the heating on."

"Your mother lives forty miles away," I said, staring at a photo on the hutch.

"Yes, but she could have helped out. I'm sure, given the circumstances, she wouldn't have minded." Then he followed my gaze to the photo.

I took pride in our hall. No matter how busy I was, it was the place I always found time to dust. The entrance to our home, the place to make visitors welcome. So even when I didn't have time to cope with the dust and chaos and clutter of the rest of the house, the hallway was always immaculate.

I had an antique hutch I'd bought specially to stand where it did now, holding our family photos in silver frames. I'd picked it with great care to go with my lovingly restored Minton mosaic tiled floor. I chose the photos that went there with even greater care, to reflect the years together and the children as they grew.

The photo of Becca last summer on the beach was center stage. A complete picture of uninhibited joy, her face raised to catch the sun like an open flower, her hair wet and tangled from the sea.

I dropped to my knees on the hard tiles.

I heard Portia's scared voice behind me. "Mum?"

And then I let the grief pour through me. I didn't know what I was doing and I didn't care. I forgot that Portia and Dan were grieving too. I was too lost in the enormity of losing Becca to consider them. In the hospital, I could shut it out—except at night—because I had to focus on Portia's recovery. But here in the house, Becca's shadow was all around me.

My head met the cold, hard floor I'd spent so much money restoring. Dan tried to haul me up, but I shoved him away violently, screaming at him to get the hell off me. It seemed a distant place where I could hear Portia sobbing and being led away by her father, and then I was alone in my own personal hell. They say hell is being with other people; that's wrong. Hell is being locked inside your own head with your own demons.

"I had to go," Dan was to say later. "Portia was terrified. I don't think you know what a state you were in. I couldn't leave her to help you."

"You should never leave her for me," I'd replied. "She needs her daddy right now."

Eventually, I had dragged myself, exhausted, onto the couch and fallen asleep there. I couldn't face going upstairs and having to pass Becca's room.

The next morning, Dan packed us and our bags into the car and drove us to his mother's house in Swindon. "I want you to stay here for a few days," he said. "Lounge around and let Mum do the cooking. I've got some things to take care of at home, and then I'll come and pick you up."

Portia was still too upset to argue, and when I looked at her white, drawn face, I didn't argue, either, but shut up and took it. From his attitude, it wasn't up for discussion. He had gone into that mode of action and emotional shutdown in order to cope.

He came back for me two days later; Portia was to stay another couple of days with her grandma. When I went back into the house, all the photos on the hutch were gone and in their place was a vase of flowers. I walked silently through the house. He had stripped away every trace of Becca. I went upstairs to her room. All her toys and books were gone. Even the furniture had been taken away. The room was empty and smelled of freshly painted walls.

I covered my mouth with my hand to stifle a sob. I had wanted her bed here to bury my face in, to see if I could still smell her. But he had utterly taken her away. There was nothing left of her in here, not a single sign. I turned to find him watching me, his face hard and shuttered.

"There is not one thing we can do to bring her back, Lizzie. We have to find some normality again, for Portia's sake."

The tears spilled down my cheeks. "You didn't have to *erase* her, Dan. For God's sake, it's only been a few months."

"Do you know what Portia said to me in the kitchen while you were losing it down there? Do you know what she said?" he demanded. "I'll tell you, and it broke my heart to hear her say it. She said, 'I bet Mum wishes it was me who died, not Becca. She's always loved her best.'"

If it broke Dan's heart to hear that, mine shattered like a mirror. Great long, barbed shards and splinters tore and cut into my flesh inside my chest, ripping me open, slashing at everything.

Dan takes Portia to school the next day on his way to work. She's only just gone back. He doesn't want her tiring herself out, so he's running her to and from school whenever he can fit it around work. She certainly isn't back to her old energy levels yet, so I'm relieved, too, although it should be me as the parent not back at work yet. But of course, I can't get behind the wheel. It's not easy for me to get in a car at all now. I've had to cancel any work I had on, to tell the lawyers wanting me to pick up cases that I'm just not available now and no, I don't know when I'll be back. Word had gotten around about my accident, so no one was surprised I was taking some time off. There'd been an article in the local paper, but the legal-world jungle drums had passed the news around quickly, and many of my colleagues had sent messages of sympathy that, unfortunately, I couldn't stand to read.

I potter about the empty house, clearing up the remains of breakfast. We all force ourselves to eat at the moment, and doing it together at a table at least ensures we do have a meal. When there is nothing left to tidy, I get my phone out and do some searching online. I know Dan said he'd do this, but it has to be me who makes this step. I cannot be dragged into it. It must be something I choose for myself, or it won't work.

It doesn't take me long to find someone, but it takes a lot longer for me to check out their credentials and testimonials, and then even longer for me to dither around, staring at the kitchen wall until my mug of coffee is stone-cold.

Eventually, I make the call. Thankfully, it is answered. Had it gone to voicemail, I don't think I could have left a message.

"Hello. Stella Carson speaking."

"Ah, uh, hello. Um, I'm making an inquiry about your counseling service."

"OK, sure—have you lost someone, or is it an inquiry on somebody else's behalf?"

She has a calm voice. I should have expected that. She sounds around my age. No real accent, a neutral and almost-beige voice.

"Er, yes, it's for me, and yes, I have."

"And you need some help dealing with that? Could I make a practical inquiry, please? How long ago did you lose them?"

She doesn't say she's sorry for my loss or anything ridiculously trite. And for that, I am glad.

"Three months ago."

"OK, thank you. That gives me an idea of how to structure a program if you decide I'm the right person to help you. I normally recommend an initial meeting, and then we go from there. Would you be interested in us arranging that now?"

I think of Dan's desperation as he held the tissues for me last night.

"Yes. Yes, I would."

14

"I CAN'T TELL YOU ALL of it. Not yet. I'm not ready to."

I am perched on the end of a gray sofa, almost ready for flight. I caught the bus over here to Stella Carson's house this afternoon. I haven't told Dan—he would have insisted on driving me. Her counseling room is in a wing to the side of her house, a large Victorian semi-detached on a tree-lined street. She has a brass plate on the gatepost, and that reassures me. It's silly, the things that make you feel better sometimes. The room is tastefully decorated in shades of gray. The art on the walls is unchallenging—muted watercolors of birds, a heron in flight, a kingfisher on a branch. It has a soothing effect, and the large French doors at the end of the room that lead into the garden add to that sense of calm. The bare skeletons of the trees are starkly beautiful, a little frost still clinging to the twigs, and the lawn crisp beneath them.

Stella and I are arranged opposite each other on two sofas bisected by a coffee table.

"You don't have to tell me anything you don't want to," she replies in that well-modulated voice. An anywhere-voice for an anywhere-woman. She is in her late forties and dressed in slim-legged black trousers and a long-sleeved, black jersey top. Slender, high-arched feet are clad in ballet pumps. The black effect is relieved by a gauzy, pale-gray scarf scattered with white stars. Her hair is a dark, precision-cut, jaw-length bob.

"I don't know what to say, then."

"Start with why you are here—as much or as little as you want to tell me."

"What do people normally say at this point?"

"Whatever they want. It really is up to you."

"I'm a barrister. I practice family law. I specialize in child custody cases, especially in representing fathers wanting fair access or even full custody. I'm forty-five and…" I pause. "This isn't what I'm supposed to say, is it?"

"Yes. Because it's what you want to say. There's no script." She smiles slightly, in a reassuring way.

"I've been married to Dan for over twenty years. He's also a barrister, but he specializes in criminal law. We had two daughters, aged fifteen and seven. Now we only have one." I have to stop—I'd choke on any more words after that.

She nods. "You lost a daughter. That's why you're here."

"Yes."

"Do you want to tell me what happened, or is that too much?"

"There was a car accident. I was driving. She…died." And I realize she is the first person I have had to say those words to. Everyone else already knew, or Dan told them when I wasn't around. This is the first time I have said it aloud.

The words feel alien on my tongue, and I can feel my pulse beginning to speed up. There's a rising bubble of panic forming inside my stomach. It tells me I'm not ready for this. Saying it myself makes it real again, and I don't want that. I want it to go away, but it won't. It never will.

"Both my girls were in the car. I could only get one out. The car went into a lake. We all nearly drowned." My voice catches in my throat. My words are like the ghosts of sailors marching up a beach to drown the wreckers in the sea. When I speak, they will undo me completely.

Stella's brow creases faintly as she meets my gaze. "So it was impossible for you to save both of your daughters. Do you think you've accepted that?"

I nod, my head leaden.

The light is fading from the garden. The trees darken to silhouettes as we sit there, and the clock on the mantelpiece marks my failure to talk to her as the minutes tick by.

"I chose." I force the words out, and a ghost sailor grabs a pickaxe from the sand and buries it in the back of the wrecker, filling his pockets with dead men's treasure.

"But it sounds like if you hadn't made that choice, both girls would have died. You could have died yourself." She rises from the sofa. "Take a moment to think about that before we go on. Really absorb that. I'll give you a few minutes." And she goes over to the window to look into the garden. She walks like a dancer, I note, as though her weight is carried by the air, not the ground. I've always envied women who can do that, but those feelings no longer seem important now.

Only the ticking of the clock breaks the silence. I can't do what she's asked me to because I've not been truthful with her. She only knows part of it. Of course, what she's said makes sense—when you don't know what I've really done.

Am I ready to tell her? No, and I don't know if I'll ever be. So I hang in this in-between place where I don't fully exist. I'm supposed to want to get better, but I don't deserve to.

She sits back down after a while. "Do you want to carry on now?" she asks with a gentle smile.

"I don't think I can."

"I'm going to ask you a question, then. You don't have to answer, but maybe it will help. You said you made a choice, and you said that as if it makes you feel guilty. Am I right?"

I am the wrecker; I taste sand and brine in my mouth as my broken body crashes to the sand. My life bleeds out on a midnight beach.

"Is it too difficult to answer?"

It's too difficult even to move. I am frozen.

She reaches across the table and touches my hand with the gentlest of fingertips. "OK, that's far enough for today. We'll stop now."

She turns to more mundane matters and discusses a chart she shows me about recovering from grief, and she explains more about how she works with her clients. By this time, I've calmed down a little, and she attempts to get some more background on me.

"So, you said your husband is a barrister too. Did you meet through work?"

"Sort of. We met at a social event, but we were there through work." I can still taste salt in my mouth. The imagination is a powerful deceiver.

"And you've been together twenty years." She smiles broadly. "Well-done!"

I smile back—a conditioned response. "We're practically unique among our colleagues for that."

"I'm not surprised. Too few marriages make it with that kind of work pressure. Quite a few of my clients come to me over the grief of a relationship breakup, you see. I don't just deal with bereavement."

"Oh, I didn't realize. But yes, of course. That makes sense."

I don't tell her I had times before the accident when I wondered if the only reason Dan and I hadn't split up like our friends had done was because we were both too stubborn to give up on each other. I couldn't remember the last time we'd been out together, just me and him, or when we'd gone out for a meal as a family, like we used to.

"Do you want to tell me a little more about your work? It sounds as if you have quite a stressful job."

I shrug. "It can be traumatic sometimes, especially if there's potential abuse going on. I'm usually representing the fathers. As I said before, that's my specialty area. I did a pretty high-profile case some years back that got me a lot of attention. After that, I got more and more approaches from fathers who wanted more contact than they were being allowed."

"Do you find that difficult, as a mother?"

"Sometimes. But I also see the state some women are in, and that doesn't put them in a good position to be the parent with main responsibility. I try to look at it less from a mother's perspective and more from the child's best interests."

She nods. "That's a good viewpoint."

"It's not always that easy," I find myself saying. Perhaps it's to fill the gap left by my failure to talk about Becca's death. "It's been a rough ride at times."

She smiles encouragingly.

"I've had a few cases where I've felt for a mother, and she's lost custody because her defense lost the battle and for no other reason. That's hard. I think the worst was a little girl whose dad took her abroad when he got custody. The mother didn't have the wherewithal to get a lawyer who could win, and she lost the case on that basis. I must admit I try to avoid taking too many cases like that. I still remember that little girl, but she must be in her teens now."

"Do you think it's harder or easier than your husband's work?"

"Oh, I couldn't do Dan's job," I tell her frankly. "It's never attracted me, having to defend people who you know without question are guilty. But as he says, everyone is entitled to a fair trial, and it's his job to make sure that they have a fair defense and that any conviction can't be overturned by a technicality."

She pulls a face. "I don't think I could do it, either, but I can see what he means."

"It's the jury's job to convict, he says, and his to make sure he has presented the right defense case. But, no, you do have to be able to shut off and walk away in his line of work. It's not for everyone."

"What's he like, your husband?" she asks, and I know this question is part of her job in piecing together the puzzle that is me.

"Dan is very driven and very focused. He likes to solve problems. He's not a big socializer, but he has a few very good friends, and his family is very important to him." I think for a moment. "He's a very loyal man but not always Mr. Empathy. He likes to find a practical solution, and he lives in a house of females—he must feel outnumbered by emotional beings sometimes. I think it makes him itch. Like an allergic reaction."

She gives a snort of laughter, and it seems like genuine amusement. A sense of sisterhood.

I smile, and the corners of my mouth feel rusty with disuse. "He's a decent guy," I add, and I feel, as always, that faint glow of pride on his behalf, because he *is* a good man.

When our time is up, I book in another appointment. She suggests I will need around six over the next couple of months. "Be prepared that it may take longer, though," she warns. "The journey after the loss of someone you love very much is not a straight road, and sometimes you will find you are going backward for a while in order to move forward in the end. I don't transport you there—think of me as a compass giving you directions as you walk."

That makes a kind of sense. And in as much as I can see myself talking to anyone about Becca, I could possibly talk to this woman.

"I chose you for your name, you know," I say suddenly, aware I am being ridiculous in this unasked-for honesty. Am I testing her? Maybe.

"Really? Why?"

"Stella. A star." I swallow hard. "It's dark where I am. I need a light to guide me out."

She stares at me. I think for a second that her eyes are tearing up, and then she holds out her hand for me to shake. "We're going to do this," she says. "Hold on to that thought."

When I leave, I am calmer. The urge to curl up into a ball and scream is quieted for a while. It's still there, buried inside as it always is these days, waiting to rise up and claw its way to the surface again, but at least I am superficially functional, and I bid a polite farewell until my next appointment.

I walk home through lamp-lit streets scented with winter, the faint taste of salt still in my mouth.

15

THE DAY AFTER MY VISIT to Stella, Portia arrives home from school, and it's clear that something's bothering her. She frowns as she passes me on her way to the kitchen. It's one of the days Dan isn't able to collect her, so she's come back by herself on the bus.

"What's wrong?" I ask her nervously. I'm constantly on edge around her since I realized how much I've let her down. And sometimes I catch myself wondering if she remembers more than she will tell me of what happened in the accident. Did I do something to cause it and she can't face telling us? I can't strike away the fear that she's hiding something from me.

"Something weird just happened," she says, getting herself a glass of water. "I don't know. Maybe I'm imagining it."

"What is it?"

She turns away. "I'll talk to Dad about it later. I've got homework."

She goes upstairs, checking her phone as she walks off, and I am left sitting there, feeling as though the door has been slammed in my face. She's still up there when Dan arrives home two hours later.

"What's up?" he asks, knowing immediately from my face that all isn't well.

"Portia," I say with a hopeless shrug. "You'd better ask her. She wants to talk to you, not me."

He gives me a sharp look, knowing how much I'll hate that attitude from her right now, and then goes to the foot of the stairs. "Portia!" he calls.

She comes down dressed in an oversized sweatshirt and leggings. She looks half-asleep, as though she's been napping. She's not been eating enough since the accident, and it's no wonder she's tired. "What?"

"Your mum says you want to talk."

She scowls. "Yeah, but it's not urgent. Nothing to make a big deal about."

He rolls his eyes. Grumpy teenage Portia never seems to get to him on that wounded, visceral level that she gets to me. "Hurry up and tell me, then, if it's not a big thing."

She rolls her eyes right back at him. "I just had this weird feeling on the way home, like someone was following me."

Dan's immediately all attention. "What?"

"But then I decided it's probably my imagination."

"Come into the sitting room," he says firmly.

Portia shoots me a resentful glance for telling him and follows. Dan sits opposite her on the sofa while I hover by the door, aware she probably doesn't want me there.

"It was when I was waiting for the bus. I was standing alone, and I got this odd feeling that somebody was looking at me. I turned round, but I couldn't see anyone doing it. Then it was like an itch. Like I said, it's probably my imagination. Everyone at my stop got on the bus when it came and it was really packed, so I was standing at the front near the driver."

"Who was at the bus stop?" Dan interrupts.

"Just some people from school and some other randoms. Nobody weird-looking, if that's what you mean."

And I'm left wondering why she was standing on her own. Why wasn't she with friends?

"Anyway, I forgot about it until I got off at my stop and I was walking home. Then I suddenly remembered it. And I don't know why, but I turned 'round. There was someone walking behind me, but right back up the street."

"A man? What was he wearing?"

"I don't know if it was a man. They were too far away, and whoever it was had a big raincoat on with the hood up, so I couldn't tell. It could have been a boy from school."

"What was this coat like?" Dan's voice is sharp.

"Black or dark gray. Just one of those waterproof things you wear on a country walk."

"And did he follow you?"

"It's hard to say. He went the same way as me, yes, until I got onto our street. And then I did check before I came in the front door, but I didn't see him then."

Dan chews his lip and frowns at her. He's tapping his knee with his fingers in a fast, agitated kind of way. It makes me uncomfortable. I've never seen him doing that before.

"But it's probably just a coincidence, Dad. I was just a bit spooked when I came in—that's why I told Mum. I'm not sure it was anything. If I hadn't had that funny feeling at the bus stop, I would have never looked 'round when I got off the bus. Honestly, maybe it was just someone walking the same way."

"Did he get off the bus? I mean, was he on your bus?"

"I didn't see anyone wearing a coat like that, no, but it was really crowded. But I don't remember a guy at the bus stop wearing it either. It may have been a kid from school messing around."

"Why would they do that?" I ask from the doorway.

She avoids my gaze. "Some people are idiots sometimes," she mumbles.

I'm not convinced that's all there is to it, but Dan cuts in before I can say anything else.

"OK, so here's how it's going to be. I'm not taking any chances. It's winter, and the nights are dark. You're not traveling home on your own at the moment. I'll rearrange things at work, and I'll go back to dropping you off and collecting you again."

"But Dad, it's probably nothing," she protests and shoots me a filthy look. Yes, it'll be all my fault.

"Probably it is, but I'm not taking any chances," he says firmly. "There are some weird people out there, and to be followed once is enough for me. I'm going to move my calendar around so I can take you to and from school all the time—at least until the nights get lighter—and that's that."

She doesn't argue with him. It's fruitless arguing with Dan when he's in this kind of defensive mode, and she knows that. They both go off to the kitchen together, talking about the logistics of the next few days and what times he's free and when she needs collecting.

I linger in the sitting room. This is not just his natural paternal defensiveness. Dan has that in bucketloads, but this is more. He wasn't there to protect her last time. He wasn't there for the crash. That's why he's doubly determined not to take any chances now.

That knowledge settles like a lead weight on my chest. The repercussions from that accident will never leave us, any of us. They will follow us forever.

If Dan is worried, however, my maternal anxiety is going into orbit. Portia might well say it's nothing and she may be right, but she was a lot less sure when she came in. He's right—there are a lot of strange people around, and if even a scrap of attention has been paid by one of them to our teenage daughter, then yes, we do need to wrap her in cotton wool. I hope it is someone from school messing about, because that's far less threatening than a strange man following her. I don't like any of this one bit. Dan's right. She's not going out alone for the foreseeable future.

Apart from going to school, when did she last go out alone? She never goes out to see friends now. She doesn't actually have anyone around anymore either. At first, I'd not noticed how odd that is, assuming it was her way of grieving and that she was still recovering physically. But too much time has now passed, while I've been absorbed in my own hell. She should be mixing with her friends again by now. How could I not have seen this? What's going on with her? I've assumed all that time in her room, she's on the phone or texting them, just like she would have done before the accident. But is that true? And then her appetite seems nonexistent. An uncomfortable feeling assails me that there may be more going on here than meets the eye.

But what?

16

SHE IS PRETTY, THE ELDER *girl, but in that unshowy way that needs a second look. Or perhaps it's because she's so unhappy that you don't notice her prettiness immediately. There's never any life in her eyes as she walks home from school, no sign of a smile for anyone around her, and no friends. She's always so alone.*

She saw me that last time. She knew I was following her. I'd been so careful, but still, she got wind of me. They don't let her out much on her own now. I wouldn't, either, if I were them. After all, they've already lost one daughter. It stands to reason they'll take much more care now.

She slips out to go to the local shop, though, one Saturday afternoon. She trudges down the front steps and along the street. A girl of her age should have a lighter, more carefree step, but of course I know why that is. I take good care to make sure she doesn't see me this time. She walks slowly to the shop, and she's only in there a few minutes. She comes out with a soft drink and a bag of crisps. I expect her to turn for home, but she doesn't. She walks to the park and sits on a bench there to eat her crisps. Is she waiting for somebody? Is this a meeting spot?

Half an hour passes as she sips her drink and eats the crisps slowly and thoughtfully, not wolfing them down like a normal teenager. She's killing time, not waiting for a friend. At first, I'm not sure what it is about her just sitting there that strikes me as off, but then I realize that unlike every other girl her age, she doesn't attempt to look at her phone.

She simply sits, lifelessly.

Such a sad little face. And she walks home as disconsolately as when she left. There's a taste in my mouth like spoiled meat.

I will watch, and I will wait. Watch her, watch all of them, until I know what to do next.

17

IT'S ANOTHER OF THOSE INTERMINABLE days when I am alone in the house. I know I'm not nearly ready to go back to work, which is a source of shame to me, as Portia has gone back to school and she was sicker than me after the accident.

"Children bounce back quicker," Dan replied when I said this to him. "Besides, school and your job are very different things." He didn't add that of course, she has less to torture herself about than I do, but I knew the thought was there.

Portia wasn't at all bounced back, though, and I wished he would do more to reach her. She is so her daddy's daughter that perhaps he can understand her when I can't. But all he would say was, "Leave her to come to terms with it."

A male view, I told him. But he would get that shuttered-down look if I pushed him, the one that tells me he doesn't have a clue how to deal with the matter so he will run away from it and bury himself until it hopefully passes.

At times like that, I really do get angry inside. Genuinely, the thing that I feel is anger, but I can't let it out. He is letting Portia down by insisting she can cope, and I am too lost to step in.

Without them both, in the silence of the morning house, I mooch around, supposedly tidying. I realize why I'm so mad with him. What he's doing with Portia now is what he's slowly been doing with me for years.

Leaving me to come to terms with things, with the frustrations that have built up, with the regrets, as he moves further and further away. His tactics didn't work, just left me with a sad and persistent dissatisfaction that's dragged me down. I can't let that happen to Portia.

My body feels old and tired from lack of normal use, as it has never done before. Perhaps that is to be expected and is still part of the physical recovery—I've had extreme hypothermia, and I was warned that it is like recovering from a major operation, so to expect fatigue and bad days for some time. Possibly, though, what I feel is due to me no longer doing any of the things I used to. The gym, the yoga, all that has gone. Now I just mooch—wandering from room to room, trying to make the time go, trying not to think. That's my only occupation. If I had a different job, I might feel more like going back to work, but to go straight back into defending which parent has the right to keep their child? That really would kill me at this point in time.

The doorbell rings, shattering the silence and making me jump. I check the clock, and it's ten thirty. I'm not expecting anyone, but it's a respectable enough time for solicitors to be about. I put my best disparaging face on as I open the door and prepare to say, "No, thank you," with a repressing firmness.

A man stands there. I know what he is immediately. I know from the way he stands and from how his colleague waiting by the parked car stands too. My stomach jolts in fear.

He smiles—a professional expression with no warmth in it. "Good morning, Mrs. Fulton. I wonder if we might have a word."

And he knows I know. Even before he shows me his badge.

"You'd better come in," I answer, but mentally, I'm trying to remember if I put Aidan's work number in my phone and then realize he could well be in court and uncontactable right now. I know Dan is. Perhaps this policeman knows that and the timing of his arrival is deliberate.

I open the door wider and gesture them both inside. My heart is playing a drumbeat on my ribs.

I show them into the sitting room and politely offer tea or coffee, which I am relieved they decline.

"Detective Sergeant Booth and Detective Constable McKinnon," the older man—the one who rang the bell—says to me as he shows me his ID. He's from the Reading station, like the others were. He has a hard face with close-cropped hair, just starting to show a touch of gray at the temples. Some would say it's a good-looking face, but it's not one I would want to come home to at the end of a weary day.

I nod at them both, swallowing down the ball of worry pressing into my throat. The younger of the two gives me a grimace that I suspect is meant to be a smile forced out through his nervousness. It only serves to set me even more on edge.

"So," Booth says, knitting his fingers together and leaning his elbows on his knees, "I thought you'd like to know that the recovery operation to retrieve your car will start soon. It's taken us longer than we wanted because of the depth of the lake, and we've had to track down a specialist team who can work in those conditions and adapt equipment, but I've had the green light that they're ready to start now."

I stare somewhere over his head, frozen by this news. "That's good," I say, and my voice sounds distant. At least it still works.

"Yes, isn't it?" he replies, nodding forcefully.

I can't really see him, Becca's face flitting across my vision.

"Have you thought any more about what happened that night?" he asks. It's not a friendly voice, and I begin to understand why his colleague looks nervous. He really shouldn't be doing this without offering me the option to have legal representation, not after Aidan complained about my arrest last time.

I haven't got any fight, though. Let them bring the car up. Let them find what they find. There's a lassitude in my limbs and a dull ache starting in my head. It's better than the fear. Let the numbness take me; I want it to. It's safer that way. I can see Becca in my mind, and I focus on her.

"I think about nothing else."

"And do you remember any more?"

I want to reach my hands out and touch Becca. I want to be here with her, in this mirage, because at least here I can still see her. I do not want this man with his hard face and even harder voice intruding on that.

"No. I remember nothing."

I hear his hiss of exasperation. "At some point, and that point will be very soon now, Mrs. Fulton, you'll have to remember, and these excuses of having lost your memory aren't going to wash."

"Really."

Oh, go away. I don't care about you.

Another exasperated sound. "Do you not think it might be better to tell us what you know now? Rather than wait until we find out?"

"You know what I know."

Does he think he'll rattle me? With this? I focus for a moment on his face. On his barren and tedious face that takes me away from Becca. And then I turn away again. He's no opponent for me, and I'm not going to dignify him with my time, let alone any trepidation.

"Oh, come on, Mrs. Fulton!" He's cross at my dismissal, and I'd be pleased—or, perhaps amused—if this was in court. As it is, I'm simply weary of him. "Don't treat me as if I'm stupid. You remember perfectly well, but you don't want to face the consequences of your actions. You might be clever, but you weren't clever enough to know you were falling asleep at the wheel that night. If you were, you might still have two daughters, not one. Poor little thing, not even eight years old. I guess people would think you'd have the decency to admit it—her own mother. Let her rest in peace and give her some dignity in death by admitting what you've done."

His companion gives a sharp cough, and I glance at him. His forehead is sweaty; he's not at all comfortable with this. And neither, I think, would this man's superior officers be. He's so far out of line that he's dangerous.

I pull myself into the here and now with reluctance. "I think you need to leave." My tone is icy. He starts to speak, but I cut him off. I find an autopilot of my old self to deal with him. It switches on readily enough when confronted with his hostility, and I am grateful, at least, for that. "I think we both know that this conversation is not one you should be having, and you're lucky that I don't view you of enough importance to do more than escort you out of my house. But let me make something very clear—if you come here again and threaten me in this way, I will report you, and it will be very much the worse for you if I do."

He glares at me. I know his type, and he'll try to brazen it out. "A little girl died because of what you did. How do you live with that?"

His colleague runs a finger around his collar and looks at his feet.

How do I live with that indeed? In truth, I live with it very badly. I hardly live at all, and I would still be very grateful if I could simply cease living and leave this pain behind me. But here's the funny thing: the more he talks and accuses me of killing Becca, the more that stubbornly forgetful part at the back of my mind hardens into a resolution that he's wrong.

So what did happen?

I just don't know. But that nagging feeling tells me that when I do remember, it's not going to be good. I can feel anxiety coil around me like a snake. My mind pushes back abruptly, forcing any lingering memory away with violence.

Whatever it is, it's bad. My hands begin to shake.

I stand up abruptly. "I really must get on," I say, walking pointedly to the sitting-room door and opening it for them.

He rises, glowering, and his companion follows, looking anywhere but at me.

I show them to the front door. He turns on the doorstep to look at me. "They are bringing that car up, and when they do, I'll be straight back here, and I'll have a warrant."

I smile and nod as if he's a guest I'm seeing off, and then I shut the door in his face.

My knees give out, and I sink onto the bottom step, shaking. Oh, he'll be back. I don't doubt it.

18

⌐

"WHY DIDN'T YOU CALL ME?" Dan demands, running his hand through his hair.

"I thought you were in court."

"I was, but you didn't even leave a message!" He sits down heavily at the foot of the stairs, immaculately polished shoes resting on my once-precious mosaic tiles. "Lizzie, you shouldn't have spoken to him."

And I know it. I knew it at the time, and I knew he'd tell me off about it. I had thought of calling Aidan and letting him deal with it, but eventually, I'd plucked up the courage to face Dan's frustration.

I can't imagine having a thought like that a year ago. I'm so unequipped now to deal with any little ripple life throws at me that my husband's annoyance appears to me as a tidal wave I can't deal with.

I can see him trying to rein himself back in. In a detached way, I'm curious as to how my face looks and what he reads in it when he can obviously see something of my fears there. How does that make him feel? A man who fell in love with Lizzie Trethanon, who told her that he knew she was the right one for him when he saw her in action in court, who loved the woman who once won an award for Junior Barrister of the Year, who sat proudly by her side when she went to receive it.

She and I feel like very different women now.

"They're trying to rattle you," Dan says with considerable annoyance when I retell him more slowly the full account of what happened with the police. "I suppose it's not entirely a bad thing, now I think about it—though you mustn't speak to them again like that. But we can use it to demonstrate that you're not trying to hide anything and that there's an ongoing impact on your mental state. You're obviously not fully recovered, and the doctors at the hospital did say that your amnesia could just as easily be linked to the physical trauma as to the mental strain. I'm going to call Aidan and set him on them. And you know what, I won't be surprised if some of this attitude you're getting is because of what we do for a living. Some of those police officers view barristers like the public view tax collectors. They can't treat you like this!"

He calls Aidan and rants his annoyance out to him through the phone. From what I can hear, Aidan's in full agreement. Besides, I'll be relieved if my lack of memory around the accident is due to the physical effects of what happened to me and not because I'm trying to block out something terrible. Dan reminding me that the doctors were perfectly comfortable with the idea that the physical ordeal could be responsible helps a little when I reach the edge of panic, as I am now.

They are always there at the edge of my mind, those lingering fear mists waiting to swirl around me. One day, I'm afraid they'll trap me inside them completely, and I won't be able to come back. I'll be lost inside them forever. It's dark in there, and cold.

I can feel my breath freezing inside me, and my chest goes tight, tight with the cold.

"Lizzie? Lizzie?" Dan says sharply, and I come back to myself to recognize he's finished on the phone.

I still can't breathe, and he's looking at me strangely.

I shake my head and make an excuse to go to the bathroom. There, I sit on the floor with my head pressed against a warm towel on the rail, and its gentle heat revives me.

I want to give up, but I can't.

I am still a mother. Portia needs me. Maybe she won't care so much about the fate of a mother who killed her sister if she believes that I did fall asleep at the wheel, but there'll be nobody to take care of her. And no matter how much she pushes me away and resents me, I know in my inner heart, with a truth that burns me as harsh as acid, that she needs me. Dan loves her, but he can't notice what I do, and he can't make sure all the little things are in place for her. Who would pick her Christmas and birthday presents if I were gone? I remember when she was little and Dan would not know how to fold her white ankle socks down but would just scrunch them carelessly, how she would never let him brush the tangles out of her hair because he couldn't do it without tugging, how he never could plait her hair into pigtails. She needs me just as much now. Portia is lost somewhere, too, in all of this, and Dan hasn't worked out how to help her back. I'm scared because I don't think he will. He isn't made that way.

So it has to be me. I have to fight them, not let them take me down. I have to fight again, and I have to do it for Portia. I *will* do it for Portia.

19

SO THE POLICE VISITED, AND *I'm left wondering what for. Have they found something out? Should I expect a call?*

But a few days pass, and there's nothing.

What does she actually know? That fascinates me, but I have no answer. There must be something going on, and I check the local newspapers, but there's never anything relevant in them. There hasn't been since those first days after the crash.

I may learn more by simply watching, and that's what I'll stick to. I know so much more about them now, but none of what I learn gets me closer to my goal.

I can't stop, though. I have to be here. Any other option is impossible.

This is what my life is reduced to.

It can't go on forever—even I know that.

20

THE NEXT DAY, WHEN PORTIA gets home, I pluck up the courage to attempt to make right a little of the damage I've done.

"Would you like a hot chocolate?"

She looks surprised and shrugs as she unpacks her bag. "Guess so." She sits down at the big pine kitchen table that I inherited from my parents after they died. I love that thing—it reminds me of a simpler life. Sometimes I think it looks faintly ridiculous in our Reading house, but neither Portia nor Dan has ever voiced that; they know how much it means to me.

I get a small copper pan and measure the milk out into it. And then the tin of grated chocolate. If you're going to have hot chocolate, you may as well do it properly—that's always been my view. There's no need for cream and marshmallows with really good chocolate. It's enough on its own. I whisk the chocolate into the milk as it heats, and then I pour the rich, scented liquid into two mugs for me and Portia and sit at the table opposite her.

Every time I look at her, I want to cry. This is one reason why I went to Stella. It's just not fair on Portia to have me around her in this state. She's been through enough. Like I told myself yesterday, I have to do it for her.

"How was school?"

"All right, I suppose."

In some ways, her standoffishness is a comfort. The comfort of familiarity. Portia rattled into her teenage years with a typical transition into no longer wanting to share anything with me, even mundane news of her day.

I miss the little girl who used to coil her arms so tightly round me when I picked her up from after-school club.

"Are you feeling tired?"

"A bit." She sips her hot chocolate, and I experiment with not saying anything to see if she fills the silence.

And it's a long silence.

Then she clears her throat. "I still don't feel back to normal yet. But I don't know how much of that is the physical stuff and how much is just… everything else."

With a horrible, sinking feeling, I realize that she's trying to avoid talking to me about Becca.

I can't talk to Portia yet about her sister, and I don't know how I will ever get to that point, which I suppose is why I need to keep seeing Stella. But if I can't talk to Portia about Becca, I need to find some common ground.

School is out—she always hated talking about school, anyway, as if I was intruding into her private space.

And then of course I realize there's another elephant in the room, one that maybe I *can* manage.

"Were you worried when they took me to the police station?" Thank goodness she wasn't here when Booth came around yesterday.

"No, I sat making daisy chains." She looks at me as if I am utterly stupid. "What do you think?"

I think you don't really care about me at all, Portia. I think you stopped loving me and started resenting me—that's what I think.

But I can't say that.

"Do you want to ask me about it?"

Now that does surprise her. She puts her mug down and thinks. "Why did they arrest you? I thought they only arrested people if they're sure they're guilty?"

"Generally that's true, but not always."

"And they didn't believe you didn't fall asleep?"

"They can't find any other reason for us to have gone off the road, and it doesn't help that I can't remember that part."

My daughter snorts, sounding just like her father. "You had an accident. Why are they so surprised?"

"Because unlike you, I didn't have an obvious head injury."

"But you still had hypothermia and shock. You were still unconscious."

"I know, but they don't seem to understand what effect that can have. Or maybe I just didn't seem convincing." I don't feel convincing, after all, and I wonder if the old me would believe the mess I am now if I was up in court.

Portia eyeballs me. "Is there any chance you fell asleep? Any even faint possibility?"

It's a hard question, and her swift coldness as she asks should not be surprising. After all, she's asking if I caused Becca's death and if I nearly killed her too.

I blink away the burning sensation in my eyes. "No."

"But if you don't remember, how can you be sure?"

Panic tightens my lungs for a moment. Does she know something I don't? Is that why she always looks so suspicious?

"I can't, I suppose."

And she flinches, her face falling in disappointment. I've let her down again. Perhaps she really doesn't remember anything and she simply wants me to reassure her. I need to do better, and I grasp for words.

"It just doesn't feel like the right explanation. I keep grasping to remember, but it's lost somewhere past the back of my mind, and I can't reach it. I keep saying this, and I know it's not making sense to anyone."

My daughter stares at me, her brow furrowed, but her eyes have softened again. "I don't know… Maybe I get what you mean. Is it like when you try to remember someone's name and you can't, and then people make suggestions and you're like, 'No, it's not that,' and, 'It's not that'… You know they haven't said the right name, but you still can't remember what it is."

I feel like crying in relief that finally, someone does understand. "Yes, darling, that's it exactly. It's just like that."

For a few seconds here, we have a rare unity. I want to put my arms round her and hold her because she is still here, but as soon as I think of it, the guilt surges, choking off the urge. What I have done will always lie between us, even though Portia and Dan know nothing about it.

"I should cook dinner," I say, getting up and bustling about the kitchen. When I look again, she has gone.

I hate that look she gets in her eyes when she turns away from me. I'm glad I missed it this time. I've seen it too often now, and it always, always reminds me of the first time I saw that expression on her face. It hurts me just as much now as it did then. And I hate myself for it too.

The first time Portia looked at me like that was on the day Dan found me locked in the bathroom. He knocked, but when I wouldn't come out, he twisted the lock with a coin and came in. I was sitting on the floor with my head in my hands and tears streaming down my face.

It was our eighth round of IVF, and it had failed.

"We can try again," he said, crouching beside me and putting his arms around me.

"No, no, we can't. We said this was the last time. That there had to be a point at which we accepted it." And I howled my despair and rage into my husband's shoulder. We had wasted so many years now, and we would never get that time back.

I could hear Portia downstairs with the radio on to drown out the sound of her mother crying. All this time, I could have focused on her instead of chasing a dream that was never going to be.

But oh, how I still wanted that moment when my newborn peered up at me, knowing me more by scent than sight, and I pressed her to my face and inhaled that precious baby smell again. Little wrinkled fingers exploring mine for the first time. That rush, that incredible rush of the most overwhelming love it is possible to feel.

No, instead I was sitting on cold tiles, my tears dripping into my husband's sweater, and it was over.

It was over.

I would never be a mother again.

And nobody, nobody understood.

There were those mothers at the fertility clinic doing this for the first time. I saw it in their eyes: *You already have a child. What are you complaining about? Be grateful for what you have!*

And the women like my best friend, Annika, who didn't know what it was like to hold your baby in your arms and for them to be your entire world—they didn't understand either.

And the older women, who I had thought might have some comprehension—no, I was wrong again. Dan's mother had merely said, "Well, we all have to stop having them at some point, and it's no different then, I can assure you. You've got Portia—count your blessings."

I hung on to Dan's shoulders and sobbed and sobbed. Downstairs, the stereo was turned up louder.

"Lizzie," he said into my hair, "I know how upset you are, and I am in pieces about this, too, but please—this is hurting Portia."

I don't care! I'm too broken by this. I can't go on.

All those comments, too, from the multiple-kid mummies—"Ooh, are you only having one?"—followed by the disapproving glances, hastily rearranged when I glared back. One had even said once, "Don't you think that's a bit selfish?" assuming I'd put my career first.

"Which was none of her damn business, anyway," I yelled into Dan's shoulder, not caring that the moment was long gone and he wouldn't understand what I was talking about.

He held on while I raged. I could feel the tension in his body as I shouted my fury into him. And he carried on holding me when it finally subsided.

Eventually, when he was sure I'd finally stopped, he let me go and wiped my face with a towel.

"We'll adopt," he said firmly.

I had no strength left to argue. And I wasn't sure I wanted to.

A baby was a baby, right? A baby would make us better.

I looked up and Portia was watching us from the door, her eyes big and solemn and disappointed.

"It's OK," I said with a tremulous smile. "Mummy's OK. She was just a bit sad. But it's all right now. Everything's fine."

She nodded, but that look lingered in her eyes.

Portia knew, I finally admit to myself now. She knew she wasn't enough for me. She's carried that all these years, and I don't think she'll ever forgive me for that. I saw it in her face that day, but I didn't want to acknowledge it. She began to draw away from me then because she felt she was a disappointment. Because she couldn't be enough. How could I do that to her? I let it consume me. I let it affect her childhood too much. Children need unconditional love, and I let Portia down.

The truth hurts: I wrecked my relationship with her before I ever drove the car into the lake. Can I ever fix that?

21

A WEEK PASSES SINCE BOOTH'S visit. Dan and Aidan kick up a stink about the way Booth behaved, and Dan rages at the neutral response he receives.

"This is because Lizzie's my wife," he says to Aidan.

He won't elaborate on that to me, so I take Aidan to one side and ask him his opinion instead.

"I think he's got a point. Guys like Dan aren't favorites with some coppers," he says. "You know this—you saw what they were like after he kicked off with them the night you were arrested. He's a lawyer, and he makes more money than they do by being on the opposing side to them. Add to that that over the years he's made some of them look stupid in the witness box in order to win his case, and there you have a pretty strong brew of resentment toward him."

"Yes, but they're supposed to be professional," I protest. "Obviously, they rub along better with prosecutors, but his is a job, just like theirs."

"And most get that, Lizzie. Most coppers are straight-up, salt-of-the-earth types. But not all of them. And this guy dealing with you is one of the latter, I think. But I'm not letting this lie—I'm putting in a serious complaint about him. It's not OK to let this go."

He might be right, but that's what I feel like: letting it go. I'm worn down by it all. Those words Booth said about Becca's death—I hear them over and over again in my head. The contempt on his face… I don't care about him, but it's just a mirror of what I feel about myself.

And then there's what I've done to Portia with my own blind stupidity, my selfishness.

I cancel an appointment with Stella because I can't face her. I can't talk about this.

At night, Dan and I lie on opposite sides of our super-king bed, pretending to be asleep so we don't have to interact with each other. We seem to have established this as a bizarre routine. I pretend to be tired at about nine, and Dan stays downstairs working. By the time he comes up, his breath usually wine-scented, I lie with my back to the door and my eyes closed. He creeps about so as not to "wake" me, and I wonder if he really does know I'm faking.

Within a few minutes, he's in bed and asleep faster than me—the wine makes sure of that. The dark and I are old comrades now; I spend so much of the night staring into the darkness, wondering whether the only real end to any of this is that I simply stop existing. Maybe without me, Dan and Portia would get along better. And I don't know how long I can keep bearing those visions in my mind of Becca trapped in the car.

When I finally sink into a restless sleep that night, I dream that Becca's real mother comes to find me. I've never met her, but in the dream, she has Becca's eyes, filled with menace. And then her face morphs into Detective-Sergeant Booth's. I hear his abrasive voice saying again, "You might still have two daughters, not one. Poor little thing—not even eight years old."

I wake up with a jerk, my heart racing impossibly, and I am drenched in sweat.

I know what those eyes were telling me. If Becca hadn't come to live with me, she wouldn't be dead now. I'm supposed to learn to live with that. How in hell does a mother ever come to bear that? How?

And Portia—she hates me too. I've let her down so badly. What a God-awful mother... No, actually, I don't even deserve to be called a mother.

Maybe I am wrong and the police are right. Maybe I did fall asleep at the wheel. They seem so convinced that I did. Perhaps Portia knows too.

If I let the police prosecute me, if I went along with this story that I fell asleep at the wheel, that would be a just punishment, wouldn't it? Maybe if I knew I was being punished, I would be able to cope with living.

I've lost people before. Both my parents died while Portia was still young, and that was awful. I felt so alone—an adult orphan. But it was nothing, *nothing* like this. This grief is an animal with sharp claws and talons. It rips through you as it eats you alive from within. You think it has quieted for a few thankful hours of relief, but no, it merely slumbers awhile and then wakes to consume you again.

There is no escape. This will go on and on and on.

I can't live with it. And I can't live with hating myself this much. The pain is physical. It's not just in my head; it hurts everywhere. There's no release from it.

I get up and go downstairs. There are no tears. I think I've cried them all away.

I take a carving knife from the block. I wonder how much it hurts and whether I'd be able to make the cut deep enough to do the job properly. I can't do it here, not where they will find me. I could go out, find somewhere secluded, and do it there. That would be better.

"What are you doing?" Dan's panicked voice behind me makes me jump.

He grabs the knife from me.

"What are you doing, Lizzie? What on earth are you doing?"

"I—I don't know."

He puts the knife back in the block and pulls me away by the arms. "What were you going to do? I need to know!" His eyes are clouded with fear. He's afraid of me, I realize. He's afraid of what I've become.

"I don't know what I was going to do. I was just thinking that maybe you would both be better off if I wasn't here."

"Why?" His cry is anguished. "Why would you ever think that?"

"Because I can't cope with this, Dan. I can't do it, and I'm destroying both of you along with me. I dreamed just now about Becca's real mother— and she hated me for what I did." Just thinking of that again traps the breath in my throat. "I can't stand this pain anymore."

He shakes his head. "Lizzie, you need to talk to me. There's something here I don't understand, and I can't help you if you won't tell me. You tried to get Becca, too—I know that. Of course you're grieving. Of course you're traumatized by what happened, but I know there's something you're not telling me."

I lean against him, my head on his chest. He puts his arms round me. He's so solid, and I need that. I need an oak tree to shelter me from the storm. It's been a long time since I let myself lean on him. Maybe years.

"You're right," he says softly. "You can't go on like this. What is it? What happened?"

I still don't fully understand how the distance crept in between us over the years, but it did, stealthily, until we were too far away to notice the loss, other than that sense of longing for something unobtainable that neither of us could recognize or name.

"What happened, Lizzie?" he repeats.

All the time we have grown apart, has it been this? That we no longer touch? Too busy, too unobservant of each other, and perhaps something else—too strong in our own skins. We stopped understanding that we needed each other.

The cold from the kitchen tiles creeps up my legs through my bare feet, making them ache. I don't mind so much. It reminds me that I am still alive, even if ten minutes ago, I didn't want to be.

"I did something awful, Dan," I say into his chest.

He pulls back a little to look down at me. "*Did* you fall asleep?"

I shake my head miserably. "No, Dan, it's not that." And I gather all my courage to tell him. "I chose."

He stiffens, and a part of me wants to grab the knife back when I feel that. I can't do this—I can't tell him. His eyes are veiled; I can't tell what he's thinking.

"What did you choose?" he says in that same soft voice.

I shake my head at him.

"You need to tell me. You have to do this, Lizzie. It's the only way through this. What did you choose?"

All those years together…years of marriage…he already knows. I'm not telling him anything now that he hasn't put together for himself from what I've just said. I know that from the way he guards his eyes, from the control in his voice.

"Tell me," he repeats with gentle insistence.

"I chose which girl to save."

He holds me away from him a little further, but he rubs my arms at the same time. "Explain it to me. Keep going, Lizzie. You need to do this."

I am in this so far now. Maybe he's right. This could break us, but I can't hide it forever. I close my eyes. "In the car, down there with the water pouring in, there was a moment when I knew—I couldn't get them both out. They were unconscious, and I had to save them quickly before we all drowned. There was a split second where I realized it was impossible to get both of them. Where I had to grab one and go. So I chose, and I chose Portia."

He pulls me back against him again, but my eyes are dry as he strokes my hair. My fear of what this will do to us is riding too high for tears.

"You saved one of them, Lizzie. You couldn't have gotten both of them out. You can't beat yourself up about not being able to get back for Becca. It took trained divers with full gear a week to get her out, that lake was so deep. You didn't stand a chance."

"But you know why I chose Portia," I say, muffled against him.

There is a long silence. I hold my breath, trying to notice any signs of rigidity in him. He is tense, I can feel that much.

Finally, he sighs. "Yes, I do know."

I wait. I feel the barely perceptible shifts in his muscles as he wrestles with this new knowledge of why our daughter died. I feel them like earthquakes against me.

"I loved Becca, you know I did," he says eventually. "It was an impossible choice, one you could never win with. You have to accept that."

"I don't know how to."

"Have you told this counselor you're seeing about this?"

"I told her I chose. I didn't tell her why."

I can feel my secret lodged within him now, an unexploded bomb. I'm waiting for it to detonate.

I straighten up and search his face. It's as blank as I expected. He's keeping how he feels carefully locked up. He's good at that. Once, I was too. Anxiety fizzes inside me, little bubbles through my blood. *Pop, pop.* I can feel them while I wait for his reaction.

He knows why I'm looking at him, and he swallows hard. He feels differently about me now, I think. I'd expected that. It's not a big explosion from him I fear, but the small and silent discharges that will come as he processes what I have done over the days and weeks. The slow death of what he thought he knew of me.

"See her again. You need to talk to a professional about this. And Lizzie…" He looks down at me again. "You must tell her about this, too—with the knife, I mean. We have to get you through this. Portia and I need you. Please don't do this again."

Oh, I wish it were true, that they did both need me. I wish I could believe that.

He puts his arms back around me and holds me. Do I imagine that he's more distant than before? I don't know.

He tugs my hand and motions to the stairs. "Come on, back to bed. We'll get there, Lizzie. I promise. I'll get you through this." And then he hesitates. "We shouldn't tell Portia. She's struggling with losing her sister. She needs to know you're not sorry it was her who survived, but at the same time, if she knows you chose her, I think she'll blame herself."

He's right. Portia adored Becca. It won't help her to feel the kind of guilt I do. This must remain a secret between Dan and me. I've caused her enough suffering already.

And yes, bed is the safest option. Talking now is too dangerous. There's too much risk we might tell each other how we really feel. Some things are better unsaid.

He takes my hand as we lie next to each other in the dark, and he holds it fiercely tight as if he can anchor me back. "Promise me you won't ever do that, Lizzie. Promise me you won't try to. We *do* need you."

"I promise," I tell him, because if that really is the truth, I can't do that to them. I can't let them fall into the kind of hell I'm in right now.

22

BY THE TIME HE EMERGES from the shower the next morning, Dan has obviously decided how he's going to deal with this—for now, at least.

"OK," he says with purpose, after he's dressed. "I'm going in late this morning. We can call your therapist and make sure you can see her today."

I nod, taken aback but too numb to argue.

"I'll make breakfast. You take your time."

The anxiety bubbles start to pop inside me again. He's not dealing with this—he's just *doing*, the way he does when he can't cope with emotions. There's no fallout for me in that—not yet—but when will that come? I can feel my nerves tingling already with the strain of waiting.

When I do go down, Portia is there eating scrambled eggs on toast, and Dan is chewing on a bagel. He's toasted one for me, too, and the toaster pops, making me jump. I can't meet his eyes right now, so I busy myself putting cream cheese on the bagel.

He's a little too hearty in the way he chats to Portia. She's monosyllabic in response, but that doesn't seem to faze him.

As soon as he returns from dropping Portia at school, he passes me the phone. "Will you make the call, or do you want me to?"

He's not giving me a choice, and I feel a spike of resentment.

"You've got to do this," he tells me firmly. "And after what happened last night, I'm not taking any chances." He checks my response and then adds, "I'm not talking about what you told me but what you *did* yesterday."

Picking up the knife. Yes, in the cold light of day, it chills me that I was in that state. And it terrifies Dan. He may be good at shuttering his face, but I know what's behind that and why he's developed this false heartiness.

I make the call. Dan wanders into the hall to give me some space, but I know he can still hear. Is this oppressive or supportive? I'm beyond discerning that. I'm in what I call "plug in and go" mode now, where I am so far beyond being OK that I have to tell myself to act and then blindly follow through without thinking. Thinking at times like this leads to nowhere good.

"She can see me this afternoon," I call to him when I hang up. "She's juggled something around to fit me in, but I'll be late home."

He appears in the doorway quickly. "That's great! Don't worry about dinner—I'll sort that out." He smiles too cheerfully for the situation. "So she did think you needed to see her today, then?"

I nod glumly.

"Good," he says again with that same forced brightness. "It's good she's taking it seriously." And then it seems to strike him that perhaps that isn't quite the right tone to take as he pauses and abruptly changes the subject. "So, I don't have to go in for another hour. Is there anything you want me to do to help around the house?"

I can't think straight. I just want to be alone at the moment.

"No, it's OK. I've made the call now. I'm fine. You go into work. I want to have some time to think about what I'm going to say to her."

"Yes, of course," he replies, and I can see him looking at me sideways, assessing how much of a risk I still am. "How are you feeling now?"

"I'm fine. It...it was a mistake, last night. I won't do it again."

"You need to talk to Stella properly about it. Are you sure you wouldn't like me to come with you? I don't want to intrude, but if you need some support—"

"Dan, it was a mistake. I've just told you. I didn't do it. I just had a thought."

"But I stopped you from doing it. What would you have done if I hadn't come in?"

"Nothing, and that's the truth. Nothing at that point. I was thinking, and I wasn't going to do it there and then, anyway. I wouldn't do that to you and Portia. That's actually what was going through my head. I will talk to Stella, I promise you, and I'll sort myself out."

He doesn't know if he can trust me and I can't stand seeing that, so I make an excuse that I need to go to the toilet and make my escape. By the time I come back, he's ready to go. He hugs me, and I avoid his eyes carefully. He's reluctant to go, but he can't avoid it now without telling me he doesn't believe what I've just said to him. I tell him I'll text him so he knows I'm OK.

Later in the day, I decide to make an effort when going to see Stella. I spend time doing my hair and makeup, which I haven't done for some time. My hair has grown completely out of what was a shoulder-length bob and it looks dull and lifeless, more muddy than blonde. My eyes look piggy and tired, and my skin is flaky. I do my best with moisturizer and concealer, but I still look far removed from how I did six months ago.

To my relief, Stella doesn't appear to think my behavior last night is a reason to call the hospital and have me committed. "I don't think, from what you've described, that you would have gone through with it at this time. It's not abnormal for someone to consider what you did in an abstract way. Suicidal ideation is a continuum, and although you picked up the knife, you're describing some strong messages you were sending yourself to prevent yourself from following through with it. What we need to look at is opening the box now and making sure you're able to talk about what you've been repressing. Your pain was telling you that you must do that, and now that you have, it will be a release of that pent-up pressure. We need to make sure it doesn't build up again like that."

That makes sense.

"Your reaction about what the policeman said is understandable. You're already struggling with guilt, and he has layered more on top of that. But that doesn't make him right. You know in your heart he's wrong and you didn't fall asleep. Let that burden go—it's not yours to carry."

"But what if it's worse? Why won't my mind let me remember? You said last time we spoke that it could be its way of protecting me when I'm not ready to remember. Well, if it is that, then it must be something awful. Did I do it? Did I do something worse?" My voice grows shrill with agitation.

"Do you think you did?"

I breathe in deeply and then out again in a sigh, trying to calm myself. "No. No, I don't, but it's more of the same. I don't think I did anything to cause the accident but because I don't know, that fear is always there. And that feeling that therefore, it must be something terrible. It's silly, isn't it? I don't think I fell asleep, but really, I've got no idea. I can't trust some vague, nebulous feeling, not over something so important."

"And that could be your anxiety talking."

It could, but it doesn't feel that way. It feels real. I grasp after the memory, but it skitters away again out of my reach, always just too far ahead for me to catch it.

What are you trying to tell me? I scream silently at my subconscious. *What happened?*

"And how did you feel after you told Dan about your choice?" she asks.

"I felt sick and empty, to be honest. It would be lovely to say I felt better and that everything suddenly became right between us again, but it isn't true. This morning, I just felt hollow, and I couldn't look him in the eye."

"What is it you're afraid of? He sounds as if he's coped well with what you've told him."

"He hasn't coped at all," I reply. "He's focusing on fixing me, and that's how he's distracting himself from dealing with what I've told him. Dan's like that. It's the same with grieving for Becca. He doesn't let himself stop to do that—he buries himself in doing things, always busy, never allowing the grief to control him. He's always in charge of it because he has to look after us, and that's what drives him. But slowly, those thoughts about what I did will creep back to him, and he'll be shocked. He'll see me differently. I won't be the same Lizzie he married, or the wife he thought he had last year."

Stella purses her lips. "We're none of us the same people we were last year, let alone twenty years ago. Perhaps you're having more trouble dealing with that than he is."

Is she right? *Is* she?

23

I SPEND A LOT OF my empty days now thinking about the past. It keeps me from dwelling on how awful the present is, from thinking about the police and what will happen next. From chasing that elusive memory that brings a paralyzing terror with it as it circles the perimeter of my mind. Sometimes I find I've sat for hours and not noticed that an entire morning has gone. I've never had this much time to fill before, and I don't know how to do it. I've no energy to do anything useful.

I can't even face going out. Every turn of the street makes me tremble at who I might see, because the sight of a small, fair-haired girl walking alongside her mother tears a savage hole inside me again. I want to fall to my knees right there on the street and howl out my pain into the uncaring concrete. I'm afraid that one day, I might do that.

I think about many things, trying to make sense of where my life is now, but of course I mostly think about Becca—both those long years of waiting for her and when she finally did arrive.

When we made the decision to stop IVF and adopt, it seemed as if we'd exchanged one kind of torturous waiting for another. I'd never been fool enough to think adoption would be an easy process, but the waiting and not-knowing takes it out of you in the same way IVF does. Waiting without certainty is the hardest to bear. You can wait forever if you know you'll succeed at the end of it all, but waiting without knowing is a special kind of torture.

We gritted our teeth through the interviews and spent long, anguished nights talking about our limits as a family around what kind of child we could take on. That made us examine the very depths of who we were, and it wasn't comfortable. It was an awful thing to have to decide who we might be saying no to, but the adoption worker told us how important it was.

"You already have a daughter, so it is vital to consider how another child will fit into your family and affect the dynamics. We want this to work for all of you, so, hard as it may be, you must be absolutely honest with yourselves."

And I really, really wanted a baby. Not an older child.

"Then you must stay true to that," she told me.

And I heaved a sigh of relief that she didn't try to persuade me that another, older child would really need us—though she did tell me the chances of getting a baby were much lower, and I had to cling on again in the void of waiting.

Portia's eighth birthday came and went and still, we were waiting.

I watched her blowing out her candles on the cake, and she looked up with a beaming grin and mouthed, "Thank you!" And then came the sinking realization that she hadn't looked at me at all as she did that, but at her father. I might as well have not been there.

I lay in bed that night, thinking. When had she stopped being pleased to see me when I picked her up from school? When had she stopped wanting to come with me all the time, even to do the supermarket shopping? When had she stopped telling me excitedly about her day? I'd thought she was just growing up, but she wasn't—she was growing away.

Not away from her dad, though. Just from me.

The next day, I rang in sick after Dan left for work and I told her we were playing hooky for the day. I made us a picnic and drove out to the forest with her.

"Why?" she asked.

"Because we need some girly time together, just me and you, like we used to."

Her eyes didn't light up as I'd hoped they would, but she dredged up a smile of some kind.

She gave me an odd look when I insisted she sit on the tailgate so I could help her on with her boots. Had I not done that for a long time? I wrapped her up in her mittens, scarf, and hat, and then pinched her nose and pretended to steal it. She did giggle then, and the tidal wave of relief knocked me back on my heels. She was still in there—we just needed to reconnect.

We walked along the children's sculpture trail, looking for carvings of badgers and foxes and elves hiding from plain view. We took pictures of each other in front of the giant sculptures of hawks and eagles. Portia dragged me into the den-making section. She actually grabbed me by the hand and pulled me in, and I laughed like a child. I had missed her so much and never even realized.

We had our picnic under an oak tree, its wide trunk protecting us from the gusts of wind. I wanted to ask her how she felt about the last years, the trying for a baby, her mother's hormones everywhere as she lurched from one fertility crisis to another, and now the adoption. I should have asked her—but I didn't dare. Her little brown eyes were shining, and I didn't want to dim them.

I was going to try harder. I was going to make sure she knew she was loved so much…

And I swallowed down the guilt, because we both knew that no matter how much I loved her, she hadn't been enough. I had still wanted another baby.

I could tell her about biology and hormones, and perhaps if she had been sixteen or seventeen, if she had had periods and PMS at least, she might have understood. But she was a child, and there was no way I could get her to comprehend what it was for a grown woman to want a child and what the force of nature could do to you.

Best now to make up for it. Best to give her all my attention. At least, then, when she was older, it would make sense to her, as long as I made amends now.

We arrived home, exhausted and grubby. I checked my messages while I ran her a warm bath.

"Hi. This is Adele from the Adoption Trust. Can you give me a call, please?"

And all of a sudden, there was Becca.

24

SHE HASN'T LEFT THE HOUSE *for days now. The curtains open and close and he comes and goes with the girl, but not her. She stays inside.*

I catch a glimpse of her from time to time at a window. She looks out but doesn't linger, as if nothing out here in the world interests her. She has imprisoned herself in there with her grief.

Nothing and no one touches her, not even her own family, it seems.

I see enough to know that. I can tell so much from shadows passing the windows, from the lights flicking on in the evening. They are three people living separate lives in there. Each locked away inside themselves.

I did that.

They say the loss of a child is the worst kind of suffering for a mother. I believe that is true. That's what I did to this woman.

He suffers, too, and so does the older girl. I did that, too, but I think it hurts the mother most.

I knew it would.

The other two go back to daily life, but she can't. And destroying her destroys him. He hurts all the more because she hurts. I hadn't known this about their relationship before, but I can see it now as I watch out here. I watch their every move.

25

IT'S AROUND THREE WEEKS AFTER what I now mentally refer to as the "shameful" incident with the kitchen knife. I see daily what it's cost Dan to find me in that state, the way his eyes constantly check me for signs I'm not coping again, for something he might have missed. He rushes home whenever he can, dropping in on me during the day with minor excuses, so it doesn't seem as though he's spot-checking on me. Stella has helped me cope and helped me see that some of those thoughts I was having are not necessarily true, but I'm still not sure what is reality and what's the product of my own self-torture.

The police will be back soon with the results of their investigations, and I still can't remember what happened that night. Can I trust my own feelings? Can I? Or are they right after all? If I don't remember soon, we could all be plunged further into a living nightmare. My blood chills a little whenever the doorbell rings during the day now. I'm constantly waiting for them to come back to tell me they've recovered the car, so at ten past eleven today, when it rings with force, I drop the cup I'm holding onto the tiled floor. It smashes into shards.

The bell rings again insistently as I stare at the broken pottery.

I dither, not knowing whether to go and answer or pick up the pieces. A third and longer demand from the bell sends me down the hall with my heart pounding.

I open the door.

"Oh my God, Lizzie! Why didn't you call me?" a voice demands, and I suddenly find myself enveloped in cashmere and perfume.

"Annika," I say weakly, returning her hug.

She bustles me into the house and holds me at arm's length. "I flew over when I heard. I can't believe you didn't call me."

And then I burst into tears. Loud, noisy, awful tears of complete gratitude.

She spins me by the shoulders. "Come on, inside! Now!" And she frog-marches me to the kitchen. "Oh!" She steps over the broken pottery and sits me at the table, then fishes in her expensive, oversized bag for a tissue.

I scrub my face with it as she gives me another big hug. Annika and I met at law school, and we've been close friends ever since. She was the girl with the loudest laugh in the room and the biggest hair, and back then, she was absolutely not my little Cornish girl's idea of what a lawyer should be. I sat next to her in the lecture hall because she was much less intimidating than those smooth, glossy girls who I could easily imagine eviscerating the defense in court. She later told me that I was infinitely more terrifying than any of them, but we were sharing a bottle of very cheap red wine at that moment and thinking how grown-up we were for doing that. We both laughed uproariously.

I haven't seen her face-to-face in nearly a year, as she's been on a sabbatical in the U.S.—a change of scenery after a bad breakup.

"Who called you?" I sniff.

She flicks the switch on the kettle and begins picking up the smashed cup. "Dan. Who else? He told me what happened." She gives me a stern look. "He told me everything. I cannot believe this has happened and I've only just found out. Why didn't you call? They're my goddaughters, and you're my best friend. I would have dropped everything to be here."

"I couldn't face seeing or speaking to anyone, not anybody, not for weeks. We had a closed funeral a month after we got out of the hospital. Just me and Dan and Portia and his parents. I don't think I could have handled anything else. I was on tranquilizers for the whole day as it was."

"You?" Annika exclaims as she tips the cup into the bin. "You never take anything. Are you still on them?"

"No, only that day. I would have never made it otherwise."

"Do you think you do need to see the doctor and get something?"

"No, I need for this all not to have happened. Is there a pill for that?"

She goes to answer, then stops, nods her understanding, and makes the tea. She sits across from me and holds my hand in a firm grip while we drink it.

"I've been trying to get in touch with you for ages, you know that. I thought you were just super busy at first, but then it went on too long. I got worried and called Dan."

I shake my head. "I didn't know. I deleted the message app on my phone when I got out of hospital. I haven't opened emails. To be honest, for a month, I hid my phone in a drawer so I didn't have to look at it. And the longer I went on shutting everything and everyone out, the less I wanted to have any contact. I couldn't...I couldn't deal with any of it." I look her in the eyes. "I still can't. I just want her back."

Annika scoots her chair next to me and wraps her arms round me again. "Of course you do, of course," she murmurs into my hair, stroking it to soothe me as one might a child.

I have needed her so badly, and I've been so far gone that I haven't even known. Apart from Dan and the girls, she's been the person closest to me ever since we met, and having her here is such a relief, one I didn't know I'd been wanting so desperately. I lean against her, exhausted.

"So what can I do to help?" she asks, and I'm relieved she doesn't suggest talking about the accident or Becca. "What do you need me to take care of?"

"You know about the problem with the police?"

"Yeah. Like I said, Dan told me everything."

"I don't know what to do about that, but Aidan's helping." I sit upright wearily. "Portia, though—I don't think she's coping too well, but she won't talk to me."

She nods. "OK. What's worrying you?"

"She's not herself. It's not just missing Becca. It's something else. She seems to have shut herself off from everyone. She never goes out, never talks to her friends..."

"A bit like you, then?" Annika quirks an eyebrow at me.

It's a fair enough point, but I know it's more than that. Something's wrong—my instinct tells me that. I shake my head. And I still have that fear that she remembers more than she's telling me.

"So I'll come 'round and have a catch-up with her. Maybe take her out shopping, stuff like that. See if I can draw it out of her. Will that help?"

Yes, it will. I'm hanging on here by my fingernails for what's left of my family. If I know Portia is all right, if she's taken care of when she won't let me do it, then that's the biggest weight off my shoulders. And I can keep hanging on.

"What about America? When do you need to go back?"

"I don't. I'm not going back. I told them I had more important stuff to do over here, so I took my chunk of leave, and I'll get back into work here next month." She leans back and smiles. "So you're not getting rid of me anytime soon. I'm here for you now, and I'm not going anywhere."

When she leaves in the afternoon, the life goes out of the house with her, but I still feel unaccountably calmer—and somehow as though there is more hope than there was yesterday.

26

DAN IS AT HOME WORKING on some papers when the police arrive. "Mr. Fulton?"

I hurry out into the hallway to see what's happening.

"Come in," my husband says with weariness. "What is it now?"

We go through to the sitting room, me hovering nervously by the door.

"We've recovered your car, and our investigations on it are concluded," the police officer tells us. He's younger than the others have been, with a frank and open expression, the kind you warm to when he isn't in your living room bringing bad news. "Mr. Fulton, could you accompany me to the station, please? We'd like to ask you some questions."

Dan raises an eyebrow. "Voluntarily?"

"Yes, Mr. Fulton."

"And will you be asking my wife to go down there?"

"No, sir, I don't believe so." He looks slightly taken aback, so I assume he hasn't been informed of what's gone on before.

This doesn't make sense. Why do they want to speak to Dan? He wasn't even there.

Dan taps his finger against his lips thoughtfully. "Are you able to give us any information about what's been found?"

"No, sir, I'm afraid not."

My husband gives a resigned smile and nods, and I'm confused. Why can't they tell him what they found? He's not a suspect.

It's only as Dan moves to the door to leave with the police officer that I grasp what he has known from the start of this visit: they want him at the station because he *is* a suspect.

"Whoa! Stop! Why are you taking him?"

The officer glances at my husband to answer, but no, I'm not having that. He may be young, but he's the one who invaded my house and disturbed what little peace we have.

"Why?" I demand.

My heart is thumping with the sudden stress, but with the adrenaline comes a surge of the old Lizzie, and I let her take over.

"Why are you taking my husband for questioning?"

"I'm sorry, Mrs. Fulton, I can't reveal any details at this stage, but we do have some questions we need to try to find answers to. We're asking Mr. Fulton to assist us." The officer gives me a polite smile. "I'm sorry to disturb you both, and I hope we won't inconvenience you for too long."

I don't trust a word of his engaging manner. He's been sent precisely because of it, I'm sure of that, to prevent more complaints and to lull us into a false sense of security.

"Lizzie, I'll go and speak to them at the station," Dan says as my guts clench in fear. "It shouldn't take long."

"I'll call Aidan. He can meet you there."

"That would be really helpful, thanks," Dan replies and adds to the officer, "He's my lawyer."

He gets his coat and leaves with the policeman, who apologizes again for disturbing me. Dan gives me a kiss on the doorstep. "Don't worry—I'll be back soon."

As soon as the door closes, I call Aidan, my skin chill with a cold sweat. Inside, every nerve I have is screaming in fear and frustration. His phone goes to voicemail, so I call Annika too.

"Dan's what?" she says. "Hang on—I'm on the other side of town, but I'll come over."

"Thanks. Oh wait, I've got to go. Aidan's calling back."

"I'll be with you soon."

I swap calls, relief flooding through me at the sound of Aidan's voice. "They've finished the forensics on the car. A policeman has just been here."

"Did they try to question you?" Aidan's voice sharpens at the news.

"No, Dan was here. But they've asked him to go with them."

"Right. Which station? Reading?"

"Yes. Can you get there?" I'm trying to stay calm, but I know it's clear to him how worried I am.

"I'm turning the car round now. Did they give anything away?"

"No, the officer wouldn't tell us anything, but they've obviously found something unexpected." And the unexpected terrifies me. I've been lost in this world where I have no control for so long now. How much worse is it going to get?

"Don't panic. You know they always question the people closest to a victim first. It's standard."

"So why not me?" And as soon the words leave my mouth, I know the answer. It's because they think I was a victim too.

No longer a suspect now, but a victim.

What's going on here?

"I'll call you when I know something," Aidan tells me.

It's an hour before Annika arrives. An hour during which I pace the carpet endlessly and stare out of the window in the vain hope that I'll see Dan suddenly return. It's illogical—it's far too soon, but I keep hoping he'll have smoothly cleared everything up and be sent on his way.

"I'm so sorry," Annika says when she does arrive, looking harassed. "The traffic was terrible. Any news yet?"

There isn't, and after I fill her in on what happened, there's nothing for us to do but sit and wait for when Aidan can call to update us.

"How long do you think they'll be?" I ask Annika.

We're interrupted by the doorbell ringing again. I recoil as I open it and see who's there.

"Hello again, Mrs. Fulton. Detective Sergeant Booth, remember?"

"How could I forget?" I reply dryly. I'm a little bit tougher and more together than the last time he was here, and he's not going to cow me so easily now. I've already worked out why he's turned up—Aidan is tied up with Dan, and he thinks I'll be alone. This guy plays dirty. It's a dangerous game, and Dan would take him apart in court over it.

"Can I have a quick word?" He gives me an encouraging grin. "It really won't take long."

I can tell he's trying to play me onside. And he has a different sidekick with him today.

Annika is lurking behind me. "What's he up to?" she hisses at me, her suspicion flaring to match mine. "Is this the guy Dan complained about?"

"Hi," he calls to her brightly. "Just need a little chat. I won't keep her. I promise."

I stand aside and let him in.

"Lizzie, what are you doing?" Annika says, appalled.

"You'll find out. Come on." This might not be Annika's usual line of work, but Booth doesn't need to know that, and she'll carry it through well enough to fool him.

"Oh," Booth says, "I—"

"She's staying," I say firmly. "She's my legal adviser. Anything you want to say to me, you can say in front of her."

He's nonplussed, which is exactly how I wanted him.

I gesture to everyone to sit down. "So, why are you here?" I say pleasantly, and I see Annika pull a face halfway between a wince and a smile.

"The forensic investigations on your car are complete, Mrs. Fulton."

"I know. So are you here to apologize for accusing me of falling asleep at the wheel and killing my daughter?"

He gives what he hopes is an appeasing smile, I expect, but it doesn't cut it. "Sorry, Mrs. Fulton, you know how it is—we have to pursue those angles."

I raise an eyebrow. "You didn't have to pursue them as you did. And what exactly is going on with my husband now?"

He flashes that wolfish smile again. "That's what I wanted to talk to you about."

I nod at him to go on, my arms folded and the impatience I want him to see clearly displayed on my face.

"Mrs. Fulton, the forensic report showed something we didn't expect. It appears the brakes on your car may have been tampered with." He pauses to let that sink in, and my arms drop to my sides in shock. "I'm afraid the report is inconclusive, as it's also possible that the damage could have occurred during the descent into the lake, but on the balance of probability, our forensics expert feels that there's a strong possibility the car was deliberately damaged. That's why I'm here."

I go numb. My ears are ringing with his words, but they make no sense. I cannot take this in.

"I'm sorry, I don't quite follow," I say in a voice that sounds very unlike my own. It doesn't even feel as if it comes from me. On the opposite chair, I see that Annika is sitting equally stunned, her mouth agape.

"Somebody may have deliberately caused your accident, Mrs. Fulton."

I let the words play again in my head, over and over. *Deliberate.*

Someone tried to hurt us? Someone. Hurt. My baby.

It's not possible. Who would do that? Why?

No, this isn't right. They've got it wrong again, just like they got it wrong about me falling asleep at the wheel. They have no idea what they're doing, and they're fumbling blindly.

"May have caused it? What do you mean, may?"

He purses his lips. "I wish I could be more definite, but the damage to the brakes is too marginal. They weren't cut through—that would be easy to identify. Our investigator reported that they look as if they've been weakened by abrasion, making them less effective, so in the event of an emergency stop, they would fail. But it's also possible that what he's found could have been caused as you skidded down the bank. He's the expert, though, and he thinks that's less likely."

I swallow hard. I don't know what this news makes me feel yet. And it's inconclusive. Booth has his doubts, I can tell. "Is there anything else?" I ask him.

"It would explain why we didn't find a braking pattern on the road, as we'd expect to. It would also tie in with your assurances that you didn't fall asleep at the wheel." He's watching me so carefully as he says this that I know he's personally still not convinced.

Annika, however, is watching me equally carefully. She has my back if I stumble.

"So what now?" I ask.

"We'll be looking into any possible motives someone might have for damaging your car."

I nod slowly, a calculated gesture. It'll give him the impression I'm more in control than I feel. It's a move I've used often in court, and I know its effect. "And that's why you're questioning my husband, I take it."

His eyes narrow imperceptibly. He's still trying to judge my reactions, and he's struggling. "We always question close relatives. You know that."

"Of course." I give him my best professional smile. "But Dan didn't have anything to do with it. He is not responsible in any way; I can assure you of that. It would be a far better use of your time to get on with investigating elsewhere."

He accepts that without demur, even though I can see he doesn't believe me. "So is there anyone else you think we should look at?"

"No, I really can't think of anyone, but Dan may be able to. Why don't you ask him that instead of what you *are* questioning him about?"

He starts to answer, but Annika cuts in. "I think you've got what you need now," she says, getting up. "Thanks for your time. I'm sure you understand this has been a shock for Lizzie, and she needs time to think about it. If she has any thoughts on who might be responsible, we'll come back to you."

He hesitates but then gives a curt nod and allows her to show him out.

Annika comes back in. "Are you OK? What the hell is going on? What haven't you told me?"

"Nothing! I don't know what's going on either. I can't get my head around this."

She sits down opposite me. "Lizzie, this is serious shit. He's saying he thinks someone cut your brakes—"

"No, damaged, not cut."

"Yes, whatever—damaged, then. Oh my God, who would want to do that to you? You seriously have no idea?"

I'm still struggling to take it in. Dan and I, we're just a normal couple. We work hard, we pay our taxes, we bring up our kids as best we can. This doesn't happen to people like us. Why would anyone want to hurt the girls and me?

"No, I really don't. Not off the top of my head like that. If it had happened to you, could you just pull the name of someone who wanted to kill you out of the air?"

"No, because—" She stops herself. "OK, fair point. I don't know why anyone would want to do this to you either. But this changes everything, Lizzie. You all have to be really careful, and we have to figure this out."

I take a deep breath. "Assuming their theory is correct. Maybe this is just another cock-up. I don't trust the police anymore."

Is this why I can't remember, though? Has it got something to do with this?

I need time to think. I need time alone. I dispatch Annika to collect Portia from school because Dan obviously won't be able to collect her as usual. She's hesitant because she doesn't need to leave yet and she wants to stay and talk, but she accepts my excuse that the traffic could be bad and goes. Portia can't be left alone out there, not after what the police have just told us.

And that feeling she had that she was being followed fills me with a whole new level of alarm.

This is the last thing I expected. If I weren't a lawyer, I might have panicked more about the fact that they're questioning Dan, but Aidan is right. In any suspected foul play, the spouse is always the first one under suspicion, but I know he'd never do anything to hurt the girls.

Think, think, Lizzie. What is going on here?

So they no longer suspect me of falling asleep at the wheel. In any other circumstance, I should be relieved. I've been waiting for this moment to feel free of guilt, but instead, something awful has come to take its place. There's no relief, only a new kind of torture as I realize the implications of what DS Booth has told me.

I might not be responsible, but someone else is. I've swapped one kind of hanging in limbo for another—one that's perhaps even worse.

If I had fallen asleep, it would have been an accident. A dreadful, monstrous thing to live with, but...

But a deliberate act? That's another league entirely. Someone tried to kill us.

I still can't believe it. But it all comes down to this: someone killed Becca.

I can feel a bubbling of rage inside that threatens to overpower me, but again, now is not the time. Now I need to think and be logical; anger and logic don't go together. They will question me again. After they have spoken to Dan, whatever his responses, they will speak to me.

I don't know what happened to that car, and I don't know exactly what they've found with those brakes, but I know one thing: Dan did not do it. Oh, we've seen the full gamut, between us, he and I, the things people will do. There are times I've cried over cases and wondered what it is that makes us human, because too many people seem to be lacking it. I've seen Dan lose sleep over some of the defenses he's had to mount. You don't work in our jobs for so many years without seeing some of the most horrible aspects of humanity.

But Dan would never, never hurt his kids. If he wanted out of our marriage, he'd divorce me. He'd put up a fight in court over custody. And I know the police are going to be all over the state of our marriage now. But he would not harm a hair on Portia's or Becca's heads.

They've got the wrong man in for questioning. Of that I'm sure.

But how do I help him prove that? And how do we find out who really did this?

27

I SAW THE POLICE TAKE *him. I didn't think that would happen. What do they know? I can only guess.*

She's not come out yet, but another policeman comes and goes.

Is this the beginning of the end? Will they start to understand now?

28

AIDAN CALLS ME AT 5 p.m. "Can you come to my place? They've let Dan go and he's here, but we need to talk—and not in front of Portia. Can you get away?"

"Yes, Annika's here, but I'll need to call a taxi."

"Don't do that—I'll pick you up. Be there in twenty."

I'm outside waiting when he arrives, and I hop into the car as he pulls over.

"What's happening?" I ask anxiously as he pulls away again.

"Well, they've let him go, but they've not ruled him out by any means."

"Has he got an alibi?"

"He was working at home all day, but he's told them that will match up with emails he's sent. And they'll ask the neighbors about his car and check his accounts to see if there are unexpected transactions. It would be easier if he had a straightforward alibi, but he's given them access to his laptop and his email accounts so that they can go through everything."

"Did that shut them up?"

"It made them stop in their tracks a bit, but they still appear to be keen on pursuing the angle that he had something to do with it. There was a suggestion that if he didn't do it himself, he might have hired someone."

I lapse into silence to digest this and let him negotiate the busy traffic until we get back to his flat. What are they up to? Is it possibly a countermove to unsettle me because they still think I'm responsible? But that wouldn't make sense if the brakes were actually damaged before the accident. Perhaps Booth thinks they weren't, though, and he's still going down the route of it being my driving. That would actually be a relief now, as at least it would mean nobody out there tried to kill us.

Dan is waiting inside for us, his face haggard and shocked.

"Are you OK?" I say in a rush, taking his hands.

"Yeah, I think so," he replies in a dazed way. "I just can't take it in. I keep thinking they must be wrong and the damage must have been done during the crash. I can't believe somebody could have done this on purpose to you and the girls."

We're both in shock, I recognize that. We sit together, reeling from it, while Aidan discreetly leaves us.

After a while, Dan kisses my hand, as if he'd meant to do so before but had forgotten. "Are you OK?" he asks.

"Yes." I can't actually say anything else. I'm too stunned. It takes me several minutes to ask him, "Was it awful?"

"The questioning?" He shrugs. "It wasn't pleasant. I could have handled it better when they were asking me about why I'd wanted to hurt you and the girls if I hadn't kept thinking about how someone out there, someone unknown, had tried to do just that. I feel sick. I can't get it out of my head."

His hand is trembling in mine. That's what scares me—that my hyper-sensible husband is so shaken. I'm not able to ground us now—I need Dan to do that, and if he can't, I don't know how I'll cope. He's held us together these past months. If he falls apart, we all will.

Seeing him like this rocks me completely, but I can't let him know that. He's in no state to deal with me being weak. I have to at least pretend to be something of who I was. "Dan, if someone did do this, they'll find them."

"If I did something to cause this—to make someone want to hurt you that much—I'll never forgive myself," he says, and suddenly his eyes frighten me. He looks like he's just been plunged into a private hell. I know that look.

"Dan?" I say, and I hate myself because my voice wobbles, betraying me. "We don't know for sure it was deliberate. They said it might have happened when the car went down the bank."

"I know." He quickly turns away. "I'm all right," he says. "It's just the shock."

It's not, and I know it. We're both in uncharted territory here, with no idea how to navigate this or how to help the other. I wonder if he feels, too, that terrible anger that I had brewing inside me earlier. Has that reached him yet, or is he still too stunned? The latter, I think—he seems more numb than enraged.

Aidan checks back in on us. "So, look," he says, taking in the state both of us are in, "let's think about some practicalities here. We need to get some logic applied to this. If it was a deliberate attempt to damage the brakes, it's a funny one. They weren't cut through. The brake lines seem to have abraded in some way to do enough damage to function for a while but then give out. I can't understand why somebody would do it like that."

"It's the *who* that matters," Dan replies. He turns to me. "You know what they asked me? They asked me if I was having an affair and whether it could be my mistress trying to hurt you all. An affair—me, after all the years we've been together. It made me so cross, and I kept thinking, *I bet they've asked Lizzie that too*. I told them I had no desire to have a bloody affair, and even if I did, I have no time to, anyway!"

That is so utterly Dan that it breaks the tension a little, and I manage a smile. No, Dan wouldn't have an affair. If he wanted to be with someone else, he'd do it in the right order and leave me first. That's just how he's made.

"I'm so sorry they suspect you," I tell him.

He shrugs. "Par for the course, isn't it? And it's the same as they did to you. I just wish I knew who did do it. It's driving me insane, thinking about it. If it is something to do with me, I think that'd finish me, after all we've been through already."

And that is so unlike him that the marrow freezes in my bones. Dan's too stoic to be defeated. Isn't he?

"You're assuming anyone did it. They could be wrong. They've been wrong with everything so far. Maybe this is more of the same. It's perfectly credible that the brakes got damaged when I went off the road. We could be worrying about nothing." And sitting here in Aidan's brightly lit flat, with my husband and his friend around me, that seems a more likely prospect than it did when DS Booth broached it. I can't believe that anyone has done this deliberately. Why would they? Of course I reacted in panic at the start, but it seems so improbable now, and it has an air of unreality.

Dan's not quite caught up with my line of thinking. I can tell that from his face, but then he's just been grilled at the police station for hours, so of course he'll feel differently.

I draw a deep breath in and then breathe out to calm myself. If only I could remember what happened, this would all be different, but I can't. And we both know that the harder I try, the more difficult it is for the memories to return.

"We can't tell Portia," Dan says. "We need to make something up. She mustn't know. And she mustn't go to school on her own either."

"Why do you think it's something to do with you?" Aidan asks.

"It's got to be, when you think of what it must have taken to plot to damage brakes like that and then carry it out. That's criminal intent, and those are the kind of people I deal with—the type who'd do that and not lose a minute's sleep. To do that to a family, to children, you have to operate on a different level than the rest of us. There can't be much humanity left in you, and that describes some of my clients." He's shivering from holding back his emotions, but the horror of what he's thinking shows in his eyes. "It might be someone getting back at me. It might be my fault."

I look at my husband as he sits with his head in his hands. Dan believes it. He thinks someone did this to us. And my sudden burst of optimism is at an end because, of all of us, he is the least likely to overreact.

So who did this, and why?

Fears trickles down my back like the slow drip, drip of water from an icicle, and this time, it won't be dismissed.

29

THE FRONT DOOR OPENS AND I hear Dan say, "Well, if you won't talk to me, then talk to your mother." Then there is the rapid stamp of feet up the stairs.

What's wrong? Dan's back from school with Portia on time, but something has happened. I go out into the hall, and he looks at me helplessly. "She's upset," he says, "but I can't find out what it's about."

My hand flies to my mouth. "You don't think she's been followed again?"

"She can't have been. I was at the gates waiting for her."

"Do you think she went out at lunchtime? Maybe we should say something to her, given—"

He puts his finger to his lips to shush me. "Be careful. She might be listening."

It's only been a couple of days since the police took Dan in, and we're still trying to come to terms with the news. We've been racking our brains since then, trying to think of someone we know who could do something like that, but the weekend has gotten in the way of Dan's plans to pull out all his old case files and go through them. He's had to wait until today to have them brought out of office archives. He has a box of them under his arm now.

I wait for a few minutes to see if Portia comes back down and then walk slowly up the stairs. Her bedroom door remains shut when I knock, so I tentatively try the handle. The door's locked.

"Portia?" I call. "Is everything OK?"

"Go away!" Her voice is muffled, and I can tell immediately that she's crying.

"Portia, please let me in."

"Get away from me!" she screams back, clear as a bell now and furious.

I take a step back in shock. I'm not sure what to do next.

"I'll give you a little while, and then I need to see you're OK," I tell her through the door, and I go and wait in our bedroom. I'm not sure if this is the right thing to do or not, but attempting to placate her through a closed door doesn't look as if it's going to be effective.

The minutes tick by, and she shows no sign of coming out of her bedroom. Maybe I'm overreacting and this is just a trivial teenage thing, but I need answers and I don't have the tolerance levels to wait. My anxiety flares these days like a forest fire after a tinder-dry summer.

I brace myself to try again.

"Portia, are you OK?"

"I want to be left alone."

"Well, I can't do that until I know how you are. Can you open the door, please? Just speak to me, and then I'll leave you alone, if that's what you want."

There's no reply.

"Portia, please. Don't make me go and get the key."

After a moment, I hear the lock turn. When I try the handle again, the door opens, and Portia is lying facedown on her bed.

"What's wrong?"

"Nothing." Her answer is almost lost in her pillow.

"It doesn't look like nothing." And then I notice something. "What's this bruise on your neck?" There's a long, thin, purple welt just above her shirt collar. It starts at the side of her neck and extends to the front. I flatten the pillow down to see better.

"For God's sake. It's nothing!" She whirls her head around, and her face is screwed up in a snarl, awash with tears. "Will you just leave me alone!"

Her ferocity rocks me. "Not until you tell me how you got that bruise." I can see it clearly now—a vicious line across her throat.

"I got hit in hockey. It's nothing. And I'm fine. I just had a row with somebody."

"Did the school send a note home?"

"No, because I didn't tell them. Because I didn't make a great steaming fuss like you're doing, because it's not a big deal!" Her voice rises to a screech. She rolls back into her pillow, her fists balled up into the quilt. "Please just go away. I'll be fine. I just don't want to talk to anyone right now."

I want to touch her, to stroke her back, her hair, anything to make her feel better. But I'm terrified of making things worse.

"I'll be downstairs then," I tell her. "Come down when you feel like getting something to eat."

But she never does come down for dinner, and when I check in on her later, she's crawled under the covers and fallen asleep.

"Leave her," Dan says as he looks in over my shoulder. "If she says it's nothing, we'll just have to trust her and take her at her word."

But I'm not so certain. That bruise… I'm not sure I believe her.

30

I RUN DOWNSTAIRS AS DAN drops Portia back from school the next day. Once he's seen her through the front door, he goes straight back out to work. Portia eyes me warily as I go toward her.

"Good day?"

"Yeah, OK."

She's just going to go up to her room now and shut herself in and me out, as she always does these days. This isn't normal, even if she is upset about her sister. Something is wrong, and I need to find out what. Dan and I may be facing the most horrible situation of our lives, but I still need to hold my daughter together as best I can. She spends all her time alone. I'm certain now she isn't going up there and chatting to her friends. She's flicking around on her phone constantly like all girls her age, but I've been watching her carefully. She never seems to text. Whatever she's doing on there doesn't seem to cheer her up either.

"Would you like to make a cake?"

"What?" She stares at me as if I've grown another head.

"I thought it would be nice. Something to do together. You used to love baking with me."

She screws up her face. Such a pretty face—sharp-featured like a little vixen, but delicate. Annika says she looks elfin and I can see what she means. "When I was six, maybe."

A little piece of me dies another death. "Oh, OK then."

I walk past her and into the kitchen, where I put on the kettle. I don't really want tea, but it's something to do to relieve the ache inside.

"I suppose we could, though."

Portia's voice behind me makes me jump. I hadn't realized she was still there.

"What?"

"Make a cake," she replies in an ungracious voice. "We could, if you really want to."

It's on the tip of my tongue to tell her it doesn't matter because obviously, she doesn't want to, but I catch her eye and think I see an awkwardness there. It reminds me of her father.

Maybe I'm wrong about her not wanting to do this.

"Yes, let's," I say, trying to sound cheerful and enthusiastic as I would have been if we'd been doing this when she was six. "Come on, pick a recipe."

I herd her through the kitchen like a lost sheep, and perhaps that's exactly what she is. We flick through a recipe book together, and she chooses banana loaf cake. I'm relieved because I know we'll have the ingredients. She tells me her choice in the same graceless tone she used earlier, but I brush that aside.

We work together on the cake, and while it bakes, I make us that cup of tea I'd been intending to make earlier. It isn't the same lighthearted fun as it would have been when she was six. We don't flick flour at each other or laugh uproariously or hug with greasy, dusty hands as we would have done then. Neither of us is ready for that. We are too raw for fun.

Fun is what we did with Becca.

I stop halfway across the kitchen, aghast. Portia doesn't notice, as she's looking at the cake through the oven door.

It's true. Somewhere along the way, Portia and I stopped having fun with each other, and only when Becca was there did we do that.

I feel sick. How could I have let that happen?

I sink into a chair in front of the table with my cup of tea. It can't be true. It's the grief talking, that's all. If I think hard enough, I'll remember. When was the last time we had fun together, just me and her?

She looks questioningly at me, and I go over and over memories with frantic speed but draw a blank.

Later, later... I can't waste this time with her now.

"I'd never had banana loaf until I gave birth to you," I tell her, and I see the interest catch in her face. "I always thought it sounded disgusting—you know I don't like the texture of bananas. And then when I got home from the hospital, a friend brought one 'round that she'd made. And it was amazing—the best I've ever tasted."

Portia raises an eyebrow at me. "Mine might be better," she says in a mock-haughty voice that makes me smile.

"It may be," I reply, my smile broadening at her uptilted nose trying to look superior.

The comical look fades quickly from her face, which crumples up as her voice cracks in a sob. "When does it get better?"

I reach across the table and grab her hand tight. "It gets bearable one day, but it never goes away." For her, that will be true. That's how it was for me when I lost my parents, and that's how it will be for her over her sister.

It's different for a mother. I don't know what the truth will be for me.

"I heard someone at school saying today what a bitch I was for not being the one who stayed behind in the car to let my little sister be rescued." Her dark eyes plead with me to understand.

"You were unconscious!"

"She didn't know that."

"Then I'll damn well tell her. Who is she?"

"She doesn't matter. She's not a friend."

"She's certainly not. She's an idiot."

Portia takes a deep breath in and holds it for a moment. And I think, with a horrible sinking feeling, that I know what she's going to ask me. And I go dizzy and faint at the thought of having to answer.

"Mum—"

The oven timer buzzes.

I leap up gratefully. "Oh, I think it's done. Can you get the cooling rack, please?"

By the time the cake is out and cooling, the moment is lost, and Dan comes home soon after to the smell of warm cake wafting through the house. He sits in the kitchen with us, and we drift around making supper after a while. It is pleasant. It's not like it used to be, not at all, but it's something worth having.

It *is* something worth having. Despite what might be waiting out there to threaten us all. Despite the shadows.

For this moment, though, as we sit round the table and eat impromptu fajitas with what we happened to find in the fridge and the pantry, while we make vague conversation about how the day has gone and Dan relates an amusing anecdote about the judge's frustration with a counsel, it is enough for me to take in a kind of normality and find some comfort in that.

Portia is smiling at her father. It's a faint, weak version of her old grin, but it's still there. She picks at her food, but she manages to eat enough for me to feel relief that she's had a decent meal for once.

There is no script for grief, Stella says, and we all find our way on our own terms. We may not be dealing with Becca's loss spectacularly well, but we are learning how to deal with it and the new versions of each other. We have made baby steps.

I get up and cut the banana cake. Portia takes a mouthful and chews thoughtfully, then looks over to me and raises an eyebrow in question.

I finish my own bite and nod. "Yours is better," I tell her.

She grins, and for a moment there, I have my little girl back again. It is enough.

31

I WAKE IN THE MIDDLE of the night in that sudden, alert way that tells me I won't be able to go back to sleep. I toss and turn for a while. Sleep is going to evade me for hours, and I will have to face that lonely journey from 2 a.m. to 3 a.m. to 4 a.m. on my own as Dan is curled on his side, dead to the world in the sleep of the utterly exhausted.

Eventually, a memory worms its way into my conscious mind. It's the one that probably woke me in the first place.

It was ten years ago, and I'd picked Dan up after court. His face was white. "What's up?" I asked.

"Tell you later," he said. "Can we just get to the garage now, so I can pick my car up?"

It should have been a no-effort thing—I was working from home, so I'd driven him to work after he'd dropped his car off to be serviced. I picked him up later, after I'd collected Portia from school. She sat in the back of the car playing with a dolly, with the complete unconcern of a five-year-old to the weird moods of adults.

Dan jerked his head back toward her for emphasis.

OK, I got it. Not now, with her in the car. I shivered—what was going on?

When we got back to the house, he disappeared into the study. "Need to arrange something," he muttered before shutting the door firmly.

Portia and I stared at the door in confusion. Then I shrugged. "Daddy has some very important work, darling. Would you like to help Mummy make cheesy pasta?"

Dan emerged for supper, a grim line about his mouth, but he put Portia to bed as usual. When he came down the stairs, he scuttled back into the study, but I wasn't going to be put off that easily.

I poured us both a whiskey and followed him in.

"What happened?"

He grimaced as the fire of the whiskey hit the back of his throat. "You got the big hitter out, then?" he commented, referring to the expensive single malt I'd bought him last Christmas.

"You looked like you might need it," I replied, curling up in the leather armchair. I always found it a touch clichéd in a barrister's study, but he liked that traditional kind of thing. I went along with it. "Go on, what is it?"

He sighed. "A rough case."

"Yes?" I prompted. He wasn't going to get away that easily.

"It didn't go well. OK?"

"You've had other cases that haven't gone well. There's more here. Come on, Dan—what happened?"

He took a swig of the whiskey. "My client didn't get off."

"It happens," I acknowledged. Dan was good, very good, but even he couldn't win all of them. Some people were just plain guilty, and no jury in the land would find them innocent. I wasn't sure yet why this seemed to have affected him so much.

"Not to him. He was determined he wasn't being sent down, so he didn't take it well when he got a unanimous conviction."

"Has he been sentenced yet?"

Dan rubbed his eyes. "No, and after his behavior in court today, he's likely to get a lengthy one."

"Why? What happened? Can you start at the beginning, please?"

Dan looked cagey, as if he wasn't prepared to disclose all of it. That wasn't like him.

"I really don't—"

"Dan!"

"OK, OK. His name is Timothy Vaughan. He's a businessman, and by that I mean he's got too many businesses to count, all of them dodgy, and most of them fronting a drug or prostitution racket. He was up for the attempted murder of a business colleague."

"You sound like you weren't comfortable representing him from the outset, but you've never said anything about him before. Why not?"

"No, I wasn't happy taking him on. There's something about this guy I don't want to be around. But that's the job sometimes, and he was paying well. He was prepared to pay silly money."

"So?"

He wouldn't meet my eyes. "So we needed it."

I put my drink down. "And why did we need it so badly?" This was unexpected. I didn't think he was worried about money.

"We *might* need it." He swallowed. "For treatment. You know."

"Oh, Dan, you said we were fine."

"And we are, but IVF costs a lot."

I got up and put my arms around him. He felt tense, and that unnerved me. "So what happened?"

"He went for me in court once the verdict was announced."

"He went for you? You mean he attacked you? How?" Even in Dan's line of work, this was unheard-of. No wonder he was reacting oddly. My husband wasn't the dramatic type, but anyone would be shocked that that could happen in a courtroom.

"I don't know. He took everyone by surprise. He launched at me past the police, and they didn't stop him in time."

"He hit you?"

"He had me by the throat, yelling in my face."

I pulled his collar open. There was a horrible ring of mottled purple round his neck. I could even make out the finger marks. "Oh my God, Dan!"

He tugged away from me. "Yes, I know."

"What did he say?" Because I sensed this wasn't just about the man's actions. He was keeping something from me. How much worse could it get? I had a bad feeling about this now.

Dan looked away. "Just sound and noise. Nothing important. I couldn't make out most of it. He was all but frothing at the mouth. Look, forget it. It's not a big thing. It just took me aback that court security could be so lax."

And no matter what I said after that, he wouldn't tell me any more. So the next day, I made some calls. It didn't take long. Attacks like this were rare in court, and our little world was buzzing with it. He was going to kill Dan; that's what Timothy Vaughan had said. He was going to make sure he never felt safe in his own bed again. He would make him pay.

I was frustrated with Dan for not telling me, but of course he would try to protect me from that.

Was I scared? I was certainly unsettled. Half of me thought it was just bluster on Vaughan's part. A lot of temper and shouting as he was taken down, coupled with some slack security that allowed him to get further than he should have. It didn't really mean anything.

But I was a mother, with all the anxieties that come with motherhood, and it wasn't as easy to shake off my fears. When you have a child, you fear so much more for them than for yourself, and I did fear he might try to hurt Portia to get back at Dan. The man hadn't said that. All his rage had been directed at Dan himself, and there was no mention of hurting his family. All the same, that was what my mind leaped to. It was nearly a year before I stopped looking over my shoulder in the street when I was out with Portia.

It's a decade ago now. It can't be anything to do with Timothy Vaughan, surely? He'd have gotten to us from prison if he were serious. His kind knows how to do that. But how many more Timothy Vaughans have there been?

It's as if a shadowy crowd lines up before my mind's eye, all silent and darkly threatening. An unknown army of people who might want to hurt us. It's overwhelming.

I lie still and try to breathe as panic, like asthma, assails me.

32

WHEN DAN GETS OUT OF the shower, he gives me a questioning glance. "What is it? Why are you looking at me like that?"

"I woke up last night. You know when your subconscious gives you a prod? Well, you remember that guy Vaughan?"

Dan freezes in the act of toweling himself dry. "Yes," he says, his voice suddenly hoarse. "What made you think of him?"

"I told you, my subconscious." I remember what Dan said after he was questioned *If I did something to cause this, I'll never forgive myself*—and I wonder if it was this he meant. "I still think it could be accidental, and Booth definitely still suspects I fell asleep. It's written all over him. I just could not imagine why someone would want to do this to us deliberately. And then I remembered Vaughan. Do you think he could have something to do with it, after all this time?"

And I can tell immediately from the way his face shuts down that I am right and that he's been tormenting himself with this question. "I'm afraid," he says slowly, "that it could be one of my clients."

I take a deep breath. "Is there anyone specific, other than him?"

"No." He rubs his eyes as if he's trying to force some image away from them, and I wonder what that might be. "I've thought and thought about it, but there isn't just one on the list—that's the problem."

"You have a list? Or is that just a turn of phrase?"

"No, I have a list," he replies glumly. "When I started going through my case files, I wrote down anyone I thought might have a grudge against me. There's been a lot over the years."

I digest this news with difficulty. It's one thing me considering it, but another to find my levelheaded husband so rattled.

Only perhaps this time, maybe it *did* actually happen.

"Isn't that true for me, too, then?"

"Maybe. Who knows? None of this makes sense." Dan slumps down in the chair, watching me. "I went through everyone, Lizzie. People I've defended who didn't get off. People on the other side—victims—who might blame me. I don't have one name, I just don't. I've tried and tried."

"Have any of them made outright threats?"

"No, nothing like that."

"But Vaughan did. And it may be years ago, Dan, but I think we should go to the police anyway. It's the only lead we have right now."

Dan drives us there. I sense a certain ripple at the reception desk. It feels like hostility, and by now, I'm not surprised by that, only that the people on the desk know who he is. I'm not used to thinking of the police in this way. All my life, they've been on the right side.

Dan sits silently next to me in the interview room.

After around ten minutes, DS Booth comes in. I see his hackles rise as soon as he sees Dan, but my husband shows no reaction. That's odd. It's almost as if Booth knows him already, but Dan doesn't appear to recognize him.

"So, how can I help you?" Booth asks in a voice that sounds as if helping us is the last thing he wants to do.

"We've been trying to figure out who might hold a grudge against us. Who might have damaged the car."

He pulls an expression that can only be described as a smirk, directed at Dan.

My husband's had enough of the attitude and gives Booth a hard look. "Do I know you?"

"The Karl Hennessy case. I was the investigating officer."

Dan frowns. "Yes, I remember it."

"And do you remember what happened after you got him off?"

"I do. But what you need to understand is that anyone accused of a crime in this country has a right to be defended against that accusation, and my job is to defend them to the best of my ability. Yours is to gather the evidence against them. You didn't do that well enough in this case."

Booth looks like he's about to explode, and Dan remains as unruffled as ever.

"What's going on here?" I demand.

"DS Booth's referring to a case I defended about five years ago. My client went free."

"He was a rapist. And he went free to do it again to another woman," Booth snarls. "How do you go home and face your wife after that?"

"Excuse me!" I bark at him. "The accused have a right to a defense, and it's a lawyer's job to do that. We don't commit the crimes. I think you're getting confused with your professional roles here!"

"I'm confused about nothing," he says, giving me a scathing look. "So what was it again you wanted to tell me?"

"I don't think it's you we need to speak to," I reply. "Is there someone else we can see?"

He sits back in his chair, folding his arms. "Nope, there's no one else available, so it's me or nobody."

"You have a conflict of interest—"

"I'm a professional police officer. Now, can we get on with this?"

Dan takes over. "After what you told us about the car brakes, we've been trying to think of who could do something like that. There was a case around ten years ago in which a client made some serious threats toward me. Could he be involved, even after all this time?"

"I see," Booth says, "and can you give me the name and the circumstances?"

Dan fills him in quickly on the Timothy Vaughan case. "Now, as far as I know, he's still in prison, but that wouldn't present him with an impossible barrier. He has a lot of contacts."

"OK." Booth rubs his chin thoughtfully. "You're right. He can give instructions from prison with those kinds of connections. I'll check if he's still inside—that's simple enough. But yes, it's a long time ago, and why now? He could have done it much sooner. Why wait?" He eyes Dan with something that borders on the kind of professional respect I would have expected before I knew the history between them. "Do you think he'd go after your kids or after you?"

"It was me he threatened," Dan replies. "But honestly, I think he's capable of anything."

Booth gives a quirk of his eyebrows that says, "Serves you right," but then he shakes his head, as if at himself. I guess he remembers a child died, and that's too much for him to bear malice over. "OK, I'll look at it. But my professional hunch is you need to look at a more recent offense you might have caused. Guys like that don't usually wait a decade."

"So you also think it could be one of Dan's clients?" I ask.

"Of course," he says, and then he smiles. "Or it could be one of you two."

Booth leaves us then to run some checks, and we wait in the interview suite for him to return. Dan is silently furious.

"I can't believe he's allowed to be associated with our case when he's so clearly got a grudge against you," I mutter to Dan, and I wonder for a moment whether another complaint would serve any purpose. Dan's next words scatter that wondering asunder.

"I could probably go into several police stations around this city and come up with more than a dozen officers who feel exactly the same as he does. A lot of coppers view my end of the profession like he does. To them, we're just parasites who are in it for the money and feeding off crime. We're on the other side—that's how they see it. And when I come up against someone like him in court, who hasn't done his job well enough to get a secure conviction, that just adds fuel to the fire."

I understand that. I never liked Dan's type of work myself, but then, many people would say the same about mine.

After a while, Booth comes back, frowning. "Vaughan is still inside," he says. "I did some reading up on him. I still think the timing is out, but if this is the kind of guy you think is after you, then we'll have to talk about whether you need protection. If that's the case, though, I'll need more to go on. If you have any other suspicions, you should pass them on. In the meantime, I'm going to look into this Vaughan in more detail."

"Show him your card," I say to Dan quietly.

He shakes his head at me, and Booth shoots me a questioning glance.

"No, show him, Dan." My voice is firm, because this idiot needs to understand something he clearly doesn't get.

Dan shrugs and takes a laminated card out of his wallet. He hands it to Booth. On it are written eight names.

"Are these people you suspect?" he asks.

"No," my husband replies.

"Then why—"

"Those are the names of innocent people," I cut in. "People who were found to be absolutely blameless of the crimes they were accused of. Incontrovertibly and without doubt. And yet they were charged and taken to trial."

Booth's chin goes up as he realizes where I'm coming from.

"Without a defense lawyer, those people would be in prison now for crimes they did not commit. Because in those eight cases, the police got it wrong."

Booth looks over at Dan, who adds, "They were my clients. I keep their names to remind me why my job is every bit as worth doing as yours."

Booth scowls. "Eight in how many, though?"

"Eight is enough," Dan replies. "They're people—innocent people— not collateral damage."

The police officer's hard face grows even stiffer, but he looks at the card before he hands it back to Dan, and he reads the names. "My best advice to you now is to go home and sit down together. Come up with a definitive list of people who you might have upset, both of you. Consider all angles, not just work. And then we'll talk." He hesitates. "And call us if you see anything suspicious."

33

TODAY I AM ANGRY AGAIN. *I'm too mad to watch them for long. Some days, it gets like that. Some days, the hate is overwhelming. I never know when it will be this way.*

It's irrational. It distracts me from my main purpose, from my goal.

But I can't help it. Not today.

I want her to burn like I burn.

34

"I'M GETTING SCARED, DAN," I tell him when we're in the safety of our own sitting room, the lamp lit to dispel the gloom of twilight outside. "I'm scared this is real. That the investigator is right, and it was deliberate. You've thought that all along, haven't you?"

He nods. "Booth may have played you slightly in the questioning. If there was still the possibility you fell asleep, he needed to give you an out, and me being a suspect might make you more likely to confess. But I think he knows that's highly unlikely. They were a lot less ambivalent with me— they're pretty sure those brakes were damaged on purpose. And that means all this is because of me."

I know what it's like to feel that blame, and my heart sinks for him. I can see that hunted look in his eyes again, and I know how hard he's fighting to keep control, to hold that guilt in and keep functioning for all of us because we need him.

"No matter how many possibilities I consider, it always comes back to that. It's the most logical option. It's almost always someone you know. It's very rare for something like this to be a random act by a stranger who just wants to kill. It can happen, but it's unlikely."

And I have to take him at his word about this. He's more of an expert than me on crimes.

"So who? The police turn to me first, obviously. That's procedure. They'll rule me out soon enough when the information I've given them checks out, but at the moment, I'm their main suspect. I'm half-surprised Booth took us so seriously today, because I expect he thinks it may be a diversionary tactic on my part."

"But it was me who thought of Vaughan."

"And that might have convinced Booth more. So, if it's not me, who could it be? We have to go through people close to us first. No, don't say it's stupid. It's a logical process we have to follow. Annika was in the U.S., so she's out. Aidan was here but has no motive I can think of."

"Of course it's not Aidan!"

"Yes, I know, but we have to eliminate logically and not assume."

"But not by going through all our friends, Dan. I understand what you mean, but I am absolutely confident without going through all our friends and family that none of them would try to kill our girls."

"So who would?" he asks. "The girls are too young for it to be someone with a grudge against one of them, not someone with the skills to damage brakes miles from here. Have you thought about how premeditated that is?"

"Yes," I reply soberly, "I have. And also about when it could have happened. It must have been when we were up there on holiday, don't you think?" A thought strikes me. "Dan, it might not be anyone we know at all! It could be somebody from up there. Maybe someone who hates tourists or—"

"That's not the most probable assumption, though."

"But it could be. At least consider it."

"OK, fine. I'll add that to the list of possibilities. But my point is this—by far the most credible option is it's someone who has something against one of us. Now, which of us deals with people with the capacity to do this kind of thing—you or me? Because it *is* premeditated. It's a calculated thing to do. And it could have happened when you were alone or when the kids were in the car. Whoever it was didn't care how many people were hurt, as long as somebody was. So yes, it may have been done when you were up there on holiday. They may have followed you."

I feel sick at the thought of someone creeping around the cottage while we slept, crawling under the car and smiling as they filed away at my brakes.

"It's also untraceable. If nobody was seen doing it, then how can you tie anyone to it? It could have happened days before and miles away. This is somebody who thought long and hard and planned this in cold blood." He shudders. "A lot of hate went into this."

My whole body shakes at his words. So much hate, and my poor little girl was the victim of that.

"The kind of people who could do that, Lizzie—that's the kind I deal with." And he puts his head in his hands. "It's got to be my fault, and I don't think I can live with that."

35

MY HUSBAND SELDOM CRIES. HE'S not a man who's afraid to, but he's generally too stoic for tears, so to see him racked with sobs is terrifying.

I try to put my arms round him, but he brushes me off and heads blindly into the garden. I can make out his shape in the growing darkness as he goes down the long path to the trees at the bottom.

He wants to be alone, and I understand that.

I'm going to tell him when he comes back in that it could be someone associated with me. We need to look at that possibility too. He's going through his client list. Well, I'm going to pull mine up as well. I might not deal with criminals as a routine, but I've upset people, too, in my line of work.

I look out into the darkness of the garden, and it all feels horribly real now. As if someone's malevolence hangs out there, waiting to catch us. A shiver of fear runs along my spine. How long did the killer sneak about in the dark, waiting to file my brakes? Did they watch us before doing it? They must have to know they wouldn't be caught. If it happened when we were on holiday, that means they lurked around outside our cottage. We may have even spoken to them. They might have pretended to be a friendly local.

I scour my brain, trying to remember back to anyone who it could have been. It hurts to push aside the memories of Becca skipping about and laughing, helping me light the log fire, smiling up at me. And all the time, somebody was out there in the dark, plotting to hurt us.

We have to catch them. I don't know if I'm ever going to feel safe again.

Dan comes back in slowly, as if all his bones ache. His shoulders are slumped over. The effect this is having on him is physically obvious. He's been so strong so far, keeping Portia and me going, and I wonder, with a growing sense of fear, how long he can keep it together.

"I'm going through my cases too," I say as he sits at the kitchen table. "We have to work out who it is and make sure they're caught."

"If he exists," Dan says wearily. "It's like looking for a needle that might not even be there."

"But you said—"

"I know, but it doesn't mean I don't have doubts too." He looks away from me. "If only you could remember what happened that night."

The slam of my mind in resistance to his words is like a shotgun going off in my face. I reel backward. It's like a physical pain.

"What is it?" Dan asks, his voice raised in concern.

I have my hands out, as if to fend off something.

"It won't let me," I mumble. "It won't let me remember."

The brain block is real. There's something here my mind is trying to protect me from.

A key turns in the front door, and Dan swears under his breath. Portia and Annika burst into the hall, laughing. It's the first time I've heard Portia laugh like that, in that uninhibited way, since the accident.

Dan hurries out to the study before they come in to join us. He's not in the mood to deal with teenage emotions. "Going back to work," he mutters as he disappears.

Portia gives me a brief "hello" and then takes herself off upstairs, thanking Annika as she goes.

"We went to see a film and get pizza," Annika says, settling at my table. "I got some information out of her. Not much, but it's a start."

"It's not good, is it?"

"Not really, no. She's feeling pretty rubbish at the moment. She says she's been feeling zoned out ever since she went back to school. Like she doesn't fit. She described it like watching herself from above and not really being there."

Dissociation—Stella's talked about that. I'm horrified to find Portia's been experiencing it, and I haven't even known.

"She confided in a friend that she felt guilty Becca died and not her."

Annika hesitates. "She told her that she used to feel jealous of Becca because you two were so close, and she was scared that made it her fault Becca died. Like she'd brought her bad luck or something."

I recoil inside at this news.

"This girl was supposed to keep that quiet, but she didn't. Some friend, eh?"

"Which girl was it?"

"She wouldn't tell me. She says it doesn't matter now—the damage is done."

"What damage does she mean?"

"She wouldn't tell me that either. Just shrugged and said, 'Some girls can be bitches,' and that's all I can get out of her for now." Annika purses her lips. "I don't think she's happy, Lizzie. But you guys have so much going on right now, and I don't think this is going to be sorted out overnight. Maybe when all of this stuff with the car is resolved, give the school a call, but right now, I think you've got to concentrate on that."

"But if she's unhappy—"

"Lizzie, you can't do everything. Take one step at a time. What's the biggest priority now? It's making sure that if someone did this to you, they're caught and put away."

I sigh. "That's what Dan said earlier."

"And he's right. She'll be OK, Lizzie. Just don't expect too much of her right now. I'll come over and take her out again. We'll go shopping."

Once she's gone, I check in on Dan, who grunts a "no" at me when I ask him if he wants anything. He's reading through internet articles with a notepad by his side. He doesn't want to talk in this mood, so I close the study door quietly and leave him to it. I don't know what else to do.

Portia's getting ready for bed and doesn't want to talk, either, so I go into the sitting room with my laptop, open it up, and start going back through my client list over the last year.

DS Booth said to look for more recent possibilities than Vaughan, and he's right. For someone to hold that level of hatred, it's more likely to be something closer to the time of the accident. It's hard to sustain that level of desire for revenge for a decade. *Not impossible*, I tell myself. Grudges can become obsessions, and those can continue for years, so we can't discount that angle. On the balance of probability, it makes sense to pay closer attention to the last year or two. My initial reaction to my list in the last twelve months is that they are so mundane it can't be any of them, but I have to look closer. Maybe I'm not seeing something because they're so familiar.

And then, for one mad moment, I wonder if it could be Becca's real mother who tracked us down. Who decided that if she couldn't have her daughter, then nobody would.

But no, that's like something from a nightmare. I discard the thought almost immediately. Her mother might have been hopelessly dysfunctional but not intentionally evil.

It's so difficult to find an answer, but we have to keep trying. We have to find out who did this, but it's so hard. Stella says I need to accept each stage of my grief and allow it to run its course. I can't do that when I know someone took Becca's life but not who or why. Every time I close my eyes at night, every moment of the day when my thoughts are not filled by some busywork I try to find, she is there with me. I miss the feel of her in my arms as she leans in for a hug—it's an ache in my bones that won't leave. I miss her radiant smile lighting up my sad moments and scattering them to the winds. How can someone so small and so infinitely precious simply no longer be? It seems an impossibility that we can all carry on in a world where she isn't.

But we have to.

It's so cold and cruel, marooned here without her.

36

SHE'S SEEING THE COUNSELOR AGAIN. *I watch her as she goes inside the gates. She takes a deep breath as if to brace herself before she rings the doorbell.*

Unlike her daughter, she never suspects I am here. That my eyes are on her. Always watching.

And this is where I will remain, like a shadow, always behind her. Knowing her every move.

I know her so well now. I can predict what she will do, where she will go.

I bet I know her better than that therapist.

When she comes out in an hour, she will get the bus home. She will walk to the bus stop as if in a trance, neither seeing nor caring who is around her. She will be lost somewhere back there, at that lake, on that night.

She is in hell.

Both of us are.

37

A WEEK PASSES, AND WE are still no nearer to unearthing a clear suspect. As a consequence, our lives are totally changed. I no longer go out alone without Dan knowing exactly where I am. Portia is always with one of us, though it's easy to hide what we're doing from her because she doesn't venture out much anyway. Dan works from home as much as possible, so he's around more. And we both jump at unexpected noises. This morning, I caught Dan checking under the car before he got in it to take Portia to school. He gave me a guilty look when he saw me watching, and I know he was trying to do it surreptitiously. He hates me seeing how scared he is. I hate seeing it too.

Every evening, Dan and I work together on trying to solve this, poring over old notes and case files.

"The difficulty here is that it could be someone who appears relatively insignificant in one of these cases, and we can't overlook that. It's important to not just look at the obvious," he says as he makes me read through his files, too, in case I find something he hasn't. He keeps forgetting things, he says, and when I ask him what he means, he tells me the details slip through his mind like it's a leaking cup. He's afraid he'll miss something important. His words worry me, but he won't talk more about it, and the only thing I can do to help is what he asks—keep looking.

I pore through all of mine, but nothing sticks out. Nothing to generate that level of violence. I decide to look at a different angle. Could it be someone who is unbalanced rather than criminal?

Dan shrugs grudgingly when I suggest this to him. "More likely with your clients," he says, "as you don't often come across someone with a criminal record."

It has to be something work-related, doesn't it? There's nobody I know whom I've upset in any other area of my life. Dan, too, is just a regular guy. He gets up; he eats breakfast with his family if possible; he goes to work. He used to take his bike out whenever he could and burn off stress by blasting away the miles on the road. He tended to dislike the social get-together side of our work, and it didn't fit in with our family life. So, like me, he avoided those. We were just an ordinary family.

Dan and I agree that it's most likely to be a man, given the way the brakes were damaged. "To abrade the brakes rather than cut them—that feels like a male action," Dan says. "It has to be someone with some mechanical knowledge to know they'd hold out for a while before they failed. Possibly it was done shortly before your journey home with the idea that you'd be moving at higher speed on the highway, and when they failed, the accident would be worse. I don't know—the police think it's odd too."

I've always kept paper diaries—I find it easier to keep track of my days that way—so I start by working through those and then matching them up with the scanned-in case files I have in archive storage. I go over each one painstakingly in case I miss something that could clue me in. It makes for tired eyes, and my neck is stiff from sitting staring at a screen for so long. It's depressing to be faced with so much potential for resentment. Could it tip over into a desire for murder? Not in a normal person, so I'm looking for cases in which there was a query about one party's mental stability or past record of criminality. There are a couple that catch my eye.

The first was a year ago and, unusually, it was a wronged wife I was working for. My first impression of the husband was that he was controlling to the point of abuse. The court agreed with me. She got sole custody of their children and a hefty settlement. He lost his emotional punching bag. There was something about him that was fundamentally unstable; I was sure of it. It wasn't an exceptional case, as these things go. He still had full visitation rights under the terms of the order, as long as the children were happy to go, but I wonder if he's the type to seek revenge in some other way. I'd always felt she got out before he started beating her and that it was simply a matter of time before he did. It was a long stretch for any normal person to go from anger and frustration to murder, but was he normal? I make a question mark next to his name on my list.

The other name I'm considering is from three years back, so it seems less likely because such a long time has passed, and also because it's a woman. But the key here could be the mental-instability angle, so I need to think it through and not discount it on the time frame and gender alone. Maybe she snapped. I don't know, and I suppose I don't really understand that kind of thing enough to be the best judge. She was an odd woman, though. There were two children, both under the age of ten, and the father had been frankly terrified of leaving them in her care. He'd put off the divorce for as long as he could stand it because he was so scared he'd lose custody. Alana, his wife, was typical of a type I see from time to time—a trophy wife. He was ten years older than her and a successful businessman, but not the kind you'd notice in a crowded room, whereas she definitely stood out. "She has a darker side," he told me at our first meeting.

The case itself became relatively easy to manage when he finally confessed to me that she physically attacked him on a regular basis. It wasn't easy for a man to admit he was a victim of domestic abuse, he'd said as he broke down in my office, but he was terrified she would turn on the children if he wasn't there. "Her temper," he said, "it's like nothing I've ever known or imagined." The catalogue of injuries he'd suffered shocked me, even after years in this job. Some of them had left scarring, and I had to persuade him to use the scars as evidence in the case. You could see the shame he felt about it written plainly on his face when he finally consented. His wife went through the whole process with an icy reserve I knew was a mask; she certainly was very good at hiding her real emotions in public.

I show the files to Dan. He reads them and then passes them back. "I see what you mean," he says, "but look at this in comparison."

I read the papers he passes me with a dawning horror. "This man, this Anthony Tyler, he's a psychopath," I say when I've finished reading. "But he's locked up, yes?"

"Yes, he is. He was never diagnosed with any kind of diminished responsibility for what he did, though, so he's in a regular prison."

"You said you thought Vaughan had reaches beyond prison. Could this man?"

"Less likely—he's a solo player. Even hardened criminals don't want anything to do with him. He was useful, once, as a hitman because he'll kill without compunction. But then he became too dangerous, too much of a liability, and the work dried up. And that's when he started killing for pleasure alone."

"Sometimes, Dan, I don't know how you can stand to represent these people," I say with a shudder.

"There was never any chance he was going to get off," he says in a flat voice. "He was always going down. He just conned himself into believing he'd be able to fool a jury."

"Are you passing his name to the police?"

"Yes, I'm going to call them tomorrow." He yawns, and his eyes are heavy. "I'm going to quit for tonight now. This is driving me crazy. We can't go on like this. If I don't find a solution soon, I'm going to speak to the police about protection."

I think of what I've just read about Anthony Tyler and his delight in killing just for the sake of it, and I understand why we might need that. The thought of the shadows out there in the night fills me with dread. I check the locks three times before I go to bed.

Dan sleeps badly. He wakes me often with tossing and turning. I think that's what sets me most on edge, to see him afraid. As I lie awake in the early hours, I can sense the fracture lines beginning to spread through him, which terrifies me more than that nameless shadow. If Dan breaks, who holds us all together?

38

MY PHONE RINGS AT 4 p.m. It's Dan.

"Is Portia there?" He sounds frantic.

"No. I thought you were picking her up from school. Aren't you there?"

"I am," he replies grimly. "She's not."

"Oh my God!"

"I've been into the school. She's not inside either. I made the teachers look for her. Nobody's seen her since lunch. Try calling her in case she picks up for you. She's not answering me."

"OK. I'll call you back."

I make a rapid phone call to Portia's mobile, but it rings out, and I stare at my phone with dread. What's happened?

And that shadowy figure from my nightmares grabs me by the throat with very real hands.

I call Dan, but the line is busy, and I desperately hope he's managed to get through to Portia.

When I try her again, though, praying for an busy tone, there's only the regular ring, and again it goes unanswered. I wait, watching the minutes tick by. *Please call back, Dan. Don't leave me here not knowing.*

I feel so useless. I should be getting into my car and racing down there to help him, but instead I'm this hopeless shell of who I was, a woman who just has to sit and wait, too scared to get behind the wheel.

Fuck you, trauma! Fuck you!

I knot my hands in my hair and tug, needing the pain that knocks back the rising panic.

What if he's got her right now? What did Dan mean, nobody's seen her since lunch? How? How can that have happened?

Does that mean she went out at lunchtime and didn't come back? She could have been snatched off the streets. Portia's too sensible to go off with someone. That means he would have had to wrestle her into a car.

Or it's someone we know. Oh God, was I wrong? Is it someone we know?

I've dug deep grooves, almost cuts, into my hands with my nails by the time Dan calls back.

"She's not here," he says in a defeated voice. "She hasn't been in school all afternoon."

"How? Why weren't we called?" I scream down the phone at him.

"It didn't get picked up—"

"How can it not have gotten picked up?" I yell.

"Lizzie, I know, I know. I've just said the same, but this isn't helping. Listen! We need to find her."

And I'm angry with him because he's there and I'm not, and now he's yelling at me.

"Can you ring some of her old friends? I'm coming home now, but a teacher suggested trying that to see if any of them know where she is."

"I don't know who to call. She hasn't had friends 'round since the accident, and I only have a few mums' numbers. I don't think she'll be there, anyway. Something's happened to her, Dan!"

"Just call them anyway, please."

I call the few contacts I have. I can only get hold of two of them, and I have to leave messages for the other three. They're sympathetic, but they haven't seen Portia with their daughters for some time. They do go and check with their respective children, but nobody has spoken to her recently, and they've no idea where she is tonight either. They confirm what Dan said. She wasn't in class in the afternoon.

"Could it be a boyfriend?" one mum wonders. "Maybe she's broken up with him?"

No, she would have told Annika about that, I'm sure. I don't think it's that, but I call her anyway to see if Portia has said anything to her. For a moment, as I wait for her to pick up, I have a flash of hope that Portia is with her and they've forgotten to tell us they had a shopping trip planned. It's ridiculous, and that hope is dashed the minute I speak to Annika. She doesn't know anything. She offers to come round and help, but all I want to do now is get off the phone and call the police.

I ask for DS Booth because he knows our case, and he's the only one I can think of who might not just tell us to give her a little longer to come home.

I'm in luck, and he's on shift. "In all likelihood, she's fallen out with some friends, and she's taking some time to cool off," he says. "But I'll come 'round now."

I never thought I'd be pleased to welcome him into my house again, but I heave a small sigh of relief that he's taking me seriously.

39

DAN AND BOOTH NOD AT each other tersely as I offer the policeman a chair. "I was going to pick Lizzie up and drive straight round to the station, so thank you for coming," Dan tells him.

"It's a fallacy you have to wait a certain time to report a missing person," Booth says. "You can report it as soon as you become worried, especially if it's a child or a vulnerable person. Obviously, then, we have to evaluate the situation and what response to take, but in this case, I understand why you're concerned for her. So let's get the questions done quickly, and I'll get some officers out there looking. Have there been any arguments recently between any of you?" he asks, taking out his notebook.

"No, nothing like that. I mean, we've all been through a very tough time, but there's been nothing of late that I can think of that could have upset her at home. She doesn't know anything about the car brakes. We didn't tell her."

"She hasn't overheard somehow?"

"No, I really don't think so. We've been careful about that. Obviously we've been stressed about it, and yes, there's been an impact on us, but I don't think it's her reacting to that. She hasn't been going out normally since the accident. She goes to school, and she comes home. That's it."

He pauses over what he's writing down. "So what about at school? Any problems there?"

I look across at Dan for support. "She's made a few comments about school. Negative comments, that is, but she wouldn't give many details. The main thing I've been worried about is that she seems to have shut herself off from all her friends ever since the crash. And then a couple of weeks ago, she came home from school terribly upset. Someone had rowed with her, but she wouldn't tell me any more than that. It turns out that one of her friends did something spiteful, and she's taken that quite hard. But with everything else going on, we've probably not focused on that as much as we should." I've let her down again—that's what I want to say—but I don't want to upset Dan by voicing it.

"Portia's a very sensible girl," Dan adds. "This is totally out of character for her. The school said she appears to have gone out at lunchtime, which pupils are allowed to do, but she didn't come back. She's been gone all afternoon." He pauses, and I notice his hands are shaking. Then I see Booth's eyes move to register that too. "What if she's been taken?"

"Have you checked her room? Is there anything missing?"

"No, I didn't think of that." I can't believe that hasn't crossed my mind, but it never occurred to me that this might be something she'd planned.

"Shall we look now?" he suggests.

We go upstairs. I know he wants to see, too—there'll be things he's accustomed to looking for in cases like these. Portia's room is just as it always is. She's made the bed and put her things away before going to school.

"Is that normal for her?" Booth asks.

"Yes, she's quite tidy." I open her wardrobe and drawers. "Everything looks the same. I can't see anything obvious missing."

"Take your time. Have a good look." He walks round her room, scanning the surfaces. "Do you mind?" he says, nodding to a drawer.

Dan shakes his head with reluctance. The idea of this man going through our daughter's things, especially without her knowledge, feels so wrong, but it's important we let him carry out his job.

He opens her bedside drawer and looks inside, and then does the same to her desk. "Do you know if she keeps a diary?"

"Not to my knowledge, no."

He picks up her laptop. "Do you know her password?"

I shake my head.

"I'm going to take this with me." He looks at me steadily, and I see something in his eyes that might be called sympathy. "There's nothing missing, is there?"

I swallow to try to make my voice sound normal. "No."

Booth pulls out his radio. "OK, I'm going to call this in and get some people out there. Can you get me a photo and give me a brief physical description, please?"

Dan beckons him away. "Back soon," he says, and then he goes downstairs with Booth. I can hear the policeman on his radio.

I sink onto Portia's bed. He's got her. That bastard who killed Becca has taken her. Is she already dead? Oh, God, where is she? Why didn't I insist on protection for us? Why? Why?

My head is whirling. This is my fault. I should have tried harder. I should have not let her out of my sight, not even at school. How can they not have picked up that she's been missing for half a day?

I can't do this. I can't. I'm going to break utterly.

Dan trudges back up the stairs. "He's gone. He's sending someone 'round to see some of her school friends. I gave him a couple of names to start with."

"She doesn't have any friends anymore."

"He has to start somewhere."

"So what do we do?"

"Call Annika. Get her to sit in for us. We're going out to look for her."

"Dan, he's got her."

My husband shakes his head furiously. "No, he might not have. We have to try."

"Booth's got our list, hasn't he?"

"Yes, I told you—I gave it to them days ago." He clenches his jaw hard. "Get your coat. We're going to find her."

40

DAN TAKES THE CAR, AND we drive around Reading in ever-widening circles. I keep trying Portia's phone, but it continually rings out. Then, at half past nine, when I call again, I get an automated message saying that she cannot be reached.

"Has she turned her phone off?" I go cold all over. *Or has someone else done it?*

"If she has," Dan says, "it's a kind of response. Better than nothing."

But I can't agree.

"It's cold, and she's only got her school coat. Do you think we should try the hostels? The hospitals?" I ask, shivering as I think of her freezing out there. And then I think, if she is freezing out there, that's better than the alternative. Maybe the killer was after her; maybe she ran away from him; maybe she's hiding.

When I say this to Dan, he just grunts. His knuckles are white on the steering wheel.

I'm about to push him for an answer, but then my phone rings. I snatch it up to answer it, but it's Booth.

"They've checked the hostels, but no luck yet," I tell Dan after I've finished talking to the policeman. "They've left her details. She's not in any of the hospitals. Nobody from school has said they know her whereabouts either. There's an alert out on social media and the radio, and they've got officers out patrolling," I tell Dan. "He says they'll keep looking through the night."

"I'm going to drive out a bit further," Dan says grimly, and he heads for the divided highway.

We're still out there looking close to midnight, and we haven't seen a single sign. I can't keep hoping. *He's* got her. Why are we driving around pretending we might find her?

Tears roll silently down my cheeks. Dan keeps his eyes fixed ahead, keeps driving.

I text her again. I must have sent close to a hundred texts by now. As Dan drives, it's the only thing I can do to keep myself sane. "We love you, Portia. You're not in trouble. Please get in touch and let us help."

"Will you stop doing that?" Dan snaps. "You could miss her out there while you're looking at that phone. You're supposed to be watching for her!"

He's terrified, too, I know he is, so I swallow my retort and look out of the window. He's silent as he drives, and when I glance over at him on one occasion, he has his teeth gritted and his eyes are bright with unshed tears. I reach over to touch his shoulder. "Leave me," he growls, and I pull my hand back, shocked. That's not like him.

One o'clock comes and goes, and then two. We've covered a large portion of the city by this time.

Dan pulls over again. "She's not going to be out here roaming the streets now. She's got too much sense. We're going to go home, and then I'll come back out in the morning."

If I thought there was any chance she was out here walking around, I'd make him keep driving, but there isn't. Dan's right—she's too bright for that. We're doing no good here.

"We'll keep looking tomorrow. We need sleep now."

As he drives us home, we both feel we've abandoned her, though. I can see it in the way Dan droops in the car seat.

Please be OK, Portia. Please be alive. Please stay safe.

41

I FALL ASLEEP ON THE sofa for an hour, no more, and I wake to the morning light streaming through the long window with a sick emptiness inside. I walk through the house urgently, checking if she's somehow sneaked in without waking us. Dan sits in the armchair and watches me wordlessly as I pass.

No, her bed is empty. I've had no reply to my messages. I try to call her again, but her phone is still off. I send another desperate text.

Then I curl back up under the blanket on the sofa, shivering with cold and shock. All my senses are heightened with fear, and every tiny noise jolts my nerves like the crash of cymbals.

Time crawls by. I want to go out and look for her again, but what if she's waited for the daylight to come home? I can't leave yet.

Booth calls us just after nine. He wants us to go over to the school. Annika's happy to come over and keep watch.

"Don't worry, just go," she says, kissing my cheek. "I'll call you the moment I hear anything."

We get back to the school as quickly as we can. DS Booth is waiting for us in the principal's office. He looks tired, and his eyes are red-rimmed with fatigue.

"Sorry to drag you over, but I need to be on the ground here while we're progressing our investigation, and I also need to talk to you. We got a lead last night that we're following up here today. One of my officers is seeing some pupils right now. The principal is off dealing with that and sends her apologies for not being here to see you, but she thought you'd rather she helped to get the information."

He sits forward and leans his elbows on the table. "Listen, some of this may be hard to hear, but it's better news than we might have had at this stage. We all know what we're worried about here, but I may have unearthed another reason for her being missing."

Hope flutters to life in my chest with desperate wings.

"One of the girls told us that Portia's been having problems in school. You told me she'd fallen out with some friends, but I'm afraid it's more than that. There's been some bullying going on for a while, and it may have really heated up in the past few days. That's what we're trying to find out now."

Dan's gone white. "No," he says hoarsely, "not after everything she's been through already."

"It seems to have started when she confided in a friend about how she felt after the accident. I think you know some of this, so forgive me if any of it is old news. She told this friend she was afraid she'd brought her sister bad luck. She said she was always jealous of her because she was your favorite."

That hits me like a blow to the stomach. It's more than she said to Annika, much more. "No, she wasn't," I all but shout at him, and I can see Dan's face collapse with sorrow. "She wasn't our favorite. We adored them both."

He shrugs in an understanding way. "Teenagers—funny things. They get strange ideas, don't they? These girls don't strike me as much in the way of friends. When she does come back, you need to have a good talk to her about how to deal with them, and speak to the school too. Because what happened next was a group of them started taunting her that she let her sister die in the accident because she hated her and wanted to save herself." He looks disgusted, as if he's lifted a stone and found something repellent under there.

"What?" roars Dan.

"Yeah, I know," Booth says to him with as much sympathy as I've ever seen him show to my husband. "She's had a lot of trouble with them from what we've discovered so far, and I suspect there's more that we don't know about yet. And I got the impression the girls who used to be her friends didn't make much effort to stop any of it—too scared of the bullies themselves, from the sound of it."

"What, so she got picked on, and all her friends abandoned her?" Dan demanded.

"Pretty much. They didn't put it quite like that, but that was the effect. So we questioned them about what happened the day before she went missing. There was some online stuff going on—we got into it this morning and we're getting it shut down. There's some seriously vicious stuff up there. An officer is dealing with that now. But what I think we'll find is it had escalated to more than that."

"She had a bruise on her neck," I remember. "She came home upset one day, and there was a bruise on her neck. She said she got it playing hockey."

"That's not how she got it," Booth says. "It was in the changing rooms after hockey. They were taunting her about her sister, so she ran out. One of them had strung a line made out of a draw cord from a gym bag across the door, and she ran into it. We found that out this morning, just before you arrived."

"My God, what else have they done to her?" I ask, my hand going to my mouth. "How has the school let this happen?"

"None of it was reported," he says. "I know it's distressing, but we're out there looking for her. Hang on to that."

My little girl is out there, she's in pain, and I can't get to her. We drove home last night. We should have kept looking.

I should be relieved if this is why she ran away. I should feel better that maybe she hasn't been snatched off the street, but I don't. Because what if whatever has been done to her has made her hurt herself?

Booth's wrong—it's not better news. I get my phone out to text her again, but I don't know what to say. I look up and Booth is watching me. "All they ever want to know is you love them and it's OK," he says, the words incongruous from such a severe man.

And that's what I text to her: "We love you. We know now about the bullying. It's not your fault. We'll make it right, I promise you. Please come home. We miss you xxx."

And all we can do is wait. Hopelessly. Helplessly.

42

BY DINNERTIME THERE ARE STILL no sightings of her, and I'm growing beyond desperate as the light starts to fade from the sky again. "Dan, I can't stand it if she's missing another night."

"Keep texting her," he urges. "She might turn her phone on soon."

We go on and on, watching and waiting. I know now how those poor, desperate mothers on TV appeals for missing children feel. And I keep thinking about a silent, shadowy figure who could be looking right at her now, because although Booth is following the angle that she's run away, I still can't entirely dispel my fear that it's more than that.

Dan's been out driving around again, looking in other places in case she's hiding herself away. I know he went walking in the woods, and I know it was because he, like me, was afraid she'd gone off and hurt herself. He hid the walking boots when he went out to the car, but I was watching from the window. I saw him despite that. He's out there for hours, looking for her. And when he returns, his face is closed down and he can't talk to me. He sits facing away from me, staring into space.

I am curled on the sofa with the blanket around my shoulders because I can't get warm when the text tone on my phone sounds.

"Oh God, it's her, Dan, it's her!" I shout, and Dan runs over.

"What is it? What's she said?"

"She's in the park, by the duck pond."

"Tell her to wait—we'll be there in a minute!" He dashes to get his coat, and I run out with him, the blanket still around me.

We are in the car in a flash, and he accelerates so fast that the tires screech against the tarmac. We shoot through the streets to the park and leave the car on the road.

Dan runs ahead of me down to the pond, but I am only a length behind him. My lungs are bursting as I push myself harder to get to her.

I see her first. She's on a bench to the side of the pond with a woman wearing a bobble hat sitting beside her.

"Portia!"

She stands up uncertainly and comes toward us. I run over, with Dan following, and I throw my arms around her. "Oh, Portia, I was so worried."

Dan arrives and fusses around both of us. Portia is sobbing and mumbling, "Sorry, sorry, sorry," over and over.

It's ridiculous—I have been so afraid, and now the elation of finding her takes me over completely. I want to cry with relief. I want to check she still has all ten fingers and toes, just as you want to with a baby. I want to hold on to her and never let go. Portia stays snuggled in my arms, her face buried in my neck, and she is shaking with cold and suppressed emotion. I hug her tighter.

When I eventually remember the woman on the bench and look up, she's already turning away to go.

She gives me a nod. "I wanted to make sure she was all right," she says.

"Oh, thank you! Thank you for waiting with her."

She gives me a brief smile and then goes off down the footpath.

Portia has her face buried in her dad's shoulder while he hugs her to warm her up. I pick up the blanket, which has fallen to the ground, and wrap it round her.

Dan guides her back to the car. We need to get Portia inside. Questions and explanations can wait until we're safe indoors.

43

AS IT TURNS OUT, QUESTIONS and explanations have to wait until the morning because Portia is so exhausted that we put her to bed as soon as we get home. She didn't sleep last night and can barely keep her eyes open once she gets into the warmth of the house. I help her to bed while Dan calls the police, and I sleep on the guest bed in her room because I can't stand to let her out of my sight in case she runs off again.

Booth calls round. "I'm glad she's turned up safe. Be sure to make an appointment with the school. We've passed them information on the bullying. It's not a police matter unless you want to press charges." He avoids looking at Dan. He still doesn't like him, but something has shifted in his view of us. The penny doesn't drop until after he's left, and then I realize what it is—he's seen Dan's reaction to Portia going missing. It's not the reaction of a man who tried to kill his own daughter. Dan may stay calmer than me in situations like this, but that's his nature, and I suspect Booth, another practical man, understands that even better than I do. But my husband is not an actor, and the fear in his eyes was obvious to all and entirely real.

It's Dan who sits Portia down the next morning to get her to talk to us. I'm too afraid that if we push her, she'll run off again.

"We need to sort this," he says firmly. "What's been happening?"

My daughter is tearful as she tells us, but Booth was right. She'd confided in someone she'd thought was a friend that she was struggling with guilt over Becca's death.

"Sometimes I had moments when I hated her," she said, sobbing, with my arm around her, "because everyone loved her, and I'm just the moody, sarcastic one that nobody likes as much. I really, really loved her, but sometimes, I was so jealous of her too."

"Portia, that's natural. Everyone has those feelings sometimes. And you might see yourself like that, but it doesn't mean that's real." I'm too upset to say more.

We both try again to tell her that it's not her and that some girls are silly and immature at that age and don't realize the damage they're doing, but she's not in a place to understand that yet.

That's where we have to get her somehow.

"What happened before you ran off?" her dad asks. "The detective said there'd been some things on a website. It's all been taken down now, but what was that about? What's going on? All of it, please."

"I don't want to go back," she says.

"You don't have to if you don't want," I tell her.

Dan starts to speak, but I shoot him a fierce look to silence him.

Portia looks at both of us and breathes out slowly in relief, and then finally, she begins to tell us what happened.

"After I told Maria about how I felt about Becca, she told a few of the other girls. One of them is friends with Anastasia Spencer."

"Is she related to that boy you went out with last year?" I ask.

"Yes, she's his sister, and she makes out that she hates me because it's my fault we broke up. But that's an excuse—she's never liked me. And Jack wasn't bothered about us splitting up. Anastasia doesn't like anyone who does well in school."

"Well, she's clearly destined for great things," Dan remarks sarcastically. What he wants to say is "Bitch!" but he won't in front of Portia.

"She's the one who set up that thing in the changing room, and she's been making what I said sound a hundred times worse, saying that I was glad Becca died and that I'd gotten what I wanted. She talked someone into making a social media page all about it, and people could post hate comments on it. That's been going on for over a week. So finally, I confronted her about it."

And that's the real Portia, right there. There's no way, if she had been herself, she would have let things go on this long. Portia won't step away from a challenge.

"So I went up to her at break and asked her what she thought she was doing."

That sounds so calm, but I can imagine how she's toning it down for us. I can see the group of baying kids, egging them on to fight. I can see Portia's hands balled defensively into fists.

"So what did she do?" Dan asks, barely controlling his anger.

"People were trying to get us to fight each other. She threw a bottle of water in my face and called me a bitch. She was trying to get me to go for her first, so I'd be the one who started it and she wouldn't get in trouble. But I'm not that stupid. Then she said she was going to print off the web pages and send them to you in the post so you'd know what—" She stops, her eyes filling up.

"So we'd know what, Portia?" Dan says. "There's nothing that stupid girl can do that would cause us to think any less of you. We know you—we're not going to believe the lies of some silly child."

"So you'd know how evil I am—that's what she said," she replies, sniffing. "And then I did lose it. I know it was wrong, but I hit her. And everyone was filming it on their phones. And I kept hitting her. It'll look on film as if it was all my fault, and afterward, I kept thinking about how I'd be suspended and you'd both be so disappointed in me." She curls up in a ball. "It all got to be too much, and I just couldn't cope anymore. I wasn't thinking straight. I just ran."

It hurts so much to think of her going through this. "Where did you go?"

"I had enough money in my purse to buy some food, so I went to a burger bar and sat there for as long as I could. Then I went to another and did the same, just buying small amounts. I got through like that until quite late, and then I was scared somebody would ask me what I was doing. I was starting to get funny looks because I was in my uniform. I went back again in the morning and did the same thing."

"But where did you spend the night?" This is what scared me most, her vulnerability once everything closed and there was nowhere to go.

She looks ashamedly down at her nails. "I got scared, so I snuck back and slept in the shed."

"What—our shed?" It was at the bottom of the garden.

"Yes. I know it's stupid, but—"

"It's not stupid," Dan says firmly. "It was a very sensible thing to do. So was contacting us last night." He grips her shoulder. "You've done very well.

Running away wasn't the right thing to do, but I'm proud of you for how you've handled everything after that. And don't worry about school—I think they have a good picture since the police got involved."

"But I don't want to go back yet, Dad. I'm not ready."

He nods and turns away, but I catch a glimpse of his face, and he looks like he's taken that hard. She doesn't want to go back at all. I know that, but Portia knows her dad won't accept that right now, so she's playing for time. He'll want her to stand firm and not be forced out by bullies, but she and I both know she's not strong enough to face that so soon after Becca's death.

"You know the rest," Portia says. "I sat around trying to find the courage to call and come home, but I was scared how much trouble I'd caused. And then that woman came to sit with me and persuaded me to text you. She was really nice and told me not to worry—you wouldn't be cross with me. Her name was Clare, and I forgot to say thanks to her." She sniffs again. "I'm so sorry for all of it."

"Hush," I tell her, hugging her. "You have nothing to be sorry about. And I thanked her, so I'm sure she'll understand you couldn't at that point. I don't think she'll mind."

Later, when Dan and I are sitting in bed, still feeling a little shell-shocked and battered, I ask him why her comment about not going back to school bothered him so much.

"I've let her down," he says quietly. "She wasn't ready, and I pushed her into going back too soon because I thought it was the best thing. I thought it would distract her and help her get over it. I was wrong. I didn't expect you to be over it in a matter of weeks, and I shouldn't have expected it of her either."

"She'll be OK now," I reply. "We'll give her the time, and she'll recover."

"Anything could have happened to her out there," he says, lying down to try to sleep, shutting down the conversation. "Anything." I touch his shoulder to comfort him, but he shakes off my hand.

I'm stunned. I don't know what to say. I wait for him to take a moment, and then I expect him to say something, but he doesn't.

"Dan?" I say tentatively.

"Just leave it," he replies in a voice I've never heard him use with me before.

"Can we please—"

"No!" And he gets up and leaves the room. A minute later, I hear the door of the spare room close and the creak of the bed as he settles on it.

I lie awake in case he comes back, but he doesn't.

What just happened? What's wrong with him?

44

THE FOLLOWING DAY, DAN ACTS like nothing happened, so I pretend along with him.

Portia does not go back to school. I tell them she's taking some time off for bereavement purposes. They were keen to have her back so they could deal with the bullying issues, but she's not strong enough for that yet. My daughter is tough, but even tough people need their time to grieve and heal.

Grief is a kind of twilight world, I tell Portia, where you can hold on to the ghost of the person you've lost, where the worst thing possible seems to be moving on and getting over them, because then they really have gone. And she nods, her eyes filling with tears. She needs time and space to be able to come through this. She refuses to see a professional counselor—it's not her thing, she says. She just wants to be at home.

And that's OK, I tell myself. *I'll bring her through this.*

Dan, on the other hand, buries himself in work. He's now at his office for longer, and I wonder if he's avoiding being at home because he can't stand seeing Portia fall apart.

"It's part of getting over it," I tell him as he comes in one day to find her crying silently in the sitting room. "It's just happening later for her. She's bottled it up, but it has to come out somehow." But I can see his disquiet brewing as he sees her crumbling day after day. He works late into the night, shutting himself away from us.

"You need to take a break, Dan," I tell him one Sunday night, because he's been in the study all weekend. "It's half past ten now, and you've been in here since this morning. You're not even coming out to eat."

"Do you remember how scared you were when she ran away that the person who did this had gotten her?" he snaps at me. "Then stop getting in my way! I'm trying to uncover who is responsible because the police are getting nowhere. Whoever it is, they're still out there, and while they are, you're not safe."

His anger shakes me. I tell myself that it's not meant for me but for the killer, but still, I leave him in there and go to bed. When I wake at 2 a.m., he's still not come up.

I call Aidan a few days later and ask him if he thinks Dan is OK. "I don't know, Lizzie, I think this is maybe one of those things he just has to work through. He needs to do something practical, and this is his way of dealing with it."

And that makes sense, I guess.

I can feel the stress inside Dan, building. I can see it in every exhausted line of his face, and I don't know how to fix it. I can barely deal with myself and Portia right now. I have nothing to give to help him. In order to function, I have to close down my fear about the killer. I have to let him be the strong one dealing with that. My daughter and I are still in pieces. We are not over that crash, and we haven't come to terms with Becca's death. "I've come a long way," I tell Stella when I speak to her, but I still have miles to go. I can get through the day now, and I can look after Portia. Anything else is still beyond me.

I allow Dan his space to search for an answer, but as time goes on, I wonder if the killer will ever be found, and doubt begins to creep back in my mind that perhaps those brakes were really damaged in the descent down the bank after all. Maybe there is no shadowy figure out there. Maybe Dan is doing all this for nothing. It happened months ago. If the killer was still a threat, wouldn't he have struck again by now? If there is a killer, of course.

Sometimes when Dan looks at me, I think I see resentment brewing that I'm not taking him seriously, that I'm not doing more to help. And then I see the guilt come swiftly after that—when he sees Portia and realizes how vulnerable she is now.

His temper is too quick to rise these days. Dan's never been like that; he's always been on an even keel in a storm. But at the moment, he sparks up over the slightest thing. He keeps it away from Portia, and I'm glad of that, but I see his eyes flash so often at something I say or do. He begins to bark a response at me, and then he stops. He holds himself in, and he leaves the room. It takes longer and longer before he's ready to come back. And as time goes on, there's a slump to his shoulders every day that never used to be there.

He still checks under the car before he drives it. He sneaks out so Portia doesn't see him, but he's stopped caring if I do. Slowly but surely, he's becoming someone else in front of my eyes, someone I don't recognize.

I thought there was a gap between us before the accident; it feels like a chasm right now.

45

ONE AFTERNOON, ANNIKA TURNS UP unannounced at the house.

"We're going for a drive," she informs me. She ignores my questions and protests and hustles me into her car. The back seat is filled with flowers—literally filled. The car is full of their scent.

"What are those for?"

"You'll see."

And she puts her foot on the accelerator and zooms us off. It's ten minutes before I realize where we are going. My heart begins to pound, and the shock makes me shiver all over. "Annika, what are you doing?"

"Dealing with it," she says, with not even a glance at me as she continues to drive.

Five minutes later, she pulls up in the cemetery parking lot, and I am cold and shaking.

"I can't believe you're doing this," I say as she gets out.

She opens the rear door and takes armfuls of flowers out of the car. "She was my goddaughter, and I never got to say goodbye. I'm doing that now because it needs to be done. I have to, and Becca would want it. Are you coming?"

I want to be petulant at her railroading. I want to be angry and shriek at her. Or I want to fall into a puddle of grief at her feet. I don't know which. But am I going to let her walk down there alone and put flowers on my daughter's grave without me?

No, I'm not.

I get out of the car with someone else's strength, because my legs wouldn't hold me up through this. Annika fills my arms with a bouquet of old country roses, their wide and open pink blooms releasing the most delicious scent. They're my favorites, and so they were Becca's, too—she loved to copy Mummy. My eyes sting, but I will not cry now; I will not. Annika's right—Becca would want this, and that's what matters. It's not about me here. I have to hold it together for my little girl. I have to do it for her.

I guide Annika to the grave. I've only been here once, on the day we buried Becca. I can't stand to think of her in here, under cold, wet earth. I bury my nose in the soft roses to hold back the tears. When their perfume fills my nostrils, I can almost hear her giggle. She always used to laugh when we smelled roses. They just made her happy.

There's no headstone yet at Becca's grave, just a marker. It hasn't been long enough for me to have a stone set in place. Dan had wanted to talk to me about the inscription so he could order it in advance, but I just couldn't even consider it. The very thought is unbearable. It's the permanence of it. How do you say goodbye in stone?

Annika lays her flowers down at the foot of the grave to allow mine to take their place at the top. When I bend to place them, I realize exactly what she's done—the huge sprays cover the area of her little body completely.

I look up.

"Clothed in flowers," Annika says softly, and then I do cry. Not the noisy, out-of-control wailing of my breakdowns, but slow, fat, gentle tears that drop onto the rose blooms like rain.

Becca would like this, a flower-quilt of roses. If she were here, she would smile and hold my hand and tell me how pretty it is.

But she is not here. She never will be. I can't feel her. I want to feel her warm, wonderfully small fingers in mine. I want to hear her voice.

I want her back. I thought that longing for another baby was the strongest, most all-consuming desire a mother could have. I was wrong. It's nothing more than a storm next to the tsunami that this grief is.

And it will never, never end.

Annika puts her arm round my shoulders. "She's gone, Lizzie, and you have to let her go."

"I did let her go."

"I know, honey, I know, but you tried to get to her. No one could have done more. And you were the best mother to her. You gave her so much happiness."

Why us, Becca? Why did it have to happen to us? Why can't you still be here?

I'm never going to have an answer to that. I scrub at my face with the back of my hand, and Annika passes me a tissue.

Before we leave to go back to the car, Annika blows Becca a kiss and waits for me to do the same. I wouldn't have thought of it myself, but it helps me to leave, a more fitting farewell for such a little girl than words she can't hear.

As we are in the car on the way home, I tell Annika, "I didn't feel her there at all. There's was no presence of her, no nothing."

She nods her understanding, her eyes on the road. "Yeah, but it's like this: if you believe in the religious stuff, she's not there anyway. She's gone on to wherever it is you believe in. And if you think that's all a load of hogwash and there's nothing after death, then burial is just a last honor to the body. They're not there either way, not the person you knew."

"And what do you believe?" I'm curious because I've never asked her, and despite how long I've known her, I don't know what she thinks about this. It's never come up before.

She flashes me a big grin. "I believe the full monty, baby. She's not there: she's in the arms of God."

"Oh!" Her conviction surprises me.

"Yeah, I know," she says with a laugh. "You never had me pegged as a God-botherer. And no, I don't talk about it. Too many people put me off when I was a kid by constantly banging on about being saved. But yeah, I believe in all of it. I'm just crap at it. I mean, chastity—that's a concept designed for before the pill and condoms were invented, so I don't have issues with that. But like I've told you before, I'm selfish. And churches bore me senseless."

"But you believe it." I savor this new discovery like a fine wine rolling around my mouth.

"Yes, I really do. She's in a good place, Lizzie, the best."

It might be wishful thinking, but I don't care. I want to believe her. I want that for my child, so I swallow hard to keep the tears at bay, and I choose hope.

46

I HAVE MY REGULAR APPOINTMENT with Stella the next day, and I tell her about visiting Becca's grave.

"You said you had something to show me when I felt the time was right. Well, I think I'm ready now," I tell her. "I need to make progress with this, for the whole family's sake. And Becca would want that too. Help me do this."

It's a huge moment, this choosing to move on, and it takes my breath away for a beat.

Her calm voice breaks toward me—a soft wave against the shore. "OK, if you're ready."

I nod to her to begin.

"We need to look at your choice, and you need to accept it for what it is. Your decision is understandable. It had to be one of them. There was never going to be a right choice."

My cheeks flush immediately in that angry frustration still held so tightly inside me. I might have held it within for the past weeks, but it's not gone. "Do you understand how shocked I am at myself? I'm not the woman I thought I was."

"Go on—it's important you tell me."

"It's like I've told you before, or tried to. When you adopt a child, you tell yourself that you will love them like your own child. When you read stories of women who have adopted, they say they love those children just like their own. You're so careful never to treat them differently. You have to completely buy into that concept. You absolutely must or it's not fair!" I stop, struggling with what I need to tell her next, and she nods at me to take my time. I've never been able to say it this clearly before now. "So for me to do what I did, for the *reasons* I did, goes against all of that. That's what I can't live with—and that I know I would make exactly the same choice again. I would always make that choice. I should have never adopted her if I couldn't be a real mother to her!"

"You must also focus on the alternative: Would it have been right to let Portia drown because you had to think of Becca in the same way as your biological daughter?"

"No, I should have grabbed the first one!"

"And then you would have suffered over why it was that one. Lizzie, an awful thing happened to all of you, and one of you didn't make it."

I clutch my head in my hands. "But the reason—you're not understanding!"

"Oh, I do understand. And we need to deal with this now. You've made so much progress, but this always holds you back." She gets up and fetches a laptop. "So I want you to watch something. I found this for you." She clicks on a video. "Just watch."

The video starts to play. I'm looking at some kind of steep mud cliff in what looks like Africa. There's a baby lion cub caught on an outcrop on the side of the cliff, several feet down. He's crying out pathetically for help. "This is the Maasai Mara—a cub has fallen," Stella says. The camera pans up, and there's a group of lionesses on the top trying to scramble down but failing and backing up to try and fail again. "This is the family. His aunties are up there. They can't get him—the drop is just too sheer."

It's horrible to watch. The cub is so distressed, and those lionesses are frantic because they can't reach him. He calls up to them, but it seems they can't help.

And then another lioness approaches, pacing forward quickly as she passes the others. The cub is crying out, slipping and sliding, and it looks like he will lose his fight to cling on at any moment. The lioness doesn't delay. Unlike the others, there's no hesitation from her, and she descends precariously, grimly hanging on to the slippery surface with her claws. She makes her way down the steep slope slowly, the cub crying out to her. The deadly concentration on her face is painful to see, and I can feel the tension in my own body as I watch.

The cub slips and falls a little. He cries pitifully but manages to scrabble again to hold on. The lioness keeps on descending with absolute focus and determination. Then, as it seems he will fall completely, she circles rapidly beneath him and scoops him into her mouth by the scruff of his neck.

I glance at Stella in relief, only realizing then I'd been holding my breath. "Keep watching."

The lioness begins her equally difficult ascent back. I can see the muscles straining desperately in her back, and she buries her claws deep into the mud as she slithers back up. The weight and strain on those claws must be agonizing for her, but she continues on as the other lionesses wait above, watching her clamber back.

Finally, she drops the cub among the lionesses at the top of the cliff and hauls herself back over. She ushers him away from the edge to safety and then stops to lick his head and groom him.

There are tears rolling down my face.

"You know who she was, don't you?" Stella says gently.

"She's his mother." I can't stop the tears. They stream down my face and fall like rain into my lap.

"Do you understand? Those lionesses are all related. That's how lion society works. They share a role in caring for and rearing the cubs because they are all related—it's a real family bond. But even so, despite them looking after that cub daily, despite them being aunties and older sisters, the only one who can risk her life like that—without a second of hesitation—is his mother."

"Yes, I understand." I can't stop crying.

"You cannot fight it, Lizzie. Thousands of years of evolution go into creating what makes a mother battle for her child like that. And Lizzie, you went back for Becca. Remember that. And remember what you've told me about those divers—they struggled to get to her because of the depth. Divers with diving gear. And you tried, didn't you?"

I nod, unable to stop crying.

She moves to sit beside me on the sofa and hands me a tissue. "You must remember that lioness, Lizzie. And you must remember her sisters. This is the last step—you must forgive yourself."

47

DO YOU KNOW I AM *watching you yet?*
Do you see nothing?
Day after day, I am here. I watch and I wait.
But the time is coming.
It needs to be soon now.

48

A WEEK AFTER OUR VISIT to Becca's grave, Dan leaves early in the morning to get to court on the other side of the country. This is a case he's already committed to, and he can't get out of it. Once, he would have traveled the night before and stayed in a hotel, but not now. Portia and I are pottering about, tidying the house, and I am glancing out of the window from time to time, as I do. It's a habit I've developed, just as Dan checks the car in the morning. Portia comes into the sitting room as I'm hoovering and hands me a local TV guide. She points to an advert inside, and I turn off the vacuum to look.

The advert is about a theater workshop during the half-term break, but immediately, I see the time and location, and my heart sinks. Oakleigh—I've never heard of the place, but the address says it's in the next county. And it's next week.

"Do you want to go?"

"I think so," she says. "I'm sort of, you know, nervous about trying it, but I also think I want to, if that makes any sense."

"You loved this kind of thing when you were younger. I was always surprised you stopped."

She shrugs. "It was different when I was little."

"I suppose so, and it was the after-school sessions you most enjoyed, wasn't it?"

I remembered those well—it was the two nights of the week I didn't have to feel guilty about her being in after-school club so late, because the musical theater group came in to teach them and she loved it. Whenever possible, I used to try to arrange my late meetings for those nights. Dan said it never failed to surprise him that his daughter was so keen on performing. "Don't know where she gets that from," he said after watching her in one end-of-summer school production in which she positively glowed throughout.

"What do you think?" she asks, and I realize I've gone quiet on her.

"It's not in an easy spot to get to, is it? And it's half-term." Which means her father won't be able to take her because he'll be working. He's had enough time off already during the last few weeks. I see the shadow start to veil over her eyes, and something I've not realized before now strikes me with a force that makes me curse myself for being so stupid and not seeing this earlier for what it is—her protective reaction.

I swallow hard. Somehow, my adored and beloved daughter has developed this mechanism to shut herself off from us to protect herself. From what? Pain? Disappointment? I don't know, but whatever it is, I do know I must stop it.

"It's a good job I'm not back at work, isn't it?" I say before I even know I'm doing it, before I've taken in the implications of what I've said. "I'll take you."

Portia doesn't say it. She stares at me, but she doesn't say what we both know. The workshop is being held miles away. There are no buses out that way. There's no other way to get there than to drive. And of course, I stopped driving after the accident. Even though legally I was allowed to drive, as I was released without charge, I just couldn't do it. But there's only so long I can give excuses to not get into the car. What stops me now is fear. Cold, nauseating fear. The kind that leaves your muscles shaking and your skin slick with sweat.

I look steadily at my daughter, and with a deep breath, I ask her, "Do you want me to drive you there?"

Something passes over her face, some emotion that I can't read. "Yes," she says quietly.

I get my phone and text a response to the number on the ad.

I won't deny that when the time comes, I'm utterly terrified as I get behind the wheel. Dan suggested taking me for a drive round the block, but I said no, I'd manage. I spend the three days before I'm due to make the journey edging myself behind the wheel and just sitting in the car. And trying to control my racing pulse, the metallic taste of fear in my mouth.

It's Dan's car. We haven't replaced mine. He said he'll take the train this week so I can drive Portia. "You could have booked cabs, you know," he said when I'd told him about it.

"I never even thought of that," I confessed. "How stupid of me."

"It doesn't matter," he replied, "and it's good that you do try. You never know when you might need to drive again."

He's not comfortable with the idea of us going at all, but we can't stay locked up in here forever.

"The longer this goes on, Dan, the more it looks like the police could be wrong. And if we're not telling her about the car, how can we keep her shut up like this? Either we have to let her do this kind of thing or we have to tell her what's going on."

He doesn't agree about the police, I can see that, but he does say, "OK, you're right—she does need to get out. But be careful. Be very careful."

The first time I sit in the car sneakily while he's having a shower so nobody but me knows, I nearly lose it and phone a cab company to make a booking, but I need to do this.

Five minutes, I tell myself. *Work up to it.*

So on Monday at 8 a.m., I get behind the wheel of my husband's car, and I turn on the ignition. Dan was out here at 7 a.m. checking the car over, and he's been keeping an eye on it from the window ever since to make sure nobody has been near it. My pulse quickens immediately at the sound of the engine, and I don't think I'm going to be able to do this. I'm going to lose it. The thumping in my chest, the way my breathing tightens—it's all going to go wrong. Portia's watching me, and I'm going to let her down.

I *cannot* let her down. I have to do this for her.

Hold it together, Lizzie, I tell myself in the voice I'd use in court.

I'm not going to crash. I'm going to get her there safely. She needs her life back. And she needs me to be strong for her. I'm not flaking out on her now. I imagine her eyes if I fail now, and some hidden strength inside steels and takes over me.

I glance over to make sure she's buckled in, and I pull out into the street. My hands are shaking on the wheel, but I don't say anything that gives me away.

"What do you want on the radio?" she asks, and I can feel her eyes on me.

"Classic FM, please."

I let her change the station, and I focus on the road. I hold her belief that I'm going to actually do this like a talisman to keep my fear locked up carefully inside me. It takes forty-five minutes to get to the village hall booked for the workshop, and it's forty-five minutes of white-knuckled control on my part. I don't dare even look to see if Portia is nervous with me at the wheel. I'm blocking that out, and I can't bear to see her face if she is scared. That might destroy me.

Miles of tarmac filled with other vehicles in rush-hour hell face us. But that's better than empty roads, in some ways. I have to concentrate, and when we arrive at the village hall, I make the excuse that I need the toilet so I can go and run cold water over my wrists to cool down my sweat and splash my flushed face.

I look in the mirror as the water drips off my nose. I made it. I did it for Portia.

She's looking about nervously as I come back into the foyer. "I'm not quite sure where to go."

A woman hurries out of a door down the corridor ahead.

She's dressed in dance gear.

"Excuse me," I call to her. "We're here for the theater workshop."

"Oh, hi. I'm Alex," she calls back, flustered. "I'll be there in a moment. Just go through to the hall over there."

I follow the wave of her hand through some double doors, beckoning Portia to follow me. The hall is already busy with teenagers lounging around, some of whom know each other while others, like Portia, are alone. She's standing behind me, all but using me as a shield.

The woman we saw in the corridor breezes in. "Hi!" she shouts above the clamor. "OK, over here, everyone, so I can check you off on the list."

Portia hovers beside me, suddenly uncertain.

"I don't know anyone either," says a voice by my elbow. We both turn to look.

It's a boy I guess to be the same age as Portia. He's got a shock of floppy chestnut hair and a confident smile. I can't help but smile back at him. He's wearing the same kind of ridiculous, scruffy black clothes as my daughter. He scratches his head. "I don't want to go over there on my own," he tells her. "Can I come with you?"

"Er, y-yes," Portia stammers, caught by surprise.

His grin widens, and he beckons to her with a jerk of his head. As they go off to the front, he turns and looks back at me. "She'll be fine," he mouths and gives me a surreptitious thumbs-up.

I smile back and return the signal. My mother instincts then go into protective overdrive for a moment as I wonder if he's an ax murderer/druggie/controlling, abusive freak. But I check myself, because the likelihood is he's a sweet kid who picked up how scared she was when we came in. And if he does think she's cute, who can blame him? She's a very pretty girl, and he obviously has good taste.

After she's had her name ticked off, Portia looks back at me and gives me a nod—I can go.

Out in the parking lot, I'm not entirely sure what to do next. I could go for a walk, but walking alone always feels off-key to me unless I'm going somewhere. When I was a child, we had a dog, and walking a dog has a sense of purpose to it. If we did have a dog, I could have brought it today, and then a walk would have felt good and like something healthy to do. For a fleeting second, I consider getting a puppy or a rescue dog, but what would we do with it when I go back to work? And is it safe to go for a walk? A swift jab of resentment strikes me at how our lives are being destroyed by this monster out there—if they exist.

I drag some sneakers out of the car and put them on. They're too pristine for a country walk; these have only seen the interior of an air-conditioned gym. I walk off down the lane with my imaginary dog. What would it be? Some kind of spaniel? But not in the city, for those are country dogs. A friend had a black cocker spaniel when I was a child, and that was the sweetest little thing. My father had Labradors, gentle, heavily molting lumps of dogs that padded around after him and left tumbleweeds of hair floating through the house, to my mother's dismay.

I don't know what kind of dog I'd have with our lifestyle, and it would have to spend most of its day in one of those glorified doggy day care centers. As I walk out briskly along the lane, I indulge in the fantasy that it might actually happen. I've got no idea where I'm going, but hopefully there will be some signs. Or I'll stop and see if I can get a signal on my phone. It's a pretty little lane, anyway, with suggestions of spring in the hedges—green buds on the bare twigs and the strap-like leaves of bluebells shooting up beneath.

I used to love my job. Despite all the running around and the frustration at how manic our lives could be, I loved the actual work itself. All the variety and the mental challenge, that was what kept me going. And let's face it, the steady adrenaline of a battle of wits in court gave me the buzz I needed. So why do I feel sick at the thought of going back to it?

Everyone assumes it's because I'm not over Becca's death yet, but Stella has taught me I will never be over it. I've been seeing her every week, and I know now that I will learn to change and carry on in some way, but it will never be over, and I will never be the same Lizzie Fulton again. Stella's job has been to guide me through so I can find a way to go on, not make me forget.

I come to a crossroads of lanes. The signs point in all directions. There's a narrow lane ahead pointing to somewhere called Nether Cossington, three miles away. I consult my phone. It's a smallish village, but there is a farm shop with a café nearby. That will do, and I strike out again in that direction.

If I could remake my life now, what would I do?

It's the kind of question I'd expect anyone to ask after a life-changing event. It's a reasonable question for a woman of my age, old enough to know this might be one of the last times before retirement that I'll have the option to turn my life upside down and twist it around and young enough to still be able to do it.

A car passes by, and I step onto the curb. The scent of new leaves crushed underfoot makes me linger there and breathe in. I don't think I can go back to what I did. The idea of dealing with parents fighting wars over who gets to keep their children seems monstrous to me now. I want to scream at them how lucky they are that they have a living child at all.

Something will have to change.

With that realization, my mind clears as morning mists disperse to a sunny day. It's like an energy surging through my tired body as my mind stops fighting. It's OK to change. It is OK.

Even before Becca died, I was drawn to making a change. Now it's more than being drawn—it's a survival instinct. It's what I need to live.

I keep going toward the coffee shop. Nether Cossington turns out to be a little gem of a village with houses of honeyed stone and mullioned windows. The farm shop café has delightful scrubbed wooden tables, and, to my joy, it is largely empty. I'm able to get a seat by a window, looking out over fields of rich earth beginning to spring with green.

I have to be the solution-finder for this dilemma. If I want to turn us around, then I have to examine the practicalities. To begin with, what am I actually thinking of?

Number one, I want out of our house—there are too many memories. I thought I loved our house, and it turns out that when I think this through, I still do, but I also want to leave it behind now. I have sweated and scrubbed and broken nails renovating that house to make it what I wanted, and now it is no longer my choice. I choose to go. All the memories of Becca skipping through the rooms are countered with the sadness of how our family grew away from each other and with the grief that followed her death, as though that is soaked into the plaster.

Number two, I want out of the city. Maybe I'm being stupid and it's that I don't spend enough time in the country to remember all the downsides, but recently, it has made me happy when nothing else has. Not that heady, giddy happiness I had in my twenties of discovering the world and all it had to offer before the kids, when Dan and I traveled. When we would just come home from work and spill out to a restaurant with friends because we could. We'd stay up far too late in good company, burning the candle at both ends. No, this happiness is a quiet and gentle pleasure, a deep contentment but bone-deep. If I want to learn to live again, it is that I need.

Number three, I have to change my job. I can still practice law but not as I have done. It is not for me anymore. I am done with it. Maybe I could lecture or move into a different branch, something completely removed from family disputes or anything emotionally charged in that way. I can look into it.

I sit back. This is the clearest my head has been since the accident, and for a moment, I feel exhausted by the thinking, but then comes an exhilaration at taking back control. I have achieved something here.

But I can't move my family around like chess pieces and be the only one who is made happier by it. And I can't do anything with the ever-present threat hanging over our heads.

I finish my coffee and walk back through the village. It's stupid and it's impractical, but I still can't give up on considering it. I'll talk to Dan. He may not like it, but I will at least try. And if he's not as averse as I think he will be, maybe he'll know how to approach Portia about it.

A pipe dream, I tell myself sternly. *They'll both hate it.*

But I have to try.

I arrive back at the village hall ten minutes before I need to collect Portia. I sneak in and look through the double doors. She's sitting with that boy from earlier, smiling and chatting while the workshop leader sets up a scene with some props. She calls Portia over with another girl.

She clicks her fingers for them to begin, and I watch my lost, lonely daughter come alive again as she transforms into someone else. I'm suddenly taken back eight years to when I used to watch her little school productions, and I would see her light up when she got up there and performed. She has lost none of that. This *is* Portia, and it's incredible to see her return. Tears prick my eyes, but I'm smiling so hard my cheeks hurt.

I hang around, watching her, but when I see they are finishing up, I scuttle away from the door and go to lounge on one of the seats in the foyer, where other parents are beginning to gather. Portia comes out with the boy. He gives me an acknowledging smile as he leaves and waves to her as he exits. She gives me a funny look—that caginess she usually uses around me hovers over her face, but she's still flushed from the buzz of the workshop.

"Fun?" I ask her, and to hell with it, I hug her the way I want to and don't care who sees or if this is the cool thing to do. To my surprise, she doesn't pull away. "Shall we go for lunch?"

We go to a country pub. Portia orders lasagna. "I'm hungry," she says, adding some garlic bread to the order. And I could run back to that village hall and kiss the feet of Alex, the workshop leader, or whatever she is called.

"So why did you drop drama at school if you like this kind of thing so much?" She'd never shown any interest in taking the subject for her GCSE exams, and it hadn't even come up when we chose her classes. I thought she had completely lost interest.

She sighs, picking at some olives I've ordered as an appetizer. "The drama teacher is so rubbish. Everyone there hates drama and hardly anyone takes it. Most years they don't even run the course. The lessons are awful, and nobody behaves. And, if you do try to get into it, everybody just mocks you."

"Why didn't you say something?"

She shrugs. "I guess at first, I thought that's just how it was at high school and that it was always rubbish, but I was wrong."

As we drive home after lunch, she's still talking about the play they were working on, which turns out to be *The Crucible*, and I'm enjoying her conversation. I turn a corner on a quiet lane.

"It's seems incredible that people could almost catch hysteria when you look at it under normal circumstances, but it has happened again and again through history, hasn't it? And I guess that's what—"

I'm concentrating on what she says, so the next thing I notice is a horn blaring as a big BMW bears down on us at speed.

My hands freeze on the wheel, my palms suddenly slippery with sweat. I jam my foot onto the brake.

I can hear as if in the distance, the horn is still shouting at me; I can hear Portia, too, screaming and yelling, but everything has gone dark… And I can see it all again, slowly, slowly enough to process what's happening…

It is dark, so dark out here, except for the blinding headlights coming toward me.

The girls are asleep in the back of the car.

I can't see.

I try to brake, and then again, I slam my foot down, but there's no response. Something isn't working. I should be slowing down now. The brakes don't feel normal.

The blinding lights head straight for me.

It's a car coming head on.

I check my side of the road frantically. No, no, it's not me… I *am* on the right side of the road. I swerve to avoid the oncoming car, and to my utter horror, it follows my line, coming straight back at me again. Fast, no sign of stopping.

I swerve again, and it adjusts its line, coming at me still.

I have no choice. I wrestle the wheel to the side, and the car crashes off the road and into the trees—

"Mum! Mum!" Portia shakes my shoulder. "Mum, please!"

My vision clears, and I am back in the daylit country lane, my clammy hands gripping the wheel. The BMW is gone, and we are skewed off the lane on the shoulder. I rub my face hard to get some feeling back in it as Portia leans over me, anxious.

"I'm OK." My words come out thickly, and indeed, I feel drugged, as if I'm coming back from a long way off.

"Ignore him," Portia says, her voice sharp and cross. "What a pig! It was his fault—he was going far too fast. Are you OK?"

I check my mirrors. We are still too close to the bend in the lane for safety, so I start up the stalled car and move us down to a passing place, where I can pull up again and try to still my trembling hands.

"Are you OK?" Portia repeats.

I remember. I remember.

49

WHAT'S WRONG? SHE MEANS THE car… Oh yes…the car.

I'm in shock. I can't hold it back any longer, and I begin to cry.

She shakes me again. "Mum, you're scaring me. What happened?"

I respond to the panic in her voice, to that remnant of my little girl calling for her mummy. It pulls me back once more. "Nothing, nothing. I had a flashback, that's all."

"That's all? What kind of flashback?"

"The accident. Look, I don't want to talk about it. Let's just go home."

"Did you remember something?" she asks urgently.

The lie arrives on my tongue, and I am grateful. "No. No, I didn't."

"That guy was so out of order. He was going way too fast. It was completely his fault."

"Some people do drive like idiots on country lanes," I reply weakly. "Forget it. We're fine."

It's a long journey back. Portia is pale and tense and silent. It's a very strange feeling, but I know now that there was no way I could have stopped us going off the road that night—the other driver made sure of that. And now there's no reason for me to be nervous at the wheel. It wasn't my fault.

It wasn't my fault.

I am not to blame for the car going into the lake. I didn't hurt my girls. It wasn't me.

Something builds within me.

As I drive home, a quiet furnace of rage ignites inside me, its fire low in my belly. Someone *did* do this to us. Someone incontrovertibly set out to hurt us. The brake damage found by the forensics team could certainly not have been accidental. All my doubts mean nothing now. It was a deliberate act to kill us.

Someone sabotaged our brakes and then drove us off the road. Somebody out there is responsible for killing Becca and for almost killing Portia.

The flames of that fire of anger within me lick higher.

Whoever did this is not going to get away with it. I'm going to see to that.

All of the time I have wasted on guilt, on hating myself, on wondering whether it was simply a case of the police having got it wrong—I could have used that time pursuing justice for my girls. Well, there'll be no more of that. I know what I need to do now, and that is to make sure whoever did this to us is found and is locked up until they rot. While I didn't know the truth, I was weak, but no longer.

Heat rises through my body, burning. They're going to pay for this. No price is high enough for what they've done. They are going to pay and pay and pay. And I'm never going to stop coming for more.

"Mum, are you OK?" Portia asks in a small voice as we drive into more familiar streets.

I reach over and pat her knee. "Yes, darling. I'm absolutely fine. Everything is OK."

Don't be scared, sweetheart. Mummy will fix it. Just like she used to make those nightmares go away when you were small.

I know what I'm fighting now. I might not know who yet, but I will.

When we get back to the house, it's empty. Dan's not home yet, but I hadn't really expected him to be. I check my watch and estimate he'll probably be at least another hour.

I usher Portia into the sitting room and stream a film onto the TV for her, then supply her with snacks. For once she doesn't object to being railroaded in that way. When she's safely out of the way, I call Annika from the privacy of the kitchen.

"Listen, something's happened. I may need a hand tomorrow. Are you available?"

I pause as she checks her planner.

"You are? Great. Could you take Portia to a theater workshop for me?

There's something I'm going to need to do. I've remembered something about the accident. I need to talk to the police."

Naturally, she wants to know what it is, but I should tell Dan first. I explain that I'll call her later.

"Something smells good," Dan says when he gets home and walks through to the kitchen to find me making dinner. He can't quite keep the surprise from his voice. "Did Portia's workshop go well? Everything was OK? You look...different."

Purposeful—I look purposeful. Because that's what I am now. "Yes, fine. Portia loved it. She's going again tomorrow."

Portia appears in the doorway behind her father. I take in her thin shoulders and nervous stance, her dark eyes, too sad and watchful for a fifteen-year-old, and the flames in my belly stoke further.

"Dad...?" She glances over to me. Her eyes ask me if I'm going to tell him.

"We'll talk about the other thing after dinner," I say briskly.

"What other thing?" Dan asks, instantly alert. It's like he's constantly on the watch for a threat these days.

"After dinner. You go and get changed. It won't be long." I shoo him out of the kitchen.

Portia lingers, watching me work with those large, serious eyes. "I'll talk to him later," I tell her gently. She isn't convinced, but she drops it for now.

Dan comes down in a T-shirt and cotton sweats. He looks tired and his hair is ruffled from getting changed, but he hasn't bothered to smooth it back into place. He sits wearily at the table, joined by Portia, and watches me as we eat.

"So tell me about your workshop," he says to Portia.

"Really, really good," she replies, her eyes lighting with enthusiasm again, which displaces the trauma of the rest of the day's events. "I'm so glad I signed up for it." She tells him about it while I listen to them talk.

"So what was it you needed to tell me?" Dan asks as he finishes eating.

"Mum nearly had an accident today," Portia blurts out.

"Let your dad finish eating," I tell her as he looks up questioningly.

She shuffles in her seat, anxious, but she waits as I've asked until he's finished the last mouthful. "An accident?" he asks as he sets down his fork.

"Yes, while I was driving."

He sits forward in alarm. "What happened?"

"I drove 'round a bend in a country lane, and a car came round the corner at the same time."

"He was going much too fast, Dad," Portia cuts in. "It was his fault, not Mum's."

Panic crosses Dan's face. "Did you crash? Who was it?"

"No, I pulled the car over."

"The guy was really rude, Dad. He was yelling at us out of his window, and it was completely his fault!"

And I hadn't even noticed that, so lost in the returning memory of that night at the lake. I'd been oblivious to what Portia described.

"It wasn't what you're thinking," I tell Dan quickly, with an urgent look to press my point home.

He nods discreetly to tell me he's understood and tries to respond in kind to dispel suspicion. "Lizzie, that's really bad. Are you OK?"

"Let's talk about that after, Dan?" I cast a meaningful look toward Portia.

He stops and sucks in his breath. "OK, right, yes. We'll talk about it later."

Portia begins to interrupt, but Dan gets up and starts clearing the table. I follow quickly, and Dan changes the conversation back to Portia's workshop until he's loaded the dishwasher. Recognizing the subject is at an end, she goes off to watch TV in her room.

"So what happened?" he asks quietly when he's sure she's gone.

"I remembered the accident, that's what happened. I haven't told Portia, but I saw what happened as if I was still there." I brace myself to describe it again. "There was another car that night. We weren't the only ones on the road. The damage to the brakes happened before we went off road—I'm sure of that now. The other car drove directly at us. I swerved and swerved to avoid it, but it kept coming at us. It forced me off the road. The brakes failed then, yes, but the brakes weren't why I went off the road in the first place. It was quite deliberate, Dan. If I hadn't gotten out of its path, it would have gone straight into the car, and it was swerving after me to try to hit us. It didn't even try to brake or slow down."

His face drains of color. "Are you sure about this? Could it have been some kind of false memory? Maybe because that car today forced you out of the way and you projected?"

I shake my head. "No, Dan, this was the real deal. It's the part that's been missing. I could remember my fear as it happened. I was living it again, but I knew what was going to happen before it did. This was a memory, a true memory."

He slumps heavily in his chair. Does he still not believe me?

"I told you I knew I hadn't fallen asleep. I couldn't remember how it happened, but I knew it wasn't that. Well, you see, I really didn't nod off. This is why I knew. It was such a horrible thing that it even penetrated through the amnesia to tell me that something else had happened, even though I couldn't remember what that was."

He covers his face with his hands, and his lack of response infuriates me. Where's his anger? He knows now, without a shadow of doubt, that somebody attempted to kill us. What kind of reaction is this?

"You do realize what this means?" I ask.

It takes him a while to answer. Then he pulls his hands away from his face. "It means we're going to the police." He stares at me, and I can see his struggle to reassert control over his feelings. It's been a huge shock for him, too, and I need to try to remember that. What I just said to myself is right—I've had a few more hours to process this than he has. Obviously he's struggling.

"It's late," I say more calmly. "It'll be much better to do this tomorrow when we've had some sleep. A few more hours aren't going to make a difference after all these months. Let's do it in the morning."

He takes a deep breath and then nods. "I guess. And I suppose it'll be easier to keep it from Portia then."

I heave a sigh of relief. "Exactly."

But he avoids my eyes and bustles about locking the house up until I give up waiting and leave him alone. He sleeps downstairs in the chair, I think.

Sometimes I think there is nothing left of this marriage. Sometimes, in the dark times, in the early hours, I remember how I felt after the accident, and I know it was true: this family is finished.

50

THEY'RE BREAKING APART. SOMETIMES I *watch them through the night, like tonight. He stays downstairs. I don't know what precipitated this latest breach. I wonder if they have found anything out. Do they know about me yet? Do they actually suspect anything?*

The hours before the dawn—how well I know that time. They will be awake, both of them.

I'll leave just before first light.

If I'd seen them like this last year, it would have brought me so much pleasure. Now, their pain and mine are entwined in an eternal knot.

So much pain; so much death.

And it's not over yet.

51

I FEEL SICK AS DS Booth shows us into the interview room at the police station.

"Found another possible suspect?" he asks.

"No, I've had a flashback. I remembered what happened on the road before we crashed." It gives me satisfaction to see his eyebrows quirk upward in surprise.

He looks at Dan and me in turn. "Can I see you separately, please? It's important we do it like this."

Dan nods. "Probably best—then we won't contaminate anything for trial."

I don't really want to do this without Dan, but I suppose I'll have to.

"So what happened?" Booth asks me when we're in the interview room and the tape is running.

I run through my memory, seeing it again as it happened in front of my eyes. "We were run off the road," I tell him. "It was no accident, and that means those brakes were deliberately damaged."

He sits back and looks at me hard. "And you're sure this 'memory' is real? It's not your mind playing tricks on you?"

"No, it's real. As it was happening, I knew what would come next before I got to that part. And that's because I'd lived through it once already. Someone tried to kill us all."

He makes a clicking sound with his tongue against his teeth. "That doesn't rule out your husband, you know."

"Oh, for heaven's sake," I cry in exasperation. "It wasn't Dan! And you know that. I know you do."

"I have to look at evidence dispassionately. That's my job." But he says it without the animosity he had toward us before, so this time, I believe him.

"Well, maybe you could do some digging around to see if that man, Vaughan, has talked about getting back at Dan recently. Someone must know."

He nods slowly. "I am. I have feelers out, but he's not high on our list of suspects right now."

"But Dan and I are?"

"There are clear motives for both of you in coming up with this story. If it's you who fell asleep at the wheel, then you're trying to cover your tracks now with this story, and the damage was done as the car went down the bank. If it's your husband, he or whoever he hired could have driven you off the road as easily as anyone else. I can't assume anything, Mrs. Fulton. I'm a professional police officer. I have to look at all possibilities before I eliminate anybody."

"Maybe you could look in a bit more detail at the list of 'possibles' he's given you, then!" I can't prevent my infuriation showing.

He adopts a resigned expression. He's working through his procedure, no matter how much that annoys me. "If there's nothing further you can tell me, I'd like to interview your husband now, please."

"He'll need his lawyer, then," I reply sharply. And I pull out my phone, ignoring him, and call Aidan.

It's two hours before we can finally leave, and I know they're not sure they can believe my story.

"And that's what worries me most," Aidan says when I tell him this. "Because that means they're not going to look thoroughly for whoever did do this. Do you think you should request police protection now?"

"No," Dan and I reply simultaneously.

"I've had experience of a witness going into protection—someone I know from a murder case," Dan continues. "It's hell. You give up your life, your friends… Everything changes. You're in a different area of the country with no family backup. Work is impossible. Mine and Lizzie's jobs are too traceable. We'd need a complete career change. Our lives would be turned upside down, and after everything Lizzie and Portia have been through already, we need to try another alternative."

"I remember that case Dan is talking about," I tell Aidan. "They had a teenage son, and he accidentally gave their identities away to a friend online. Blew the whole thing open, and they had to start again somewhere else."

"You could ask them to put somebody on watch at the house."

"We could," I reply, "and that might make me feel better, but the killer didn't come after us at home, did he?"

Aidan falls silent.

"And the answer to that," I retort, suddenly fierce, "is not for us to go into hiding but for them to find who did it! And if the police won't try, then we need to try all the harder. Maybe we'll find something we missed at first."

Aidan runs his hands through his hair as he thinks. "You're both right," he says. "I'll help."

We spend the rest of the day at Dan's office going through every note we've made, looking again for any discernible motive. "There's nothing that stands out, though," Aidan says despairingly. "God, it has to be something significant for someone to go and do this."

"It's what we found last time," Dan says. "Lots of possible angles for resentment, but nothing clear-cut. Vaughan would be the most obvious, but it's so long ago. Tyler got sent down, so he's out of the frame. The others—it all amounts to a heap of resentment but no clear, compelling reason to go after our kids. Yes, get me worked over or a contract out on me. I could understand that from some of the people on the list, but not my children. We're missing something here—we have to be. What *is* it?"

Aidan gives him a sharp look, picking up, as I do, that Dan's tone is too agitated, too unlike him. His hands are shaking—he's holding a file, and I can see it visibly wobbling. He needs to find this person, I understand that, but it's become an obsession now. A way to smother his fear for our safety, and until he does find the killer, he won't have any peace. His whole identity as a husband and father has become tied up with this.

And he's failing. That's what he thinks—it's clear to both Aidan and me, from the desperate look in his eyes. I've never seen Dan look weak like this, like he will disintegrate at any minute. Every day we don't find an answer, he gets worse. He tries to hold on, but he's losing his grip, and I can't help him.

I feel a fresh burst of hate for the man who did this to us. I was right in the beginning when I believed Becca's death would destroy us. Slowly, we are self-destructing: first me, then Portia, and now Dan. Because of one man's hate, and for what? We still have no answer to that.

I feel the reach of that hate as if it's a real person, my shadow figure from the nightmares.

Are you out there? Do you like seeing what you've done to us? Do you? Well, I'm not going to let you get away with it. I will find out who you are.

52

ANNIKA'S INVALUABLE OF LATE. SHE'S taken Portia out again, clothes shopping this time. Dan and I are supposed to be having some quality relaxation time together. Not that she expects us to relax, because how can we in the current situation? But life has to go on, and we can't sit here in suspended animation, waiting for the police to actually catch who's responsible. Dan and I are stretched as thin as violin strings right now under the tension of it.

I watch my husband pace around. He doesn't know how to relax anymore. He used to burn off his work stress by cycling, but his bike chain is rusty now from lack of use.

I am watching him self-destruct, and I am powerless.

I haven't been able to finish grieving for my daughter. Not only did this monster take my daughter from us, he's taken my grief too. I exist for revenge now. To attack.

As my rage builds, so Dan drops further into whatever private hell he survives in. He's very careful not to let me in there.

He goes into the study and closes the door. I can still hear him pacing up and down over the parquet floor.

I gather up my resolve and go in after him. He's by the window; I'm struck by how rigid his back is, as if he'll fall apart if I touch him, as if he'll shatter.

"Dan?"

"Leave me alone, please." His voice is odd, taut.

"Are you all right?"

"Yes. I need to be on my own. Please go away."

"Has something happened?"

He begins to shudder all over, as if he's had ice water poured over him. "The police called me earlier. I went into the station. They said they had news. I can't believe it—they told me weeks ago when I gave them our list that they'd checked on him and they hadn't. They've only just found out."

I can't approach him. Instinctively, I know if I touch him, if he has to turn, he won't be able to get these words out. I wait silently.

"Tyler's out. He'd been moved to an open prison for exemplary behavior, and he went missing. He's been out on the run for a year, and I didn't know. I never knew. I gave the police his name, and they didn't check until now and they've put us in more danger. It's in their files. How can they have messed this up?"

And so the shadow man has a name. And a motive.

"They can't protect us," Dan says. "They couldn't even check on him properly when all this time, he's been on the loose." He leans his head against the window. "It's my fault, it's my fault, it's my fault—"

"Dan—"

"Get out. Please get out. I can't deal with you right now. Just please get out!" And he crashes his fist against the wall.

I hurry out of the study and close the door. I can hear the sound of my husband sobbing through the door. My blood is frozen in my veins.

53

DAN IS GONE WHEN PORTIA and I get up in the morning. I check the study cautiously in case he's still in there, but there's nothing except a half-full mug of cold coffee on his desk. Once office hours have started, I call the police station. Booth isn't available—on annual leave, they tell me—but I press the issue. I'm transferred to another detective.

"I need to know what's going on. Why weren't we told until yesterday that Anthony Tyler was out of prison? How can you make a mistake like this? My daughter died!"

"There's no evidence to suspect Tyler at the present time, Mrs. Fulton," is the smooth reply.

"That might be true, Detective, but if you'd been on the receiving end of police suspicion as I have, maybe you'd be a little more understanding of how angry I am that someone who does have an actual motive is out there and nobody told us!"

I hang up. I'm too angry to deal with them right now.

Instead, I need to do something practical. The police may be incapable of protecting us, so I need to equip myself. I don't even know what this man looks like, so I go online and search for details of that old case. Sure enough, I find a police mug shot in the newspaper report.

He's in his mid-thirties with a smooth-looking face and high cheek-bones. He's moderately good-looking, with nothing exceptional about his appearance at all, other than his eyes. They look too detached to be human, or is that my imagination because I know what he did?

I stare at his face on the screen, and for the first time in my life, I feel anger at my husband that he picked this path for a career. That he's brought us near people like this.

Ashamed, I push that feeling down deep. If I'm going to feel that, I should have done so years ago. I can't be angry with him for it now—that's unfair.

It's not that I stop fearing what's out there or I stop being furious and wanting to get it cleared up, but I have to shift focus for a while. I have to tuck my anger neatly in a drawer before Portia realizes what's going on.

Dan comes home to find me and Portia in the sitting room, watching a movie together. It's a quite ridiculous rom-com, but it's distracting both of us, so it's doing its job.

Dan looks around the room as if he's not really seeing it. "Enjoying yourselves?" he asks sharply—too sharply—and Portia looks up at him anxiously.

"Are you OK, Dad?"

"Yes. Looks like you are too!"

Her lip wobbles at the anger in his voice.

"Whoa!" I get up to fend him off. "Look, I don't know why you've suddenly come in here to pick a row, but stop. Stop right now."

"Don't tell me what to do," he snarls. "I'm glad someone's enjoying themselves around here. What's wrong with that? Oh yes, our daughter died. Did you forget?"

"OK, that was uncalled for." Portia is sitting behind us with her mouth open wide. I see the flash of temper in her eyes, and I know what's about to happen. "You are out of order, Dad."

"I'm out of order? I'm trying to sort out the shit we're in, and you two are in here laughing and joking like nobody died at all. Oh, I forgot again! But apparently, you're falling apart really, aren't you?"

Dan's eyes look like it's not us he's seeing at all but something he hates.

"Better that than sloping around pretending you've dealt with her death and obsessing over work instead," Portia shouts at him. "I actually feel semi-human again for the first time in ages, whereas you are just pretending. It's like you try to ignore that she ever existed. I mean, you even took all her photos away. There's not a single picture of her here anymore." She folds her arms at him, and in that moment, she looks so like him that it takes my breath away. "Deal with it, Dad!"

And he explodes. There's no other way to describe it. He grabs a vase from the bookcase beside him and hurls it across the room to smash against the fireplace. "Deal with it? Who do you think is really dealing with it? Me! Not you, not your mother! You have no idea, really no idea..." He knots his hands into his hair and runs out of the room.

Portia stares at me, too shocked to do anything.

"Stay here," I warn her.

He's in the kitchen, and I follow him in there.

I've been afraid of things coming to a head, and now that it's finally happened, I still don't know how to deal with it—or him. "How can you?! You know what she's been through. How can you speak to her like that? She doesn't know what you're going through. You can't blame her."

"Oh, and that's all my fault, isn't it? Something else that's all my fault. My fault Becca died, my fault Portia is like this. Nothing's ever your fault. No, always me. Never martyred you!"

"Dan, you can't lose it now, please. We need you!"

"Everyone always needs me." His face is suffused with rage. "But I can't do it anymore. I can't be everything for you all. With you opting out of life! With our poor bloody daughter falling apart in front of your eyes while you wallow in your own guilt and self-pity! You're doing nothing."

He's scaring me now. I really don't recognize who he's becoming. All our years together, and I've never seen him like this.

"If you weren't so self-obsessed in the first place, you wouldn't have taken them up there on that so-called holiday. You would have waited for a time when we could all go together..."

Before my eyes, I can see him cracking down those strain lines. The rage, the frustration, the grief leaking out like magma—burning me.

"I would have been there. I would have known there was something wrong with the car."

I can't say anything to him. I can only watch in horror and hope he comes back to himself at the end of it.

"I would have known, and I wouldn't have driven it, and Becca would still be alive—" He stops, staring at me wildly, tears filling his eyes.

But he doesn't find whatever it is that he wants from me. And I see his face morph back into rage again as I stand there, stupid and

ionIgive heraquick kiss on the head. "You stay here while I go and sort
it out."

And when I enter our bedroom, I see I was right. "Dan, what are you
doing?" My heart begins to race.

He hurls clothes into a suitcase. "I've got to go. Got to go now."

"What's wrong with you?"

"I can't deal with this. I can't deal with you. Any of you." He's muttering,
forcing the words out. He won't look at me. His eyes look stranger than ever.

"Dan? Dan, stop. You can't do this!"

"I can't stay. I can't. Don't try to stop me." He picks up the case and grabs
his phone and wallet from the bedside table. He really is about to go.

"What about Portia?" There's an edge of hysteria in my voice.

"I can't do this. Tell her I'm sorry." His voice cracks on a sob.

He hurries toward the door, and I block it with my body. To my horror,
there is a brief scuffle as he moves me out of the way and I resist. He doesn't
hurt me, but I know, as he drags me to the side with measured force, that there
is nothing I can do to stop him going. He's going to leave, no matter what I do.

He runs downstairs and I watch him go, frozen with shock. Never in all
the times I've wondered if we might split up have I ever imagined anything
like this. I want to call him back, but it won't work. And I don't want Portia
to hear me screaming after him for him to come back, and then see him go.

He walks out of the house, and he doesn't look back.

The front door closes behind him. From the sitting room, Portia cries out, "Daddy?" and then she follows into the hall. She opens the door and calls after him into the street. It breaks my heart to hear the confusion and desperation in her voice and to hear the car driving away.

I shut my eyes tight. What just happened? How did we get to this?

"Why did he do that?" Portia asks as I pull her in from the doorstep, where she's still staring into the street, hoping he will come back.

"Stress makes people do strange things sometimes. He just needs some time to himself. He's been very worried about some…issues at work."

"No, Mum, he has a suitcase. He's leaving."

"He just needs some time," I repeat firmly, because what else can I say? I don't know what's going through his head myself, so I can't explain it to her.

I think my marriage just ended.

54

IN THE EARLY MORNING LIGHT, Dan's half of the bed is still unruffled and cold. I'd half hoped he'd come back in the night and snuck in without waking me. But no, he really is gone.

I get up, and Portia obviously hears me as she comes to my bedroom door, eyes wide and scared. "Mum, what's Dad doing? Where is he?"

"I don't know. Probably still with Aidan—that's where he went last night."

I'd tried to call him last night, but he wouldn't answer. At first, I gave him space, in case he calmed down. Then, after an hour, I began to be afraid for him. I couldn't *not* call, even though he wouldn't answer. So I did call him, repeatedly. I left messages. I texted. But there's been nothing in response from him.

Aidan texted, though, a couple of hours after Dan left. "Don't worry— he's here. Can't say much now. Busy with him."

And then a little later, "He says he needs some time on his own. I'll keep you updated. Hope you are OK. I'll call you."

I have seen Dan cracking up over these last weeks, but even in my worst nightmares, I didn't imagine he'd leave us alone at a time like this.

For him to do this, he must be smashed inside completely.

It's his fault. That's what he's said over and over again through the last weeks. I know how that can break your mind. But when I went through that, he was there to help me, even though I couldn't see that clearly at the time.

I haven't been there for him in the way he needs. Or perhaps he hasn't let me.

And a shiver of fear runs through me. The killer is still out there, and now Portia and I are on our own.

Aidan calls mid-morning. "He's in a bit of a state, but he's staying with me for as long as he needs, so I'll look after him. Try not to worry too much, and remember I'm your friend as well. I'm here for both of you." He has a quick chat with Portia, too, and tells her she can call him anytime if she's worried about her dad. "He's going to be OK—everything's just gotten to be a bit much for him, that's all," he tells her. I don't contradict him because it seems to cheer her up a little.

By evening, Portia has relaxed slightly. She's still upset, and Dan won't answer the phone for her either. "But I've been thinking really hard about it, and Dad's been through a lot. He's had to be strong for all of us, hasn't he? And I think maybe he's been strong for too long. When that happens, you need a rest, don't you?"

I swallow hard because I can see the truth in that. But she doesn't know about the killer. Every time I push past the fear and reach out for some sympathy for him, my anger assails me again. How could he do this to us?

The answer, of course, comes swiftly—because he had no alternative left to him. He simply couldn't go on.

He would have never, never gone if he had a choice. Not now, not with Tyler out there. Dan would never do that, unless he was in such a state he couldn't help himself anymore.

55

HE'S GONE. I HADN'T EXPECTED that.

And so now she's alone, just her and the girl.

How will she deal with this? He's been holding it all together until now.

I keep thinking I know her by now, but I find I have no idea how she will take this. Logically, I expect her to fall further apart, based on recent months. But I think logic might prove wrong.

He'll come back, I think. He's not the type to walk out—that much I know of him.

And I will be here to see it, of course. I have to be here. I have to see this through to the end.

56

I CALL DAN AGAIN THE next day. I'm vacillating wildly now between being heartbroken for him, for us, for our marriage, and being furious he's gone when we're still in danger.

"Dan, you have a daughter, and she misses you. So pick up your phone and call her!"

I hang up. It doesn't really make me feel much better. I wish I knew what was going through his head right now. I think I could stand all this better if I did. I'm just guessing at the moment, and it's driving me half-crazy. Between that and living in constant fear—

I stop. I make myself stop thinking. I can feel the panic brewing, bubbling, rising inside me.

Stop. Redirect. Don't let it take over.

Think of something else. Something practical.

Let the anger back a little—that'll carry me through this.

Yes, I'm angry. Angry at the man who's done this to all of us. That's a good emotion right now. That'll help me do something useful.

Focus, Lizzie.

Dan spun fully off into this obsession that it's his fault because one of his clients is responsible. And then, of course, when he found out Tyler was out of prison, that just confirmed it for him.

A nagging thought at the back of my mind takes a firmer hold. What if Dan's wrong?

There's nobody else I can think of who it could be, not like him. But that doesn't mean I should discard the possibility.

The thought nags and nags at me as the day goes on until, in the end, I pull up that newspaper article again, looking for clues. Clues that might tell me why he would want me and my children dead.

Tyler enjoys killing—that is clear from the trial report. When he was found guilty, he asked for three more offenses to be taken into consideration. He was proud of what he'd done. It would lengthen his sentence, but by that point, he wanted to give everyone the middle finger.

There's nothing in the articles I read to indicate he blamed Dan in any way for not getting him off, but Dan's afraid of him. So why specifically? I was so horrified when I first read Dan's files on this man that I didn't stop to question why it might be him. It just seemed to follow from the kind of individual he is. And then the news that he's missing just cemented that further.

I need to dig deeper. Dan's not here to ask, but there has to be something I've not found here.

The murders were all of adults. He's never admitted killing a child. Of course, that doesn't mean he hasn't, but if he asked for other crimes to be taken into consideration, then wouldn't that have come up?

Child killers get treated differently in prison, though, and he knew by then that he was going down for a long time, so maybe that would be a factor. Dan might not have gotten him off, but he certainly managed to make them keep the sentence down, even after those other offenses. So why would Tyler want to get back at Dan?

There's nothing here to clue me in.

Dan's case notes—is the Tyler file still in the study?

I go in and ferret through the boxes he's left there. Eventually, I unearth Tyler's file and begin reading.

He doesn't commit gory, sadistic murder, this man—no, his calling card is the swift and simple, much like when he was a hit man. Just the removal of life is enough. He enjoys it, but there's no basking in torture like the serial killers in films. Quick, deadly, and gone—that's how he operates.

I read on. And then finally I find something. A record of a meeting between Dan and Tyler. Just some handwritten notes from Dan. At first, it seems to be nothing and I almost miss it, but then there is Dan's scrolling writing. "Tyler informed me he did not like me. I told him that it isn't necessary to like me, and I was there to do my job effectively. He replied,

'Yeah, but I *really* don't like you.' Then he laughed and asked me if I have kids—this appeared to be changing the subject. I redirected him back to the events of the evening in question."

That's it. That's all it took. Was it changing the subject? Or a threat? That will have played on Dan's mind. From that psychopath, those few words are enough.

So much weight, too heavy a burden even for my stoic rock of a husband to withstand. Even rock can crumble under pressure.

So Tyler is a very real suspect, and one who we now know was loose at the time of the crash.

But I know about him now; I am better prepared.

The shivers of fear running through me at the thought of this man and what he may have done to us are very real, but he's not going to beat me. Not again.

57

"HE'S NOT COMING BACK," I tell Stella. "I know that. I saw it coming, after all."

"What do you think has happened?" she asks.

I shrug helplessly. "Everything."

"Come on, break it down," she replies, leaning back on the sofa. "You need to understand what's happened to Dan."

"He's left us when we most need him." I didn't expect my voice to be so bitter, but I can't keep the hurt at bay any longer.

"Talk to me about him," she urges. "Tell me what's been happening to him these last months."

"I don't understand why he's done this." I'm not a woman who throws things, but at the moment, I feel like hurling something, breaking it.

"And I'll help you to understand. Trust me—take this journey with me. Tell me about him since Becca died."

I take a deep breath and try to ground myself. "In the hospital, he was there for us. Portia and I were very ill for a good while, and he stayed with us. He canceled all his work, which is a big deal for him. It might seem obvious that most husbands would do that, but he's a man of routines and keeping to his word; it took a lot for him to turn everything on its head that way. But he did. For once, he actually did."

"Did you think he wouldn't?"

I consider the point. "It would have been difficult for him. It's not that he puts work first, but he struggles to prioritize family emergencies. I could always drop everything and just go if something happens to one of the girls. Portia had a bad accident once at school and was unconscious. I just told the clerk I was going and off I went. I left it for them to sort out. Dan can't do that—he's physically incapable of it. He has to try to deal with work issues before he can leave. Does that make sense?"

Stella nods. "Yes, and I guess some people are just wired that way. But it's worked for you both in your marriage. What was he like after the hospital? You've said before that you don't think he was handling his grief."

"It's just like Portia said to him—he blocked it out. He dealt with us and our problems so he wouldn't have to face how he felt."

"Or he had to fix you before he could fix himself?"

That strikes a chord so strong it makes my ears ring with the truth of it. "Why didn't I see that before?" I ask her, blinking back a sudden surge of emotion. "I should have seen that, shouldn't I?"

"You weren't in the right place to," Stella replies. "He sounds like a fixer."

"He is," I reply miserably.

"And then he couldn't fix things to make them safe for you. How would that have made him feel?"

"A failure." I know that with certainty. "And worse, he thinks he's caused it—all of it."

"Look back to before Becca died. You said you'd been growing distant. What caused that?"

"I don't know. I just know we got further and further apart."

She frowns in concentration. "When you couldn't get pregnant, when things were hard then, what did Dan do?"

"He kept me going. He kept me hoping. He went out and sorted fertility treatment. Then when that didn't work, he organized the adoption services meetings."

"And when things started to drift, what did he do?"

"He stopped being around." I can see she's trying to get somewhere with this, but I don't know where yet.

"And when he couldn't fix things this time?"

"He left."

"He ran, Lizzie," she replies. "It's not just leaving. He's having what would once be called a nervous breakdown. It's a response to extreme pressure in his life that he just can't deal with. He's ill, Lizzie. He hasn't just checked out on you. Think of how you've described him."

"He fixes things," I reply slowly. "He has to fix everything and this time, he can't fix any of it. He couldn't fix me being unhappy with our lives before Becca died, so he distanced himself. And how could he fix it when I didn't know what it was myself? And now he really can't fix this." I look up at her. "So what do I do? What does he do? How does he get over this?"

She sighs. "It's not quick, unfortunately. But it's not uncommon, either, so hold on to that. Someone pushes themselves to their limits physically, emotionally, and then they cease to be able to function. Their brain shuts them down to prevent them from hurting themselves further. He needs rest, and he needs medical help. Can his friend help him get that?"

"I'll speak to Aidan. I'll make sure he does." I bite my lip. "He might not get better, though, not back to how he was—I can tell from your face."

"No, he might not ever be the same," she says gently. "But that doesn't mean he can't recover and be well."

It doesn't mean he can either. I'm not stupid. And it doesn't mean Dan and I aren't over. I come away from Stella's understanding this situation better, but I know the only thing I can do for Dan now is to fix this myself, because he can't do it for me anymore.

He's done enough. He's done too much. And now it's my turn.

58

I THOUGHT HE MIGHT HAVE *come back by now, but there's no sign of him.
He doesn't even visit. Is he gone for good?*

*That wasn't part of my plan. In fact, it might wreck everything.
Damn him! Damn him!*

59

IT'S A FEW DAYS AFTER Dan left, and I am walking back home from the local shop after buying milk—that's the moment I notice the car.

I am halfway along Cooper Street, a tree-lined avenue of quiet Edwardian semi-detacheds, when it happens. I get the strangest sensation, like an itch across the back of my head. As it creeps down my neck, I tell myself I'm being paranoid.

But that feeling won't go away. That feeling that I'm being watched.

I remember what Portia said when she thought this was happening to her. We never did discover whether that incident was her imagination or someone from her school. Or something more sinister.

As I turn the corner at the end of Cooper Street, I whirl around, hoping to catch anybody who is there by surprise. Tyler—is it him?

There are a couple of perfectly normal-looking people walking down the street far behind me. It's a suburban street, so there's nothing surprising in that. I bend down and pretend to fiddle with my shoe so I can get a better look. There's nobody here who looks like Tyler or Vaughan or anyone who looks even remotely suspicious, and I start walking again, feeling pretty stupid.

Nevertheless, that feeling persists. I can't hear footsteps behind me. And I know there's no logic to the feeling at all, but it just won't pass. I try quickening my pace. As I cross over the street, I spot the little coffee shop on the corner next to our avenue. That's an excellent excuse, so I dive in there and get a latte. I add a pastry to the order to prolong the event, and then I take my purchases to a small table situated close to—but not directly in front of—the window. It gives me a clear sight of the street beyond. As I sip my coffee, I look out over the rim of the mug. There's nobody hovering obviously outside. Several people pass as I sit and watch, but none of them look like the people who were behind me in the street when I turned around to check earlier.

I don't know what I think any longer. Less than a year ago, we were a normal family. Comfortable enough financially but stretching ourselves all the time to meet the demands of work and children. Now…now, I don't know what we are. We are in some kind of hell from which there seems to be no escape. I don't know how to get us out of this, and I want to throw my mug at the window in frustration. I picture it smashing against the glass, a starburst crack spreading across the pane, coffee dripping down the window onto the floor, the milky-brown liquid pooling below, and the horrified faces of the other customers.

I get up abruptly and walk out before I do something stupid. I cross the street in front of a parked red car. At first, I think there's no driver in it, but then I jump as I see a black-coated figure move inside the car. I look harder and realize they're bent over the passenger seat, trying to retrieve something. It's alarming how the slightest thing is making me jumpy now. I probably did imagine that feeling of being followed. I'm nervous enough to.

Who wouldn't be, though? I tell myself firmly. *It's only normal, considering what we're going through.*

I set off for home again and turn onto my own street with relief. I can't wait to get in and lock the door.

To be safe.

60

BUT AS I OPEN THE front door, there it is again—that prickle up the back of my neck, across my head. I spin around, but there is absolutely nobody in sight.

What is wrong with me? Do I think the neighbors are watching me now?

I swallow hard. Now that is something we haven't considered. We've been so convinced that it must be something to do with work that we've never thought about anything close to home.

A neighbor.

Oh God, a neighbor with an obsession. It's the kind of thing you read about in the papers. You never think it'll happen to you, but the thing is, it does happen to someone. I bet those victims never thought it would be them either. And all you need is one crazy with a desire to destroy…

And oh, I know about closed doors and how you'd never suspect what goes on behind them… Some of the stories I've been told through work…

I hurry inside and lock the door behind me. My heart pounds as I race up the stairs to the attic. This used to be the girls' den, but Dan even cleared Becca's stuff out of here. Portia hasn't come up since her sister died. The dust is thick, and my feet stir it into the air in a murky, choking cloud when I run across the floor.

At the end of the room is a porthole window, and from there, I can see out onto the street below. *Right, you monster, if you're out there, I'll catch you now.* The window is dusty, too, but I refrain from cleaning it. It's still clear enough to see out of, and I don't want to draw attention to myself standing up here. If I stay to the side of the window, there's even less chance of me being seen should someone choose to look up while I peek out onto the street.

Still…still there is no one around. I survey the neighbors' houses, or the ones I can see, at least.

There's the Hamiltons: two kids like we had, but theirs are younger than ours. He works long hours, and she's just gone back to work now that their younger one has started preschool. I smile at them if I see them, but then again, it's rare that I do see them. Absolutely no motive at all that I could think of for wanting to hurt us.

Next door to them, the Daniels family. A blended unit with four kids between them who come and go busily, back and forth between here and their other parents' houses. They're all between my girls in ages. Portia and Becca haven't been friends with any of them, and I'm again only on smiling terms with the parents. It can't be them. We have so little to do with them. There's no possible logical motive. I pause for a second—is this someone with a motive at all? If so, we're into the territory of some kind of psycho-pathic behavior, and I've never seen any sign of that in the people around me either. We're all so boringly normal. And busy.

On the other side—well, I don't even know their names. A young couple who remind me a little of Dan and me when we first got together. They seem pleasant enough whenever I have occasion to see them from a distance.

I can't see the house next door from my vantage point, but they're retired now, and their children are all grown-up and gone away. Occasionally, they take in a parcel for us if we're out, and they sent a beautiful bouquet of flowers for Becca's funeral. They go on holiday a lot now that they have their freedom, and they'll pop over before they go to ask us to keep an eye on the house while they're gone. It is preposterous even to imagine for a second one of them forcing us off the road.

The other side is even more unlikely. Another retired couple, both in poor health. The last time I spoke to them was well before Becca's death, as I tended to hurry in those days to avoid any neighborly conversation. But then they'd talked about moving to Spain, as the weather might help their aches and pains. I'm sure, now that I think about it, that Dan said one of them had a bad fall just after Christmas. I hadn't really been in a state to sympathize with anyone at that time, so my memory is hazy.

I stretch my neck to look out further, my heart rate beginning to slow as I discount the people living around us. I'm just being paranoid.

I shift my gaze to the next house along, and then I notice a figure coming past. It's Portia. I hadn't even realized she'd gone out. She walks along slowly, passing a parked red car, and she kicks a pebble lightly between her feet as she walks. She has a shopping bag in her hand, and she's sipping a can of lemonade.

She draws closer to the house and then disappears from view as she comes up the steps. I turn to go down and meet her before she realizes where I am and wonders what I'm doing up here, but then I stop.

No, it can't be—can it?

I turn back to look out of the window again. I must be going mad, but no, sure enough, parked up the street, there it is—a small red car. A prickle runs up the back of my neck, and I squint to see it better. That car outside the coffee shop earlier, the one with the driver bent over—that was a small red hatchback, and it looked remarkably like this one.

Oh, come on, Lizzie, how many little red hatchbacks must there be in this city?

I'm about to dismiss it and go back down to see my daughter when the car pulls away from the curb and drives slowly past my house. After it has gone past, it picks up speed and turns out of the street. The angle is wrong for me to read the number plate or be sure of the model, and I swear under my breath.

Come on, though—it's a coincidence, isn't it?

That prickle on my neck tells me to think twice. I've been looking out on this street for a while, and during all that time, nobody got in or out of that car. That means whoever is driving it was sitting in there throughout. And doing what?

Watching…

61

THAT EVENING, DAN FINALLY CALLS. I have to try to control my responses to him, I know that, but it's so hard. And I'm afraid anything I say will make him worse.

"How is Portia?"

"She's upset. She misses you. She blames herself for you leaving after the argument."

"It's not her fault."

"Whose fault is it? Mine?"

There's a long silence. "Neither of you."

"Why did you leave, then?"

"Because I couldn't stay. It hurt too much. I was scared of what I'd do."

This time, it's me who is silent for a few moments. He sounds odd, and I don't know how to deal with him. Stella's right—he's very ill. "Look, this isn't a conversation we should be having on the phone," I say finally.

"I'm sorry. I can't be there. And nothing makes sense now. I'm no good to you. I never was—if it weren't for me, this wouldn't be happening to you."

It isn't as if my anger with him dissipates immediately, but yes, years of marriage come into play. My husband begins to make sense to me again as I recognize what is driving him.

"You think if you've caused this, it's you they are trying to get back at. I understand that's hurting you badly. But why now, Dan? Why not when we first found out about the brakes?"

"It started then. It's been happening since then. But at the beginning of that, there was a doubt, and the doubt kept me sane."

"Dan, you need to be careful. I think someone may have followed me today. You need to keep your eyes open in case they know where you are."

"Have you called the police?" he says in a hoarse whisper.

"No, not yet. I can't be sure enough, and I think it's too tenuous to call them at the moment. It's not as if they've been of any use so far."

"I'm sorry, Lizzie," he says, and there's a crack in his voice as he speaks. "I can't help you. Not anymore. I can't help you, and I can't help myself."

I can hear him sobbing, and anything else he says becomes incoherent. Oh, I know exactly what he means. Of course I do. I've walked that path.

"Dan? Dan, listen to me. I'm not going to go on about it anymore. Just please answer a question—are you with Aidan now? Is he there? You shouldn't be on your own when you're feeling like this."

I can hear that he's speaking through tears. "Yes, he's here. I'm OK. I'm OK. I'm sorry, Lizzie, I can't keep talking. It's killing me."

He hangs up, and I'm left holding the phone with my heart banging. There's a slick of fear across my skin. Whoever is responsible for this doesn't need to take any more direct action. They're destroying us anyway. If they're watching us, then they know that.

Dan's reached that place where he's not truly rational anymore. He can't do anything other than run and hope that running helps us. I know what it's like to be broken, and logic doesn't come into it. That's where he is now.

The fear is like rising bile, and I try to swallow it down in the same way.

It's choice time, Lizzie, isn't it? You can sit here and panic and lose it. You can call the police and put it in their hands. But we've already done that, and they've done nothing. And while that goes on, you're supposed to live every day knowing all our lives could be at risk.

Because that's what I'm really facing here, let's get that straight.

Are our lives at risk now? Today?

Because if they are, I'm not going to sit here and panic and cry about it. That might be what Dan is doing right now, and I'm not criticizing him for that; I've been where he is right now, and it's been a long journey back for me to get even this far.

But you know what, Lizzie? I say to myself. *You might have been frazzled and tired and sometimes utterly done in from the pressure of making everything work and keeping everyone happy, but you had an intellectual life as well in your work. A job that might have been frustrating and felt like it was too much too often, but that you were, let's be honest here, amazingly good at.*

I let that sink in for a moment, because it's true and it's needed. Mine is a tough enough job, anyway, with some brilliant minds in direct competition with each other, but within that, I had managed to stand out in my field. I never took the time to boost my ego by thinking of it that way, and I had never needed to until now. I had a personal drive to do my best at work, and that had been enough.

So why does it matter now?

Because I'm at a junction. This is a battle of wits now to find out who is responsible, and I have to win it. I have to remember who I used to be.

62

SO SHE IS SURPRISING ME. *She hasn't fallen apart.*

Her face looks different from how it has for the last few months. She looks like she might put up a fight.

She still doesn't know what she's fighting for, but I do. It's her sanity; it's her future.

63

PORTIA HAS BEEN TEXTING THE boy from the theater group. There's always a quick, then carefully hidden flash of delight on her face when he texts back. Apparently they've been texting and chatting since the workshop, and he'd like to hang out with her. So she asks me if he can come down on the weekend. It's an awful time for her to want friends over—not that she knows that, of course. But I can't keep her locked up in here forever. She's lost enough already.

By Saturday, when Sam descends on us, I'm beginning to think I must have taken leave of my senses because there's no further sign of anyone watching us. If this continues, I'll have to contact Dan and tell him I was wrong. If he'll answer me, that is. If not, I'll have to tell Aidan, but not yet. I'll give it a little while longer. I was so sure about that car, and I'm not going to ignore that now, even if it does appear, at face value, I could've been mistaken.

The doorbell rings and Portia races down the stairs. I leave her to answer it. "Hi!" I can hear the pleasure in her voice. For me, that's the equivalent of coming home to a crackling log fire on a snowy day. I've waited so long for her to get to this place, and I can't let it be ripped away from her now.

She brings Sam into the kitchen to say hello. "Thanks for letting me come over," he says immediately. He has a straightforward, honest gaze, this boy, and I like that about him.

I exchange just enough pleasantries to be considered polite by a teenager and not annoying by my daughter, and then I get out of their way.

From Portia's approving smile, I know I've done the right thing. Dimly I can remember the embarrassment of parents hanging around when you had friends over, and I laugh to myself. And it's good I can laugh, I realize. It's taken a long time to get to that place.

I go up to the attic with the pretext of doing some dusting and vacuuming, but really it's so I can be near my vantage point to watch the street below. My new car is parked out there. Since Dan isn't here, I need to have something for emergencies, in case we need to get away quickly. We can't be stranded here alone with no means of escape. So yesterday, I picked up a new 4x4. Stupid for town, maybe, but I feel safer in something that size.

After an hour of looking out onto the road, I'm getting a crick in my neck, so I take a break and sit down in the chair, stretching out my cramp by bending my head from side to side.

The girls used to love to have pretend sleepovers together up here, I remember, as I sit looking around the empty room. It used to be so much work to keep all the toys clean and tidy. I can see the room as it used to be, toys strewn over the floor, and them playing happily in the middle. I can see Portia playing with her serious concentration that seldom wavered, and Becca beside her—glancing over to me often to smile and give a little wave. She always wanted that connection, my little sunbeam, and always wanted her mummy nearby. Perhaps she would always have needed that because of her background, but I never minded. I was glad to be there for her.

She hadn't had the best of starts, they warned me before I met her for the first time, and there could be issues related to that, but she was a healthy little girl of ten months. The healthy part was in itself a miracle when I learned what had happened to her; even getting to ten months of age in her home environment was remarkable. They had whisked her away then, and her mother had agreed to give her up because she was already pregnant with another child.

I shuddered when they told me that. "It happens," Adele, the Adoption Trust officer, said with a sour twist to her mouth.

Becca's mother had managed to stay largely sober while she was pregnant with her, but she had started drinking again almost as soon as Becca was born.

"What about the new baby?" I asked in horror, and Adele shrugged, her eyes telling me what she wouldn't say.

Becca had been lucky. The next-door neighbor had intervened when she saw her mother's neglect and given the baby plenty of cuddles and made sure she was fed.

"She's had some contact and affection, but you'll still need to work at it with her," Adele told me. I went straight out and bought a book on attachment parenting.

I met Becca for the first time on a rainy winter's day, but when they brought her into the room and she looked over at me and smiled—it may be trite, but it is true—the sun came out for me. She had wavy, ash-blonde hair and eyes the same color as mine.

"Hello," I said, and she held her arms out to me. Dan later said that if anyone looked at a child the way I did that day, they were bound to want to go to them. I sat her on my lap and showed her the little teddy bear I had brought for her. She wrapped her chubby fingers around my hand and around my heart. I bent my head to press my lips shyly to her hair and breathed in her scent.

"She does look a bit like you, doesn't she?" Dan marveled.

And there she was—my daughter. A different arrival than Portia's, but an overwhelming one all the same.

We connected immediately. Even Adele commented that she'd never seen a baby bond so quickly.

Dan and I had talked about what had happened to her, and when we brought her home, we put her in a side cot bolted onto our bed so I could be in contact with her as she slept. She would fall asleep holding my hand, and I would lie and watch her. I bought a baby carrier and carried her around in that rather than use a stroller.

I was very careful to involve Portia in everything to do with her. Portia helped me choose her clothes and bathe her, and she would play with Becca for ages. I wasn't the only one who connected with her instantly.

"Best little sister ever," Portia would say to her as she kissed her good night.

When I lay next to her cot at night and I thought of what that little mite had been through, I was incandescent with rage. How could anyone treat a baby that way? So many women I had seen in that fertility clinic, so many desperate for their own child and unable to have one, and Becca's mother—no, I would not dignify her with that title—the woman who gave birth to Becca treated her in this way and no doubt her new child too. It just wasn't fair.

I was going to make it all up to Becca. I took adoption leave from work. I enrolled in classes for baby music, baby movement, baby swimming. This little one needed as much stimulation and love and Mummy-time as a child could possibly have. I'd read about what happened to children who didn't have early love and bonding in their lives, and I was going to pull Becca back from whatever damage had been done to her. Whatever it took.

She didn't cry at first, and I worried frantically about that because I knew from the books that it was a bad sign. I put her on a strict feeding routine and got her used to being fed at regular times, and then one day, when I was sure she was expecting lunch, I waited, my heart in my mouth.

She did nothing for a while, and then after half an hour, she started to fuss. I hung in there and didn't respond, and then finally she let out a wail of frustration.

I scooped her up immediately. "What is it, darling? Are you hungry? Well-done for telling Mummy!" I put her in her high chair right away with her favorite rice cakes so she could watch me getting her lunch. I all but danced around the kitchen getting it ready.

It wasn't all smooth sailing, but gradually, I taught her to communicate what she wanted again. I would fall into bed at the end of the day, exhausted from being super-vigilant all the time. But I taught Portia how to help, too, and she would sit with Becca on the rug after school, showing her how to play.

And when she fell asleep in my lap in the afternoon, before we went to collect Portia, I would sit and watch her eyelashes grow, just as I had once done with Portia, and I would know our family was complete.

I am allowed to miss her, I remind myself now. *I am allowed to remember.* That's what I have talked about with Stella. I must let myself recall those happy times and all that she gave us in her short life. I am allowed to be angry, too, that she didn't have longer. But I must keep moving forward.

I have to find out who tried to kill us, not just for Dan and Portia but for her too. So I ignore the stiffness still lingering in my neck, and I get up and keep watch from the attic window again. I have to solve this.

64

AIDAN CALLS ME TO CHECK I'm OK, as he does every few days. He reassures me that Dan is still staying with him.

"He's no worse than last time you spoke to him, Lizzie, but he's struggling. I did get him to see a doctor. Maybe he needs a bit more time. It's been a terrible burden for both of you. How are you? You've not seen anything else to worry you? Make sure you call me if you do, and I'll come straight 'round."

I thank him. He's trying to do his best in a difficult situation, and I can tell he's not sure what to do to make it better.

Two weeks have passed now since I first spotted the red car, and my mind has been at war. This is the difficulty: in the past, I've been inclined to trust my instinct when it speaks to me in such strong terms, but I have lost so much that I don't know if it's safe to do so anymore. How do I distinguish between instinct and paranoia when I've fallen apart and the pieces of me being put back together are neither complete nor in all the right places?

And so it comes about that when I leave the supermarket, pushing my cart back to the car, I'm not expecting to see anyone watching me. Something, however, makes me glance past my own car and into the parking aisle beyond. My eyes are pulled by some invisible cord.

And there it is: the small red hatchback.

My heart races, and I look away quickly in case he sees me. Of course, it might not be him; it might be any old red car. It's a parking lot, for goodness' sake—there must be several of them here.

But I know. I *know* it's *that* one.

I can't see the number plate from here. I'm at the wrong angle, but if I position myself carefully, I can appear to be casually loading the trunk while I keep the car under surveillance.

I dilly-dally by pretending to repack the bags in the trunk while I peek at the car. There's no one in it.

My heart sinks. Perhaps I'm wrong and it is just another red hatchback.

As I watch, a woman comes walking across the car park, carrying a small carrier bag. To my surprise, she goes up to the red car and unlocks it.

I'm still trying to process that as she gets inside. Obviously it isn't *that* car after all. I was wrong. I take my trolley back and get in my car.

I'm about to turn the ignition when…

Wait…

What was it she was wearing?

I take another sneaky look to check I'm right. And yes, she's wearing a black waterproof jacket. Just like when I first saw the red car and the driver was bent over in the seat wearing that kind of coat. I remember the hood had a pale-gray lining. So does this one.

Is this who was following me, then? A woman?

What's going on?

She's watching me, I'm sure of it. I can't see her face, but I can see her shape in the driver's seat. The temptation to move closer for a glimpse of her face is like a tidal wave, but I mustn't spook her. It's been a full week of worrying without any opportunity to get information and flush out who she is, and I don't want to end up in that position again because I've moved too quickly.

I edge the car out of the parking space and drive past her toward the exit.

Yes, it's definitely a woman in a black waterproof coat, just like before, when I'd assumed it was a man. She looks away so I don't catch her staring at me, but that's what she was doing. I manage to get a good look at her as I pass. My skin itches as I feel her gaze return to me—it's like mites in my skin as I move off down the parking lot.

I'm unsure of her age. I suspect she's younger than me, possibly much younger, but she looks so exhausted and worn-down that it's hard to tell. But what is most important is that there's something else, and that's a sort of nagging familiarity about her features. It excites and terrifies me at the same time. *Do* I know this woman?

Her mousey-brown hair was pulled back messily as if she hadn't given any care to it, and if she had any makeup on at all, it wasn't obvious. She definitely looked like a woman who makes no effort with her appearance. Like a woman who'd given up. Something chimes within me at that thought. I think I've found a clue there. Is that the key to who she is? And what this is about? She feels more dangerous than her nondescript appearance suggests.

Who are you?

65

I DRIVE HOME FROM THE supermarket, and I can't be sure, but at one set of traffic lights, I think I see her several cars back. When I get home and out of the car, I force myself to carry the shopping bags in with no more urgency than I showed at the supermarket, just in case she's there. But once the front door is closed, I dump the shopping bags down in the hall and race up to the attic. Sure enough, there is the red car parked further up the street.

Dan has some binoculars somewhere. He got a cheap pair for the girls when they went through a phase of nature-watching on holiday. They wanted toy ones, but he said they were so useless that he'd get them a real pair—something small and cheap so nobody minded if they broke them, but something you could actually see through properly. I kick myself for not remembering them before. Now, where on earth could he have put them?

I run down and have a quick look in his bedside drawers, but they aren't there. Not a surprise—I haven't seen them for years. *Where, where would you have put them, Dan?* Ah, the junk drawer. I hurry into the kitchen, hoping she doesn't move the car while I'm gone. There's an old chest of drawers in there where we section off all the household junk that needs a home. The bottom drawer is where Dan keeps all the passports, maps, leftover sun lotion, and travel adapters. I rummage through it, and yes, there they are, a little pair of compact binoculars. As I rush back upstairs with them, I'm half convinced she'll be gone by now.

No, she's still there! It's an odd thing to find yourself relieved that you're being watched, but I need a better look at this woman. The lenses on the binoculars are dusty, and I breathe on them and give them a rub on my top, my fingers fumbling with urgency. It takes a few desperately frustrating minutes to remember how to focus them, turning fiddly little rings on the outer edges of the lenses until I get the trick of it, and then I am finally ready to look at her.

I zoom in on the car. She parked too close to the one in front for me to see the license plate, but I do have a good view of her.

So who are you, and why did you want to hurt my children?

I reassess her age. She's got relatively few lines, so I estimate her at not yet forty, but her mouth droops. There's no life in her face at all, and it's that which makes her look older. As I analyze her features further, it's that which makes her look plain too. With more effort, I would guess she would be an attractive woman, but she looks so—what's the phrase? Worn-down. Yes, that's it—that she's entirely the opposite of attractive.

What's happened to you?

Again, there it is—that pull at my memory. What am I not getting about this? What? I search her face for the answers.

I know you, don't I?

The more I look at her, the more convinced I become. I have seen this woman before. Did she look different last time? Has she changed her hair?

What is she looking at? She just seems to stare down the street, though I suppose there is nothing to watch at the moment. She's definitely got my front door under surveillance.

So what do I do now?

Maybe I should go out again and try to draw her out. Portia won't be back for ages. I could go down to the park and pretend I'm looking at the ducks or something like that. It's not too far to walk. I head outside, curious to see if she'll follow me at all, and if she does, whether it will be on foot or in the car.

It's incredibly difficult to walk along with apparent unconcern when you so want to look back to see if you're being pursued or watched. I would be terrified if this was happening while Portia was with me, but somehow, I feel invincible on my own. That's ridiculous, I know, but there's an aspect of challenge to my mystery woman in that feeling. *Come on and try me, because this time, I'm ready for you.* Maybe it's the relief of actually being able to do something proactively rather than being the victim I have been for the past months.

When I enter the park, I dodge behind a clump of bushes to check on her. And yes, she's following me. It gives me a peculiar satisfaction to know I'm right. But I have to play this carefully. If this is the woman who cut my brakes, then I can't underestimate how dangerous she is. My blood chills at what might be running through her head right now, at what her plans might be. I'm afraid, yes, but I swallow the fear down because what's needed now is action.

I can do that. I have to grit my teeth and get on with it.

Out on the pond, the swans are swimming with their cygnets. Becca would have loved to see this. The fire inside me flares, sudden and fierce. I want to run up the hill and shake and slap that woman up there. To scream, "What have you done?" in her face. To—I don't know—kill her, maybe.

Yes, maybe I do want that. Maybe that's really why I don't want to call the police yet, because I don't want that option taken from me. I can actually feel that level of violence inside me. If this woman is responsible, truly responsible, for Becca's death, I want to end her. I want her dead but to suffer first. The police can't make that happen; only I can.

But there's Portia.

Always Portia. Because if I do indulge in this briefly cherished fantasy, then Portia will lose her mother.

Only if I'm caught.

If I'm not caught, I could destroy the bitch who has ruined my life and destroyed my family, and I could walk away.

Am I crazy? Maybe. But I'm remembering that lioness in the video Stella showed me. No, I'm not crazy. I'm normal. This is how a mother looks when someone murders her child.

And then, in a flash, it comes to me. As she sits down on a bench and turns her head and I see her in profile, I realize where I've seen her before. I let out an audible gasp.

The woman from the park. The woman who sat with Portia when she was missing. It's her.

I go cold all over.

How long has she been following us? And what would she have done to Portia if we hadn't gotten there when we did?

I clench my hands into fists to stop them trembling. She didn't do anything to Portia at the time, and it seemed that she was behaving as any woman would when finding a distressed girl alone at night. But that could have been an act.

Because this woman is capable of murder. She's proved that.

How did I not recognize her immediately? I'm furious with myself, but it was dark and she'd been wearing a woolen hat over her hair. Am I sure it is her? I take another good look. Yes, it's there in the straight-lined nose, in the features that might once have been delicate and pretty. It's her.

I glance back to the bench where she's sitting. *I am going to annihilate you.*

I never thought I had it in me to plot murder. I was wrong, because that's what I'm doing all the way back from the park.

66

SHE SAW ME. FINALLY.
But did she really see *me?*
Did she?
I guess I'll find out soon.

67

I'M STILL SHAKING SEVERAL HOURS later. I'd walked back home, and she'd followed me again and parked. She'd lingered for around forty-five minutes, watching the house, and then left.

It's a woman. I can't get over this. We were so sure it was a man.

I'm struggling to believe it.

Perhaps I'm wrong, and she has nothing to do with the crash.

Which is ludicrous. So I can stop that train of thought right now. It would be far too coincidental that someone completely unconnected to the accident would start to follow me, or us. That would just not happen. She has to be linked in some way.

What I find difficult is that this normal-looking woman could possibly have damaged my brakes and then run me off the road. She looks as if she can barely get through the day, let alone plan and execute murder.

But appearances can be deceptive, and I need to remember that. All this time, we were looking for the wrong person. I remember briefly considering women it could have been, but those ideas were discarded so easily.

Portia has spoken to her. She told her a name. What was it?

It takes me a minute to remember—Clare, that was it. I doubt very much that's her real name. It'll be a false one designed to throw us off track.

I need to talk to Portia about exactly what happened with that woman and get any scrap of information I can. She's in her room, texting Sam back and forth, but puts her phone aside when I ask if we can have a chat. *That's real progress*, I tell myself. At least something positive is happening in my life. She and I are slowly learning to reconnect.

"Just humor me with this. That woman who sat with you the second night you were missing—tell me about her."

"Why?" Of course she asks. Portia always asks. I'd expected that.

"Can you trust me and just not ask me that now? I will explain eventually, I promise. But not now." I keep my voice calm and gentle so my words don't cause her any alarm.

She looks at me askance for a moment and then shrugs. "OK. If you want."

"How did you meet her?"

"I was sitting on that bench on my own, just staring at my phone and trying to decide what to do. I was there for ages. I was close to home, so I felt better in some ways, but in other ways, that made me feel worse—more anxious. And while I was trying to pluck up the courage to call, she came and sat down next to me. She said, 'Forgive me for asking, but I couldn't leave you here without checking you're OK.'"

Nothing wrong in that so far.

"I said I was fine because I wanted her to go away. I mean, I didn't know her. She said I didn't look fine and I'd been there a long time, and she just wanted to be sure I was all right. Then she said, 'Does your mum know you're out here?' and I got a bit upset."

It could have been a chance thing to say, but I suspect it was more loaded. She'd been watching us.

"Then she said, 'I'm Clare. What's your name?' and I told her. She said, 'If my daughter was sitting on her own in a park at this time of night, I'd want someone to check she was all right and help her. Do you need help?' So I told her I was being bullied and I'd run away. And I was thinking about phoning you because I wanted to go home, but I'd made such a mess of everything. Then she said, 'As a mum, I know this—your mum just wants you back safe and sound. She loves you. You won't be in trouble—just call her.'"

This is so strange. *Can* she be the one who drove us off the road? It doesn't fit with her behavior that night.

"So I texted you and she said she'd wait to make sure I was safe until you came. She said I'd done the right thing and not to worry anymore."

"OK, thanks." I need time to digest this and work out what on earth could be going on here.

If she is the woman who drove us off the road, why did she persuade Portia to come back to us? It doesn't make sense.

68

THE ONLY WAY FORWARD, I decide, is to draw this woman out and see just what she's about. I can't keep sitting around trying to make sense of the senseless. I need to find out more about her. Over the next few days, I get out and about more. Frustratingly, she seems to disappear again for a while, but then one day, my luck changes; I spot her car following me down High Street.

I park and walk down to a coffee shop, where I buy a cappuccino and sit in a corner.

Sure enough, she comes in and orders something at the counter. I pretend to be on my phone so it appears I'm not looking at her, and she sits down a couple of tables away.

I've had enough of this wondering. Time to make something happen. This is my chance to see what she'll do. I get my phone, and I know she's close enough to hear.

I pretend to make a call, and as I do, I shield my phone from her view. I need this woman to follow me to an exact location, so I have to set this up in a way she won't suspect.

"Hi, Dan. I need to talk to you. I know you don't want to see me ever again, but this is about our daughter."

I pause.

"I know we're over and it's not about that. It's about Becca's headstone. We never finalized that, and as you're her father, I need to consult you."

I pretend to be listening for a moment or two.

"So I want to discuss it with you. We need to be adults about this. I'm going over to her grave now to think about the inscription, and I want you to think about it too." I pause again. "Yes, I understand you left me because the accident was my fault and you never want even to speak to me again—you've said that before—but we do need to do this. I'll call you later. When are you free?... OK, you call me, then, this evening."

I "hang up." So far, so good.

Now for the next step, and this will be interesting. I drive to the cemetery. When I arrive, I think that she hasn't followed me at first, but then I realize she's being careful. Her car draws into the parking lot only as I exit down the path in the direction of Becca's grave. My heart begins to beat faster. We're here in the place where my daughter lies at rest, and I am playing cat-and-mouse with the woman who may be responsible for her death. There's something obscene about that, and a feeling of nausea washes through me at the thought of her walking near Becca's grave. I should have protected my daughter from her in the first place, yet now I'm bringing this woman here where Becca should have peace. It's so, so wrong. I almost turn and run back to the car, but I can't—I have to do this. I need to push those feelings away and make this happen.

I am trembling as I wander slowly between the gravestones, appearing to read them as I go, but I heave a sigh of relief when I see her begin to follow me from a distance. We are here now, and I have to have the resolve to follow through with the plan.

There's an air of unreality lying over all this, but I think her reaction might tell me something important. I'm acting on instinct here, a mother's instinct that this is going to reveal some aspect of this woman's motivation.

I cannot understand how a mother, if she really is one, could behave in such a way, could kill a child.

When I reach Becca's grave, I clear away the remains of the flowers and touch the ground under which she lies. I know my mystery woman is lurking somewhere behind me, watching. I should want to dash her brains out on one of these headstones, but oddly, my anger is stilled at this time, replaced with confusion.

I need to understand what's going on here. Whatever the answer is, I have to find it for myself. It's become a compulsion. Going to the police right now is not an option because that will only delay me learning the truth.

I don't want her to come over to Becca's grave, but... "I'm sorry," I whisper. "I don't want her near you, but I need to find this out. For you and for Portia. I know you'd understand."

I can't help myself any longer. I turn around, expecting to find her staring at me. But she's not. She's hunkered down on her knees several rows of graves away, bent over as if she's sobbing. It's a good act to hide yourself from notice in a graveyard—is that what she's up to? After several long moments, she hasn't looked up, and I edge closer, and then closer still. Ostensibly I am reading inscriptions, in case she does look up and catch me.

I'm shocked to the core when I see the tears free-flowing through her fingers where her hands cover her face; her shoulders heave with sobs. Either this woman is a consummate actress or she is genuinely crying, and crying as if her heart will break.

Shaken, I creep back over the grass to Becca's grave. If she killed Becca and then followed me here, shouldn't she be gloating? Why would she do that to us and then come here and fall apart?

I have to carry on as planned, so I say goodbye to Becca, and then I wander around for a while, looking at the gravestones. When I next look up, she's gone, and I see her in the distance walking back to her car, her shoulders rounded and hunched as if she is drawing her pain into herself. And when I eventually return to my car, she's sitting in hers, still crying.

She didn't go near Becca's grave, even when I moved away. Why not? She's oblivious to me as she sits sobbing.

And then my gut tells me why—her guilt wouldn't let her. This woman is not gloating about what she did. She's haunted by it.

69

THE FOLLOWING EVENING, I'M STILL thinking of the woman. She's not left my mind since I went to Becca's grave yesterday. I've spent the last twenty-four hours trying to fathom who she might be and what motive she could possibly have.

I even got Dan's notes out and looked through for any signs of a woman bearing a grudge against him. We were so sure it was a man when we looked together. Maybe we missed something obvious because of that, but I found nothing.

And then, as I am clearing up the supper plates, it comes to me—the missing piece that's been eluding me.

Her face.

Her face was familiar. I put two and two together and got to the woman on the bench.

But it's more than that. I've seen her before that. Clare... Clare...

It *is* her real name. Oh my God, it *is*.

I can hear bells in my ears, and I drop my head between my legs so I don't faint. I slump to the floor. For a while, I simply sit there and stare at the wall.

Clare Underwood.

It all happened so long ago. I didn't go back that far in my notes. Not far enough.

I can see her more clearly in my memory now. A slim woman, almost a decade younger than me. Pretty in a delicate but girl-next-door kind of way, as if she spent a lot of time outside or with horses—that type. The last time I saw her, her long hair was streaked blonde, and it suited her.

But then again, that last time I saw her, her eyes were red-rimmed from weeping, and her face was blotchy and tortured. Because I'd just taken her daughter from her, hadn't I?

Clare Underwood.

Could it really be her? How long ago was it? It must be seven years, easily. She looks completely different now. But it's been a long time, and the last time I came across her, she'd been a rich man's recent cast-off—still well-dressed with expensively colored hair, for all her preference for a more natural look than her successor. She wasn't this disheveled, tired woman of today. No wonder I didn't realize—she's almost unrecognizable from the young woman I faced across a courtroom.

Why now, and why after all this time? It doesn't make sense.

But it is her. I'm sure of it now. I remember the case itself quite vividly. It's one that's stayed with me over the years.

It was around a year after I first made my name for representing in paternal custody that Greg Underwood walked into my chambers one gusty autumn day. He was one of those men whose presence filled a room—a large, square man in his early forties with darkly tanned skin. Some women would have found him extremely attractive, but I didn't. My taste ran to the lean rather than his powerful build, and I found him overpowering rather than magnetic.

He held out a strong hand for me to shake. "Mrs. Fulton, thank you for seeing me." It took me a moment to place his accent, and then I got it—he was South African.

I gestured to the chair. "My pleasure. How can I help you?"

I've never had traditional heavy office furniture, choosing instead to surround myself with lighter woods and more contemporary styling. He looked around and nodded. "Not what I was expecting, but I like it."

"I like to do things my own way," I replied, "and thank you."

"I hear that about you," he said, eagerly sitting forward in his chair and clasping his hands. "I also hear you get results."

"I certainly try." I gave him a carefully cultivated professional smile. "So what's the problem?"

"I'm getting a divorce," he said with a grimace, "from my second wife. We have one daughter, and I want custody."

"OK, and will her mother contest that?"

"Yes, that's why I'm here to see you. You come highly recommended in dealing with this sort of situation."

"I can't make any promises," I warned him, "but I will certainly do my best. It's important you're completely honest with me about everything. I don't like nasty surprises in court, and they can really wreck a case, in my experience."

He nodded. "And I know your experience is extensive in this area, so I'll be guided by you."

"Thanks. Let's start by taking some history. How old is your daughter?"

"She's six."

I looked up at him. "That's going to be tough. She's very young."

"That's what the lawyers I didn't hire said. I heard you were better than that."

I gave him another cool smile. "I don't make promises. I'll give you an honest appraisal of your chances when I've got a full picture of the situation. I'm a barrister, not a magician, though."

He laughed, but he wasn't amused. There was a hard look in the back of his eyes that I didn't like.

"So tell me about your family—how long you've been married, why you are divorcing, that kind of thing—and please try not to leave out anything you think may be important." I prepared to make notes and waited expectantly.

He drew in his breath and pursed his lips thoughtfully. "Let's do this in consecutive steps, then, so I don't miss anything. I met Clare nine years ago. I was still married to my first wife, Lara, but we'd split up. And she was back in Johannesburg."

"How long had you been separated?"

"About a year. We'd not gotten 'round to divorce, but then I met Clare." He shrugged. "I guess that was that. I wanted to be with her." He scrolled through his phone to show me a picture. "That was her back then, before she became a bitch."

I winced but didn't let him see it. The woman in the photograph was very young. Around twenty, possibly not even quite that. She had a pretty, fresh, country look. And what was the word? Untouched. Yes, that described her well. I recoiled inwardly at the sudden picture I got of their relationship. He would have been mid-thirties then, and she was so very young. She looked so innocent. It wasn't the age gap, but there was something repellent about the idea of them together.

"My business was really taking off internationally. Lara wanted to stay back in Jo'burg and have kids. That wasn't what I wanted. I wanted to travel, and Clare wanted to be with me. I divorced Lara, and Clare and I married a few months later. It was great at first. We were flying between London, Paris, and Amsterdam. It was all really happening, you know—an exciting time. Even when Clare got pregnant, which we hadn't planned, she said nothing would change. We'd manage. It wouldn't affect our lifestyle."

I was frankly incredulous. Had she been that stupid that she thought a baby wouldn't change things? Or just too young to know what it would entail? Or too scared of how he'd react, so she had to set up a line for him to swallow? No woman ever really knew how much disruption and sacrifice motherhood brought until she was living it, that was true, but to think it wouldn't affect their lifestyle at all was ridiculously simplistic. Maybe she wasn't too bright, though. Somehow I doubted he'd married her for her brain—that wasn't the impression he gave at all.

"So what did Clare do before you married?"

The length of time it took him to recall the answer showed me the importance with which he regarded her past life. "She was studying. She wanted to be a journalist, but I don't know if she ever would have been."

"And what does she do now?"

His confusion with why I'd even asked told me the rest of what I needed to know. "Nothing." And then his mouth took on a sour twist. "Apart from making my life bloody difficult."

"OK, thanks. So you had a daughter. Let's continue."

"Yes, Chloe. We carried on as before for a while. I got a nanny to look after Chloe, so she came around with us. Chloe was born in London, but she has dual nationality. I flew us back to South Africa for a visit soon after she was born so she got to see her other home." He laughed. "She was about six weeks old. I wanted her to see home good and early."

I refrained from pointing out she wouldn't have been able to see much at all at that age.

"So we carried on like that until Chloe got to school age. I was prepared to get her a tutor, but Clare wanted her to go to school, and that meant she wanted to put down roots and stay put. It wasn't what we'd agreed."

Or what he'd insisted on. I was beginning to feel that was more how this marriage had played out.

"She wanted another kid, but I didn't. You know, I love my girl, but I wasn't ready to have another. Clare wouldn't drop this thing about the school, though, and she said Chloe was too young to board. When I checked, she was right. Clare said she might consider it when Chloe was seven but not yet. She said they'd only need to stay put in term times and they'd join me as normal in holidays. I figured it was only three years until Chloe was seven, so we could grit our teeth and stick it out, although I still wasn't happy about it." His grim expression recalled just how unhappy he had been too. "I carried on living across Europe, and they lived over here and joined me when school wasn't on. It wasn't the same, though. We drifted, I guess, over time, and Clare changed."

She grew up, I thought.

"We wanted different things. She became difficult."

Yes, she definitely grew up.

"Basically, it's over between us now, and I'm ending it. I'll make a settlement in reflection of the time we were together, but I want her out of my life, and out of Chloe's as far as possible."

"Why do you want full custody of your daughter?" I admit I was surprised that he did. From his description of how he came to be a father and their life afterward, I'd have expected he'd be relieved to be rid of the responsibility. Perhaps some holiday visitation rights and nothing more would have been in line with what I thought he might have asked for.

He drew his brows together. "She's my daughter." As if that should explain everything, and perhaps it did. There was a proprietorial manner about him that made my skin itch with irritation. "Look, you told me to be honest. I've met someone else—Vanessa. She's younger than Clare, and Clare's being difficult about Chloe being around her. She's trying to poison Chloe against me."

"I see. Do you have a picture of Vanessa?"

He bristled visibly. "I do, but how is that relevant?"

"I don't want any surprises," I told him with another bland smile.

He sighed in exasperation and scrolled through his phone again. And then I sighed when he showed me the picture. As I'd expected by now, she was about twenty-two, hanging off his arm and of a type. In honesty, exactly the type I'd been expecting his second wife to be when he'd begun to explain about her, but I'd been surprised by Clare Underwood. I wasn't surprised by this Vanessa.

"And her job is?"

"She worked behind the bar in a casino."

I scribbled some notes. Of course he used the past tense. Now her job was him.

"And a picture of Chloe, please? Yes, I realize this is frustrating for you, but how people present can be extremely important in these cases. You'll have to trust me on that."

The little girl he showed me was all her mother's child. There was no trace of her father's heavy features in the little freckled face and long light-brown hair. She had the same open expression her mother had worn in that first photograph. I smiled. "Cute kid," I said, handing him the phone.

He nodded and shuffled in his chair. I picked up on that sign. He was about to tell me something I wasn't going to be pleased to hear.

"I'm pulling back on the European arm of the business," he said, his eyes fixing on a point out of the window behind me. "The economy and the political climate, it's all affecting business, so I've made the decision to retrench back into the South African market."

I began, with a sinking feeling, to see where this was going. "And how will that affect your living arrangements?"

"I'll be moving back to Jo'burg permanently. With Chloe."

70

THE STUPID THING IS, I almost turned down Greg Underwood's case. By the end of that first meeting, I'd developed something very close to a dislike for him. I remember wondering if I would have fallen for what appeared to pass as charm from him if I'd come across him at the age Clare did. I rather thought not, though. Even at that age, with the naïveté of youth, my taste had not run to that level of brash arrogance. I'd disliked that sort of thing, even then. Quiet confidence was what I'd found attractive, not that full-of-himself style of men like Greg Underwood.

But I hadn't turned him down. He had offered an enormous sum for me to represent him, and I'd thought of my family and what that could provide them with. I'd swallowed down my scruples and done my job.

I am still struggling the next morning to reconcile my memory of Clare Underwood with the kind of woman who could force a car with two children off the road. I need to see her again. Maybe I'm mistaken or clutching at something that isn't there, because it seems so wrong that it could be her. I have to lure her out so I can check. I want a better look at her, now that I think I know who she is.

I walk to the local shop at ten the next morning on the pretext of needing milk again and hope she'll be hanging around. As I leave with my purchase, I catch a glimpse of a woman standing alone by the bus stop across the road, a waterproof jacket zipped up around her and the hood up.

It's her.

You are Clare Underwood, aren't you?

A shaft of fear pierces through me. She looks so inoffensive, but inoffensive doesn't damage your brakes and drive you off the road.

I'm caught in a trap of indecision. Should I go and confront her and stop her? That might make it worse. I can't exactly wrestle her to the ground and carry out a citizen's arrest. Confronting her could push her into action.

Think reasonably. How do I get a better look at her? There's a pharmacy further down the street. I'll walk down there and see if I can get her to follow me.

Thankfully, she does, and as I browse around one of the counters in the shop, she does the same in an adjacent aisle. I angle myself so I can see her in a mirror. She appears completely disinterested in anything other than the toothpaste she's looking at.

So is it definitely her?

I take a moment to study her face. I can see nothing of that carefree girl from Greg Underwood's original photo, but of course, that wasn't the final time I saw her. I last saw her at the end of the court case, when her victorious husband punched the air at the verdict. She had looked at us in shock, her eyes desolate, before she broke down uncontrollably. Those eyes, yes, they could belong to this woman.

Is this my fault? Did I do this to you? Because, if you are Clare, we both know that what I did in that court case was not fair.

71

THERE WAS A SENSE OF hushed anticipation as I faced Clare Underwood across the courtroom. I could feel the expectations of her husband behind me. I ignored her pale face and trembling hands. He hadn't paid me this much to feel pity for her.

"Mrs. Underwood," I began. "Can you tell the court your employment status?"

She looked taken aback. That obviously wasn't how she'd expected me to open. "I don't have a job."

I feigned surprise. "But you want full custody of your daughter. How will you support her?"

Her eyes flitted nervously around the court. "I-I-I…" and then, as I knew it would, her gaze shifted to Greg.

"Oh, I see," I segued in smoothly. "You're expecting my client to continue to support you."

She lifted her chin, and I felt a shaft of admiration for her that I ruthlessly quashed. "I'll get a job."

I smiled. "Doing what?"

"Objection!"

"I'll allow it," said the judge. "It seems relevant."

"Thank you, Your Honor." I faced Clare again. "So what sort of job are you planning to get?"

"I haven't thought about it yet."

I raised my eyebrows. "Dear me! Haven't you been irrevocably separated for some months now?"

"Yes."

"I see. Well, let's move on. My client needs to return to his native country for business reasons. It is impossible for him to remain in Europe, as he has done up to now. Chloe has dual nationality, and it is his desire to repatriate both himself and her. You object—is that correct?"

"Yes, I won't see her."

I held up my hands. "You don't have a job here. Couldn't you just as easily have no job there?"

"Objection!"

"Sustained!"

"My apologies," I said swiftly to the judge. "Mrs. Underwood, is your objection to Chloe's father having custody based solely on him taking her to South Africa?"

"She's my daughter. She should live with me."

"Is he a bad father, Mrs. Underwood?"

She swallowed. "No, but—"

"Has he neglected Chloe? Failed to provide for her?"

"No."

"Is he abusive?"

"No."

"Does Chloe love him?"

"Yes." Her eyes searched mine for where this was going.

"Does he love her?"

"Yes."

"And he can continue to provide for her. Can't he, Mrs. Underwood?"

"Yes," she replied heavily.

"So, if either parent should be given full custody in this case, Mrs. Underwood, can you tell me why it should be you?"

She was so young, and her lawyer really wasn't very strong. Clare kept looking at me, pleading silently for me to understand, for me to help, but she wasn't the one paying me. She was wasting her time, looking to me for aid.

"I'm her mother," she said, too loud and too shrill. "She's only a little girl. She needs her mother."

I nodded slowly. "I see. A mother who, by her own account, can't give her any degree of security, who can't make any provision for her that isn't totally reliant on her father."

"I love her! It's not just about money—she needs love."

"Which her father is also capable of providing."

"Not the way I can!" Her voice carries a note of desperation.

"Ah yes—I was coming to that. Because that's what you've told Chloe, Mrs. Underwood, isn't it? You've sought to influence her in your favor and against her father by making her believe she needs you more than him."

"No, I haven't." Her gaze flies wildly around the court as she realizes she's walked into a trap.

"Mrs. Underwood, Chloe is also a South African citizen. Nobody disputes you love her, and Mr. Underwood is not trying to deny you access to your daughter." Actually, he'd had every intention of that, but I'd told him any judge in their right mind would wipe the floor with him if he took that attitude into court without considerably more reason than we could possibly give. He'd accepted that grudgingly. "Now, while my client is obviously prepared to make a substantial settlement to ensure his daughter's needs are met, you must surely see that the precariousness of your position and the fact that you've made no attempt to ameliorate that means that Chloe's father is in a better position to meet all of her needs going forward. Unfortunately, he does need to seek full custody given the living arrangements. I understand this is hard for you, but this is about Chloe's best interests."

"I have thought of nothing but Chloe's best interests," she snapped back at me.

I rolled my eyes, a tactical move to annoy her. "Come, come, Mrs. Underwood. It wasn't in Chloe's best interests when you made her think that her father didn't love her as much as you did, that he only loved her in a superficial way because he wanted to control her, that he isn't capable of real love—"

"I didn't!" she cried out, appalled.

"You did, Mrs. Underwood. And Chloe was so distressed by that; she told her father she needed to stay with you because you loved her more. You put your daughter in the position of having to choose, and you tried to influence her to pick you. You used her!"

Clare was crying, and openly so, crying in horror.

"And that, Mrs. Underwood, now that *is* abuse."

It was easy after that. The fight went right out of her. Discrediting her after that was straightforward.

It was a clever twist on the truth—a gamble. Those were words she'd spoken to Greg, not Chloe, but in the maelstrom of emotions that runs up to a divorce, what words get said to whom get forgotten or misremembered, and I'd banked on her having given a negative impression of Greg to Chloe at some point. That was inevitable. And faced with that in court, her memory of precise words and events would fail her. She would panic and falter. I'd relied on that, and sure enough, she did.

I won the case on well-timed words and a gamble. But justice was not well-served that day; instead, money won.

72

AS SOON AS I'M HOME, I begin with a search on Clare, starting with the electoral roll. I can't find anything on her in this area, but she could have moved or married again and changed her name. There's nobody on LinkedIn that could be her and no trace of any obvious social media presence. Hers is such a common name that Facebook doesn't yield anything. However, I wasn't expecting it to be easy, so I stick at it. After hours of widening my searches into different areas and still finding nothing, I take a break and go for a breath of fresh air in the garden.

It's a clear night and warm enough for me to go outside with only a cardigan. There are still some lights on in the neighbors' houses. Does she watch me at night? I've never seen her, but that means nothing. Is that why she looks so tired? I suspect it's more than that. She has the bone-weary, dead-eyed look of a woman who has given up on everything, who has lost everything.

Hold that thought, Lizzie.

Lost everything?

Clare isn't the person I should be looking up. How stupid of me. I need to go in right now and see if I can dig up anything on Greg or Chloe.

My hands are shaking as I log back into my computer. It must be a premonition of what I'll find, and in seconds, I have my result. It takes the breath right out of me. I'm cold all over as I stare in utter horror at the screen. Whatever I imagined I'd find, it was not as bad as this.

I click on the link to open the first article. It's a South African newspaper, and it's dated the summer before our accident. I do a quick calculation—we were on holiday in Florida then and out of the country for three weeks. If it was reported in the UK press, I would have missed it.

The article finally finishes loading, and I scan the first paragraph. I feel sick. I'm trembling all over, and my heart feels as if it will burst or stop entirely. Oh, dear God, what have I done?

SOUTH AFRICAN BUSINESSMAN IN FATAL ACCIDENT

Johannesburg police have confirmed the death of businessman Greg Underwood in a car accident on Monday. Underwood was traveling to visit friends with his daughter, Chloe, when the car went off the road in the torrential rains experienced earlier in the week. Both Underwood and his daughter were pronounced dead at the scene of the accident. Next of kin have now been informed. Further details will be released when they are available.

Chloe died in a car crash just a few months before our accident. She was still with her father, and now she's dead. In South Africa, where I made sure Greg could take her.

So it *is* Clare Underwood in the red car, and now I understand why. I have destroyed her life, just as she is destroying mine. It makes hideous sense. She can't get back at him now, so the only one she can lash out at is me.

Me and my daughters.

A cold sweat forms along my spine, and I hurtle upstairs. I maintain enough control to open Portia's door quietly, but it's a battle. She's asleep, still in that side-lying, half-curled position she's always slept in, the duvet tucked right up under her neck. I'm filled with a terrible fear. What's Clare's next move?

I watch Portia sleep, my heart thumping with the very real terror that she, too, could be taken from me. Her eyelashes are so long that they still lie like feathers against her pale cheeks, just as they did when she was a little girl. She looks so peaceful. I know I can't stand here all night looking at her, and I close the door quietly and go back downstairs.

I need to make myself read the rest of the articles on the Underwoods. I don't really know what I'm looking for, but as I had such a part in this mess, it seems only right that I should know the full consequences of what I've done and, bit by bit, piece together the additional information. As I dig around, mining the internet for information, I discover the full story.

Greg had retrenched his business back into South Africa—I knew that, of course. But in the seven years since he'd pulled out of Europe, the South African arm had begun to struggle too. On further investigation, I found it was about to go under, and he was going to lose everything. There was no mention of his girlfriend, Vanessa, and I assume one of them had discarded the other along the way.

But faced with insolvency, he still hadn't let his daughter go to her mother. There was a brief mention of his ex-wife in one article, but Clare wasn't named. Had he stopped her contact with Chloe as the years went on? There was no information to answer that question.

Clare had waited a few short months before taking her revenge. If she is still following us, she isn't done with us. That means Portia is at risk, despite what happened when she ran away. I should ring the police right now. What if she goes underground, though? I've got no confidence in the police after the way they failed to check properly on that man, Tyler, and I have to get this right. Enough damage has been done already. I wish I'd dumped Greg Underwood's case as I'd wanted to. I wish the money hadn't swayed me. He would have found somebody else to do it for him—his type always do—but my hands would be clean.

And my daughter would still be alive.

I am responsible for Becca's death. Not in the way I thought, but if it weren't for me, she would be alive now and tucked up upstairs in her little bed surrounded by her teddies.

Poor Becca and poor Chloe. Both of their lives cut brutally short. Just children who deserved to be running around, carefree and loved, not lying in graves.

What is it with men like Greg? Why couldn't he have been more reasonable and let her stay with her mother? He'd have seen her in the holidays. But no, he had to win. He had to have everything. And what has that brought us to? Two little girls lost their lives because he couldn't lose a case.

My laptop is wet with tears. I don't know whether to sit, stand, or sink to my knees. It's beyond my comprehension. That poor child. At least my daughter had a happy life. Thank God I can say that. I wonder what Chloe Underwood's mother would say. That must be the worst torture, not to know if your child was happy and loved as much as Becca was. It tortures me now, just that thought. What must that do to Chloe's mother? I hug my arms around my body to try to ease the pain.

I didn't kill Becca. Clare did, but I helped put Clare in this place.

And my husband is sitting in Aidan's spare room, blaming himself for this. Falling to pieces for something I did. I can't talk to him about any of this right now. He's struggling too much to take in any more. Aidan's been clear that he needs rest and time—total mental rest from this. No matter how much I want to call him and tell him, I can't do that yet. I have to make this right first.

A few months ago, the knowledge of what happened to Chloe would have destroyed me, taken me back to the dark place and held me there.

Now, it takes me somewhere different. I have done something awful to that woman, and this is where we now are. But I will not go down with this. She has unfinished business with me, and I have a husband and child who need me to resolve this. To make it safe for them again. I remember the lioness: her fierce determination to save her cub. Nothing was going to stop her. Nothing.

I need to have that strength.

I have to go to bed now. I need to be in the warmth and the dark. Tomorrow, I'll need to be strong. I have to sleep. Right now, I feel old and very weary; my bones ache with sorrow and grief.

In the morning, I will have to make a decision, and whatever it is, I will have to act on it, but the night is no time for that. Instead, I'll use it to build the power I need, and the dawn light will bring me the resolve to go on. The last thing I see before I fall asleep is Chloe Underwood's freckle-faced photo framed in my memory.

73

BY DAWN, I'VE MADE MY decision.

I drive Portia to Annika's house at ten o'clock. Annika runs down the steps when she sees me. "Go in, Portia—the door's on the latch. I just want a quick word with your mother." Annika can see I've got no intention of going in, and she glares at me as hard as she can. I kiss Portia goodbye and hug her extra hard. Annika grabs me once Portia is out of the way. "What are you up to?"

"As I've told Portia, I have to follow up on a possible chance to get back to work. It came up suddenly."

"Bullshit, Lizzie. What are you up to?"

I get back in the car. "Look after her, and thank you." I can hear her swearing at me as I drive away.

This isn't going to be easy. I have to lure Clare out of hiding, and then I have to turn the tables on her.

I spend a frustrating hour waiting around near home for her to surface. She drives onto my street and I follow from a discreet distance, keeping the car carefully out of her sight. I'm rewarded by her only lingering for a little while after she sees my car has gone and there's no sign of anyone home. I follow her to my local supermarket. It's chilling to watch from the road as she cruises around the parking lot, looking for my vehicle. How often has she done this?

When she draws a blank, she drives off, and I follow again. I nearly lose her at High Street, but then I catch up again as she drives out of the city. I trail her for around half an hour, and then, to my satisfaction, she pulls up at a house on the outskirts of a small nearby town. It's a little terraced house, and she unlocks the door and goes in. I park further away and walk up to the house on foot. When I skirt round the back of the street, I can see over her fence into her kitchen and she's making lunch.

She doesn't take long, and then as soon as she's eaten, she goes back out in the car again, possibly to look for me.

I sit in my car and write the note. I've thought long and hard this morning about what to say. Still, it takes me some time to get those words down on paper. I hope it isn't obvious that my hands are shaking as I write.

Dear Clare,

I know what happened now, both to your daughter and to mine. I would like to speak to you, please, and would appreciate it if you could meet me. I will be at Rawlington Boating Lake at 7 p.m. this evening.

Thank you,
Lizzie Fulton

I deliberately chose that time, as I know it will be quiet at the lake, and I can't, therefore, imagine us being interrupted. Dogs are banned to protect the bird life, so it isn't an area where people will walk in the evening. I don't know what I'm going to do when I see her, so it's best that nobody is around to witness. Also, I want neutral territory. That's important to me, to feel I have some measure of control.

I seal the sheet of paper inside an envelope and write simply, "Clare," on the front.

And now for the most nerve-racking part. I have to post it.

I get out of the car confidently. Anything else would arouse suspicion if anyone is watching me. And I stroll down the street to her house. I pop the letter through the door, but I can't help looking over my shoulder as I do.

There's nobody around, and no sign of anyone in the neighbors' windows, so nobody sees me. It's as if I don't exist. That's what I am today—I'm a ghost. Not Lizzie Fulton at all.

And then after that, I drive out of the area again and find somewhere to go for lunch. I wonder if she will see the note in time. I'm not sure what I'll do if she doesn't.

And now all I can do is wait.

I keep my phone turned off. No distractions. I need to stay focused.

I go to a quiet spot where I can watch the river flow by. What I want most now is peace and quiet and time to remember.

It's such a little memory to be drawn back to, but it's what I turn to now. I need to remember when we were happy—all of us, unconditionally, even Portia that day. A cold and rainy Sunday in February, the day after a storm, and we were all sitting around the house, bored and staring out of the windows at the rain coming down, when Dan clapped his hands together and said, "Come on, we're not sitting here moping around. Let's go out."

There was an instant howl of protest from the girls. Becca was only four, but she could certainly make her feelings known at that age as well as Portia could.

"Rubbish," Dan said with a grin. "What is it they say in Norway? There's no such thing as bad weather, only bad clothes. Get wrapped up, put your waterproofs on—we're going out."

To be honest, I felt like anything but going out there in the chill and damp, but Dan looked so enthused that I went along with it, faking some cheeriness to get the girls moving. He didn't tell us where we were going but kept the girls in frustrated suspense as they tried to guess.

"Where, Daddy, where?" Becca's little voice kept piping up from the back of the car.

"You'll see," he called back, and Portia huffed her exasperation loudly.

We arrived at a forest some miles from home. There was a stall in the parking lot selling cups of hot chocolate and Dan bought us all some. "But what are we doing here?" Portia asked, voicing the question for all of us.

He quirked an eyebrow at her. "We're going on an adventure!"

I was expecting he'd booked us onto some organized activity, but no, apparently not. Instead, he led us, carrying steaming cups of chocolate, into the heart of the forest and under a thick canopy of leaves that protected us from the drizzle still falling. He put a waterproof rug down on the exposed roots of an oak tree and hunkered down on it. "Lean in so they can't hear," he said in a whisper.

It was Becca who flung herself into the role first. "Who, Daddy?" she whispered back, snuggling close into his side.

"The wolves!"

Her eyes grew saucer-wide, and Portia looked at me over her head, her lips twitching.

I sat down beside them. "The wolves?" I said in a hushed voice, and patted the rug for Portia to join me. She did so with the cynicism of a pre-teen, veiled for her sister's enjoyment.

Dan nodded. "The wolves. They're out there somewhere." He cast his hand out toward the trees, and Becca looked in thrilled fear and snuggled tighter to him.

"Ooh!" she said, delighted.

"We have a job to do. It's very important. An evil magician has put a spell on the wood, and he's made all the good fairies fall asleep. It's him who let the wolves in. They're sneaking around keeping watch for him, so we have to stay very quiet and look out for them. If you see one, hide—or he'll tell the magician what we're up to and the fairies will never get the wood back."

I chuckled quietly to myself, wondering what on earth had gotten into him. This was so unlike Dan, although he always did tell a good bedtime story. That had never failed to take me by surprise about him. He was so untheatrical the rest of the time.

"What do we have to do, Daddy?" Becca asked, enthralled.

"Well," he said, leaning in so the wolves wouldn't hear, "we have to build a den, first of all, so they can't see what we're up to. Then we have to collect as many pine cones as we possibly can, and we have to dip them in the magic potion…here!" He pulled a large tub of purple glitter from his bag. "We need to hide inside the den so they don't know what we're doing. And then we need to make some magic models of all the fairies in the wood that we want to wake up. I'll keep count and tell you when we've got enough."

"And how will we do that?" Portia asked, trying not to laugh.

"We'll collect twigs and stick them onto cardboard to make the models." He pulled a squeeze bottle of wood glue and some old cardboard from the bag and grinned. "See! And obviously, we'll need snacks while we work." A packet of chocolates emerged too.

The girls were so excited, even Portia, who gave up her air of being really far too old for this kind of thing and mucked in with gusto.

"How did you think of this?" I whispered to Dan while they were running around collecting long branches for the den.

He laughed. "Got it off the internet. A guy I work next door to put me onto it—said he did it with his kids and they loved it."

"I can see now where Portia gets her theatrical side," I said, winking at him as the girls came back hauling branches.

It was such a simple afternoon, just messing about in the woods, but I was so proud of him for thinking of it, and the girls had such fun. We laughed and joked as we built the den, and then the girls dipped the cones in glitter and made the fairies. Finally, Dan lit a campfire, and we toasted marshmallows.

"To keep the wolves away while we break the spell," he said knowledge-ably. "Wolves hate the smell of marshmallows!"

Becca and Portia threw the pine cones onto the fire, and while their backs were turned, Dan quickly sprinkled the fairy models with some silver glitter from a little pot hidden in his pocket.

"Oh, oh! I think it's working!" he cried. "Listen! Listen—I can hear them waking up."

As the crackling of the fire died down, he held his hand cupped to his ear, a beaming smile breaking out across his face. "It *has* worked. They've woken up."

"Oh look!" said Becca, spotting the fairy models with their array of fresh glitter. "Look!"

"That's thank-you dust," Dan told her. "They're saying thank you to us for helping them."

We trudged back to the car later with Becca clutching her glitter-coated fairy models happily, Portia helping her carry them, and my heart bursting with happiness. Spending time together, all of us. That's what family meant to me.

74

AND SO SHE KNOWS.

And I am relieved. I am so glad that this will soon be over.
It is time.
I don't know what she will do.
I just want it to end now.

75

I AM AT RAWLINGTON BEFORE seven. Her red car is already parked in the emergency lane, and I can see a woman's figure walking down to the wooden jetty. There's no one else around. A fine drizzle falls intermittently, peppering the smooth lake surface. I'm pleased by the change in the weather. It reduces even further the chances of being disturbed.

The path isn't muddy, despite the drizzle. When I arrive at the jetty, she's standing at the end, looking at the lake. The boats are all locked away for the night, and there's nothing to disturb the silence but the calls of birds across the water. She turns and registers no surprise at seeing me, so I think she knew I was already there.

I search her face, and behind the dark circles that run underneath her eyes and the gray skin, I finally see the remains of the innocent young woman in her husband's photograph. I wonder if she can see the difference in me, too, since she killed my daughter.

I haven't known what I was going to feel or how I'd react. That's, after all, why I got her to come out here to this isolated spot. I don't know what I'm capable of.

As I look at her now, though, I feel numb. I feel nothing but a sense of unreality. We are here but not here—this is a bump in time and not part of our lives. I could do anything here, literally anything, or I could do nothing. And I just don't know what it will be yet.

I wait to feel hate, but there is only emptiness.

"Thank you for coming," I say to her. It's such a ridiculous thing to say, but there are no protocols for a situation like this.

She nods. She's wearing that black waterproof jacket and jeans. Her hood is up.

"You've been following me."

"Yes." She makes no attempt to elaborate. Her gaze is unwavering.

"Can I ask why?" My anger sparks at her seeming indifference, but I'm not going to let that show. It's far too early for that.

She shrugs, and there really is no expression in her eyes at all. It's as if nothing touches her. Despite everything, I acknowledge that I recognize that place. "I wanted to see how you were."

"Why?" I throw it out at her as a challenge, no question about that, and I see a flicker of something in her eyes. That gives me satisfaction.

She averts her gaze to look out onto the lake again. "You said in the note that you know what happened to your daughter. What did you mean?"

"I think you know that very well. Don't you?"

"Why don't you tell me?"

"You killed her."

Her eyes return to my face, and there's a strange lagging quality about her movements, as if she's drugged. She isn't—I know what that is because I've been there too. It's when someone pulls you back from where you were, in your private place with your grief, in your own personal hell that you can't leave. Down there, in that place we have both been, you are with your child. No matter how much you torture yourself with those memories and that anguish, you are closer to them there than you can be if you let go and come back to a reality without them there.

I hate Clare, I hate her so much, and yet I understand her too. That's hard, and I hadn't expected that.

Still, it won't change my plans.

"Yes," she says.

And there's nothing, absolutely no emotion in her voice, no remorse. That fire of anger flames inside, boiling my blood, until I want it to bubble over so I can grab her, choke the life out of her, throw her into the water. Show her the same mercy she showed my poor little girl. I think some of this must show in my face, because her expression sets even harder.

"So what do you want from me?" she asks in that same flat voice she's used throughout. "If you knew, why didn't you call the police?"

Standing here, wanting to kill her, my reasons seem stupid to me now. But I will do this. "I don't trust them to deal with it properly. They've done nothing but mess it up so far. And there are two other reasons. The first is that I needed to tell you something myself, and I couldn't do that if I put this in their hands."

"And the second?"

"I'll get to that." There's no guidance manual in the world that can tell you how to face the woman who killed your child, and whose child's death you are in some way responsible for. I'm struggling here. We are two mothers standing here facing each other, and I'm caught between hate and regret. Dan would tell me I'm doing this all wrong. So would Annika. But only I have lived this, and they can't know—no outsider can.

"Go on, then." She's so lifeless it scares me.

"I didn't know about Chloe's death until yesterday."

"It was all over the papers. How could you not know?"

"We were in the U.S. last summer when it happened. I had no idea."

Something moves in that sea of awful blankness that is her face, the merest ripple, but I have touched something.

"So how did you find out?"

"I saw you following me. I recognized you from the night you sat with Portia. You told her your name is Clare."

"You remembered my name?" She sounds surprised.

"Of course. Why would you think I wouldn't?"

"People like me don't mean anything to you."

Is this why she did it? Because I'm looking at this ordinary woman, and I'm struggling to believe someone like her could damage my brakes and then force us off the road. She looks as if she can barely find the motivation to get up in the mornings.

"Yes, I remembered you. I didn't recognize you straight away, but not because I don't remember you. I've never forgotten you or your daughter. And when I looked you and Greg up online, I saw the newspaper articles, and I saw what had happened to Chloe." This is so terribly important now. Whatever happens next, whatever we both do, I must do this part right. "I am so sorry, Clare. I should have never taken that case. I had an instinct to turn it down, and I should have gone with that."

"Why didn't you?" She stares at me, cold-eyed.

I will not lie to her. I, of all people, will not lie to a mother over that. "He paid me an enormous sum of money to take it on."

She hangs her head. "Yes, he would."

"I am sorry. I'm sorry because what was said in court wasn't fair to you, and most of all, I'm sorry for what happened to Chloe."

"She wanted to come back to me. She'd wanted that for so long, and she was finally getting old enough for the courts to listen to her." She lifts her eyes to mine, and they are brimming with tears. "But he wouldn't let her, and he even stopped her visits to me, then, because she didn't pick him."

I go cold all over. "He stopped you seeing each other?" I'd suspected he might try that, but I was hoping he wouldn't have succeeded. "For how long?"

"We used to have a few visits a year, but nothing for the last twelve months. He always hated her seeing me, but her telling him that she was going to leave tipped him over the edge. He wouldn't let her come at all then."

"*Did* he love her? He said he did."

The tears spill over and run down her cheeks, mixing with the rain. "He might have said that to get his own way. He may even have really believed he did. But he didn't know what love is. He wasn't capable of it. Chloe knew what I knew, that he didn't really ever love anyone."

"He wanted to own them," I add softly.

She nods. "So you saw that. You're right—you shouldn't have taken that case."

"I'm so sorry," I say again. "It's a useless word—sorry—because it doesn't fix anything, but I am."

She wipes her face with her hands, a curiously childlike gesture. "She wasn't happy with him. Oh, he gave her everything—the best schools, her own horse, expensive dresses, anything she wanted."

"Except her mother. That poor little girl."

"He tried to stop my access after his first year in Johannesburg. He relented a bit after the second year because she plagued him until he gave in. She was allowed to come over and see me three times a year, for a total of six weeks."

It was less than he'd agreed to when I'd represented him, which was a visit every school holiday, adding up to nine weeks annually.

"I used to live the rest of the year for those six weeks. They were everything to me. We Skyped the rest of the time, but she had to hide that from him. She always said that as soon as she was old enough, she'd come home for good. She knew I could never afford enough money for a lawyer who could best her father in court, and she didn't want me to waste money trying only to lose. He had me beat on that, but Chloe kept telling me to hang in there—it wasn't forever. We were waiting to be with each other again." Her tears flow freely and unchecked. "And then he took her from me again, said he was taking her forever this time, and I'd never see her again. And that's exactly what he did. Not in the way he meant, but that's what's happened. If I could get to him, I'd torture him for all eternity. I hope there's a hell, I really do, because I want him burning in it for all time."

I swallow. "But you couldn't get to him, so you got to me instead."

And I see the first flash of hate in her eyes. "I saw you one day. It was soon after she died, and I saw you just walking across a street to your car. You were rushing, dressed in a work suit and heels. I knew it was you immediately. Every moment of what happened in court, every word you said, I remember all of it. It haunts me." She takes a few deep breaths in and out to calm herself so she can speak. "So I followed you, and there you were with your happy family life. With your kids, your husband. Everything was just perfect for you, and there I was—I didn't have much, and the only thing that mattered to me had just been taken from me in the most awful way. You'd helped to do that. I had nothing. I hadn't been allowed to start a new relationship after Greg because if I had, he'd have used it as the excuse he wanted to stop Chloe coming. I gave up any chance of that to keep the little contact I had with her. I hated you, and the more I followed you and saw you living your 'happily ever after,' the more that hatred grew." She grips her hands into fists so tightly that her knuckles are white. "I wanted you to suffer."

I can hardly speak, but I have to make myself. "So what did you do?"

She grimaces. "You said you knew."

"I want to hear it from you."

"So you can tape me saying it to take to the police? I don't care. I have nothing left. Tell them—they can lock me up."

"I'm not taping you. I just want to hear it in your words."

"I followed you when you went on that holiday. I watched you doing all the things I would never be able to do with Chloe, and I hated you more and more. So, so much. I wanted you to feel like me, to know what it's like, and then maybe you'd think again about destroying more lives. I messed with your brakes when you went out for a walk. My father was a car enthusiast, and he used to love me to help him when I was a kid. So I knew what to do.

I wanted the brakes to fail when you were on your way home, when I forced you to try to brake hard. When you were driving home, I lay in wait and I drove my car right at you."

"But my girls—why would you hurt them?"

"Why did you hurt mine?"

"I didn't set out to. You must know that."

"But you didn't even think about her. She was six years old, and you took her away from her mother. She was unhappy, so unhappy. You went back to your kids with the money you got from making my daughter miserable." She spits the words out and they are like a blow to the stomach.

I know, deep inside, that this is why I didn't go to the police. *This* had to happen between the two of us. It was necessary and yes, part of justice. I know that on some visceral level.

"I see that now, and I'm sorry."

She cocks her head to one side, and I can see her rage burning higher and higher. I understand that, because mine burns too. It may be banked now while I process my part in this, but it is still there, smoldering, waiting to flare again when it's given fuel.

"Yes, you understand now. You understand because I put you in that place." She smiles horribly. "What's it like to live in hell?"

There, right there, is the gush of oxygen needed to turn my anger into an obliterating furnace.

I don't pause. I don't take a breath. I launch myself at her.

As I come for her, she lifts her hands slightly, as if to protect her face, but she offers no resistance. I crash her to the ground, my hands round her throat, gripping as tight as I can.

I will choke the life out of this bitch who killed Becca.

76

"I DID NOT DRIVE THAT car with your little girl inside," I yell at her. "Your husband did. You were stupid enough to marry him and even more stupid to have a child with him. He was your choice. Did you think about whose fault that was?" I sit over her, gripping harder and harder, and it gives me a vicious pleasure. As she struggles for breath, she begins to fight beneath me, trying to buck me off and claw at my hands with hers. "I would never have knowingly hurt your child, but you killed mine. And you knew what you were doing when you did it."

The struggling lessens the longer I hold her.

I will kill her. I will.

I pushed life back into Portia's lungs after what this woman did to us, and I'm going to shut the life out of hers now.

I close my eyes as my hands grip tighter. I never knew I had so much strength.

How easy it is.

And then, like cinema stills projected onto the inside of my eyelids, I see the images of those two little girls, side by side—Becca and Chloe.

Chloe looks as she did in that old photo, a touch younger than Becca. Both of them with those same beautiful innocent expressions, trusting little eyes, smiling faces. Girls who have been deeply loved.

My hands lose their grip.

Becca, if she was here now, would take my hands and tell me to stop. Her gentle voice would pull me back from what I was about to do.

She would not want this, not for me, not for Portia, and not even for Clare.

I open my eyes, and Clare is lying beneath me, looking up at me with terrified eyes. Her hands are at her throat as she gulps in air.

I scramble away from her quickly before I can change my mind, bending over to rest my hands on my thighs as I catch my breath.

"I need to know," I say to her in a flat, dead voice, "that you're not trying to take my other daughter."

"Is that what you think?" Clare's voice is hoarse and faint, barely audible. "That I'm going to hurt her?"

There is nothing left for it but truth. That is all we have to save us, she and I, and there will be no lies told here—not by me, anyway.

"Yes. That was my other reason for coming here today. I needed to know if you were...if..."

"If I was planning to kill her?" Clare's voice is still choked and damaged, but she manages to sit up. "No."

"Then why did you keep following us?" And I don't know if I dare believe whatever she is going to say. My fear has overtaken my anger for a while, and I can't take in anything else but that.

Clare holds her hands up in a gesture of hopelessness and surrender. "I needed to see that...that you were both still alive."

"What?" It comes out as a shout, which is not my intention.

Clare winces. "I don't expect that to make sense, but it's true."

"Is it? So explain. I think you owe me that much." There are these awful moments where I see in her face a flash of the woman she once was, and those moments douse the rage that threatens to flare again.

"I know what losing a daughter does to you. I needed to know you and your older girl made it. And that you kept surviving. That's why I followed you, and that's why I sat with her that night in the park—to make sure she was OK." Her damaged voice is almost a whisper, and I have to strain to hear. "I watched you all that time before I did what I did. And after that, I needed to see you were going to make it. Not just that you recovered from the accident but that you could keep going after losing the little one. I watched you for so long because you were struggling, all of you, but especially you, and it's my fault. I saw you in that lake, you see. I saw you bring your older girl out, and I saw you go back for the other one. I watched you try and fail. You tried so hard." Her voice cracks on a sob.

Truth, that's what I said to myself. Truth between all of us. "I will never forgive myself for not getting her too."

"I'm sorry," she says, and she gets to her feet. "I am so sorry for what I did, and I can never say sorry enough. My little girl had just died, and I was…I was not myself. I did a terrible, terrible thing, and I'll be punished for that." She turns her gaze back to me. "You can go to the police now and tell them. I'll admit it all. There'll be no more trouble for you and your family." Her face just crumbles, and there she is as the tears begin to flow again—the Clare Underwood of her despicable husband's photo. "After Chloe died, I changed. I can't explain…I just wasn't…"

"You don't need to." And she doesn't, because in this moment, I understand her. I have *been* her.

"And then, after I did that awful thing to your little girl…" She can't go on, and she collapses again in a howling ball.

I watch as she lies there, rocking herself back and forth. It's the way a mother rocks her child to try to soothe her.

I have been you. I could be you now.

I can see those images again, of Becca and Chloe, so alike in their ingenuous smiles. And I look at the broken woman lying on the deck.

I walk to where Clare is sobbing in that animalistic way, a way I have cried myself. I sit down beside her on the jetty and dangle my legs over the edge toward the water. After a moment, I place a hand on her shoulder and wait.

What do I do?

This is the woman who killed my daughter.

This is the woman whose daughter died because of something I did.

I can go to the police. She'll be locked away. I'll have justice.

But there's something else I know, and that is that Clare is already being punished. There's nothing they can do to her that's worse than what's already happened.

And here is the thing: when you lose a child, you become another creature entirely. A creature made of rage and unimaginable grief. Your inner lioness, the one that crawls on her claws down a cliff face to save her cub, that lioness is left with nothing to protect. And so she faces that loss outward. I was caught by her lioness's rage, and I have felt that rage within myself.

How many lives will be destroyed by Greg Underwood and his brand of toxic masculinity? Maybe it needs to stop here, stop now.

But this is crazy, and I'm being ridiculous—she killed Becca. She has to pay for that—logic dictates it.

I look down at Clare, and I know: she will never stop paying.

This could end here.

She moves her hands away from her face, and I realize I've been rubbing her shoulder. She is a mess of tears and snot, and she makes no attempt to hide it. No, we are beyond that, she and I.

"I was supposed to die too."

"What?"

"I was supposed to die with you. I was supposed to hit your car with mine, and then we'd both be dead. That was why I didn't just cut the brakes. That was why I drove the car at you. But you dodged, and then you went off the road. It didn't happen how I thought it would."

Yes, I can see that. I believe her.

"I called the ambulance."

"You did what?"

"I watched you, everything that happened in the lake, and that's when I began to see what I'd done." She's still lying on the jetty, gulping words out between sobs. "I sat and watched you try to keep your girl alive, and I cried for mine. And as I watched you, some of *me* came back, and I realized what I'd done. I couldn't watch you die, and definitely not your daughter. I phoned the ambulance. Told them I'd come across you while walking my dog. When they came, I took them to you." She sobs harder. "I wish they could have saved your little one."

And I know in this moment—I know indisputably—this ends now. There has been enough pain. Nothing will be served by dragging this out. I need to mete out an unexpected justice.

"Clare, what did you want to see when you followed us?"

"That you were OK. Because when your child dies, you want to die yourself, don't you? And I didn't want your daughter to lose her mother because of me." She sits up and tries to get the tears under control so she can speak properly. "And then some days, I could only live with myself enough not to down a bottle of pills if I could follow you and see that you were both still alive and recovering. That's why I followed you—to see you were getting better. But then it all started to go wrong again, and I couldn't leave you all like that. I had to help your daughter, and then your husband left, and part of me thought that was fair because of what you'd done to me. But the rest of me was scared for you all. I wanted you to make it so I hadn't destroyed your other daughter's life too." She closes her eyes in pain. "She's a sweet kid. I don't want to see her hurting."

I am going to make a choice here, make a choice again. But this time, my choice will free me, not destroy me. I am going to let go. I am going to free us all.

"Clare, I want you to do something for me."

She rubs away some tears so she can see. I wonder what Greg Underwood would say if he could see her now, lined and weary, her face streaked with despair. He'd sneer, no doubt. He was a fool. This is what love looks like, this woman in front of me. He knew nothing; he never did.

"I want you to live, Clare."

She shakes her head. "I don't understand."

I take a moment before I speak. Am I sure? The thought comes to me— what would Becca want? What would my sunbeam child say about all of this?

I can't keep back the tears myself as I answer Clare. "I'm not going to the police. I want you to live. Really live."

They say forgiveness is a choice. Well, I'm choosing.

"We need to make a life for ourselves now that our daughters are gone, Clare. I want you to go out there and do that. Make a life. Live again."

She gazes at me in confusion. "You don't understand. I don't want to go on."

"On the contrary, I understand perfectly. But Chloe would want you to. Wouldn't she?"

She nods slowly, as if it costs her a lot to do so, and how well I understand that feeling. "She would. But what I did to your little girl—it's not the same for you. You can't understand what it's like to live with that. I'm not asking for pity or understanding from you—please know that. I don't deserve it. But it's not the same for us."

"I have to live with what happened to Chloe too," I remind her. I hesitate because this is hard, but then I take her hand in mine. "And there's something you don't know. I'm going to tell you only because I want you to take something from this. For it to help you."

She stares in disbelief at my hand in hers. I can't believe I'm doing this myself, but she called the ambulance. She made that call. She came back from that place she was in, that place I know, and she called the ambulance. That's why Portia is alive now. She did a terrible, monstrous thing to us, but then she saved Portia and me. She would have saved Becca if she could have—I know that now. Without her seeing what she'd done, finally coming back to her real self, Portia and I would be dead now. That's no small thing she did.

"You caused Becca's death, and I do hate you for that. I do, and that will never leave me, just as you will always hate me. But you saved Portia, and I won't forget that either." I squeeze her hand gently. "So you see, if you want to put something right for us out of all this mess, you have a choice."

"I do want to put it right, but how can I when I can't bring your daughter back?" she wails.

"I can't bring yours back either. And we would if we could. I know that now. All we can do now is rebuild. Make a new start, Clare. Sell your house and move away somewhere else, if that's what it takes. Or change your job, if that helps. Find someone who will love you for your real self and seize life. Because if you don't, then Greg really has won, and I don't believe men like him should win. Do it, Clare—do it for your daughter and for mine."

She's trembling as she asks me, "And what will you do?"

I glance over toward the bank, to the path that leads me to my car, which will lead me home. "I will live too."

Clare nods her understanding. "If I do it, it gives you permission too?"

"Yes, I guess it does. There's been enough hate and death, and we can't reverse it." I look her in the eyes. "I really believe we would if we could. If we could change the past, we would do it differently."

"Yes," she says fervently, nodding furiously as fresh tears spring into her eyes.

"We can only try to put that right now, in our own ways. I've come to understand something today, while I was sitting and waiting to meet you and thinking about all of this. I'm going to quit my job, Clare. I'm not taking those cases anymore—I can't now. They weren't all like yours. I helped a lot of genuine people as well, you know. I made things better for a lot of children. But I will never be able to do that work again, not after Chloe. I'll still work in law, but I'll find something different."

"Somebody else will just do it instead."

"I know, but it won't be me, and that matters to me now. What will you do?"

"I don't know." She takes my hand back tentatively. "And I don't even know how I'll find the strength to try."

"You must, Clare. You must do it for both our daughters. And you can."

"Can I? I wish I knew that. It's easier to exist to hate and fight than it is to live and let go."

"Because when you let go, she's not coming back." I nod at her, and she bites her lip furiously to stop herself crying again. "But they *are* gone, and I think your little girl would want you to let go now, just as mine would. So find a way, Clare."

She takes a deep, shuddering breath in. "For them." And then I see her gather herself, and she gets up and helps me to my feet. "You're right. We'll always hate each other, no matter how much understanding there is. I'll never bother you again. No more following, so I won't know if you're safe. But we should never see each other again—it hurts too much, doesn't it?"

"Yes. But I will be safe and you must be too."

"I know—for them. I won't dishonor their memories." She gives me the faintest of smiles. "You always did present a very good argument."

I give her that same faint smile back.

"Find a way to be happy, please," she says softly. And then she turns and walks away from the jetty.

77

THE DAY AFTER THE BOATING lake, I wake up with a heavy feeling in the pit of my stomach. I need to talk to Portia about what's happened. There's no way around that. Not only does she deserve to know, but the police investigation into our accident is now going to prove fruitless. She will want to know why I will appear to be content to live with that.

We sit in my large and too-empty bed in our pajamas and talk properly. For the first time ever, I feel as if I'm talking to her with no barriers. She tucks her cold feet in under my leg just like she used to do when she was small, and I explain what happened.

"What are you going to do about that woman?"

"I don't want to do anything, Portia. I hate her for what she did to you and Becca, but I understand how damaged she was when she did it. That's not an excuse, but I've lived some of that madness. She loved her little girl so much, and I know how that feels. It was me she wanted to hurt, not you two. She just couldn't see through her hate for me. When she knew she had hurt you, that's when she came to. It's what pulled her back into sanity."

"She can't have driven us off the road and thought me and Becca would be OK."

"No, of course she can't. But in that mental state, in those depths, the rational you is lost. There is only rage and grief. Thinking clearly would have been beyond her. Knowing that, how can I condemn her in the same way I would somebody who had done that with full reasoning?"

Portia purses her lips. "I can't imagine you saying this a year ago."

"A year ago, I didn't know what I know now about losing a child."

"Nobody is going to understand why you're doing this—you do know that?"

"I know, but they haven't walked this path, and I have." I stroke her hair. "She saved you. She would have saved Becca if she could. It was me she wanted to hurt, except really it was her husband. But she couldn't get to him anymore, so she struck out at me instead. She intended to die herself in that accident. If she'd been thinking in a sane way, she would have never done that—she'd never hurt a child—and that shows you what a state she was in. I don't expect you to understand, but you must trust me when I tell you I know what that level of derangement can do to a mother."

She's silent for a moment. "When you were telling me what you said to Clare, you said you had to choose which one of us to get out of the car. I didn't know that."

"Yes." And I know it's always going to hurt me to talk about this, but she deserves the truth. "That's a large part of why I struggled so much after Becca's death, more than you or your dad did. I had to choose down there. I could only get one of you out and I knew it, and I chose you."

She sits very still and stares at her hands. "I thought you would have picked her."

"Why?" And I know, heartbreakingly, what her answer will be.

"I thought you loved her more."

And there is so much pain and rejection locked up in those few quiet words that I want to sob it out for her. Instead, I simply say, "No."

She takes a deep breath and nods, but she doesn't reply for a long, long time. Finally, she leans her head against me and says, "You couldn't save us both, Mum. And you would have picked her over yourself—I know that."

And she's right. I would.

I hesitate. "I know I get on your nerves sometimes because I still want you to be my little girl, and you want to grow up. One day, when you have your own child, it'll all make sense. I said that to my mum after I had you. I actually called her up and said, 'I understand now,' and she laughed. She said she knew that would happen."

Portia makes a moue of uncertainty. "I'm not sure I want kids! But yeah, OK, I'll take your word for it." And her voice softens. "Anyway, you're wrong. Sometimes I do still want my mum. I...I just don't always know how to say it. The words sort of stick inside, and I feel stupid saying them."

"I think that's part of growing up," I tell her. "I'm so proud of you, you know. I'm so proud of who you are and who you're becoming. I don't always think you know that."

"No, I don't," she says in a small voice.

"Well, you do now." I hold my daughter tight, and for a moment, I imagine Becca's arms wrapping round both of us.

78

ADDRESSING THE ISSUE OF CLARE with Dan will be more difficult. The police haven't managed to find anything of material importance, and I've let it go quiet in the hope that the investigation steps down due to lack of evidence. It has crossed my mind to contact them and dramatically downplay that flashback, but a natural opportunity hasn't arisen. Discretion is the better part of valor, I decided. But the one person I can't keep in the dark is my husband.

I text Dan. "I need to see you. A phone call won't do. There's no danger—I know that now. I also know it wasn't your fault. Please meet me so I can explain."

We meet in the park near our house on a quiet afternoon. "It's over," I tell him. "I know what happened, and most importantly, I know who it was. It wasn't one of your clients."

He looks dreadful. He obviously isn't eating or sleeping. He seems depressed, clinically so, which isn't unexpected from what Aidan and Stella have told me, but it's still a shock to see it. It's strange, but in the few weeks since I last saw him, he's grown to look so unlike the man I know that I can't quite reconcile it. His cheeks are gaunt, but what's most upsetting is the absence of expression—I don't recognize my husband in the man looking out of those eyes at me.

He listens silently, but with growing horror as I tell him what happened on the jetty. And then I watch his face change to anger, as I knew it would. This much I do recognize of him.

He leaps up from the park bench, glaring. "You had to apologize to a murderer?"

"Yes, I did. That might seem crazy to you, but—"

"You were just doing your job, and if you hadn't done it, somebody else would have!" He stares at me, wild-eyed. And I'm afraid of who he is now.

"A child died, Dan."

"Yes, our child."

I'm not getting through to him, but I have to find a way. "She was a lovely little girl. Her name was Chloe. She didn't deserve to die."

"And Becca did?"

"No! But what I'm saying is that none of this would have happened if Greg Underwood hadn't had some sick need for control. She would have been here with her mother."

"Greg Underwood—so that's his name. Right, I'm calling the police!" He whips his phone out of his pocket.

You idiot, Lizzie!

"If you do that and they arrest her, I swear to you, Dan, I'll speak in her favor in court. I'll tell them I forgive her, and I'll plead for clemency."

He looks at me as if he hates me, and I recoil. "Why? What about Becca? Doesn't she deserve justice?"

"Dan, you have to believe me—she is a broken woman. No good will come of locking her up."

"When did you grow a bleeding heart?" he snarls. "She killed my daughter. She's going to pay."

"She's already paying. I know that. I know the signs, and I know them from the inside."

"Oh, that's what this is about—you and your guilt." His face is twisted in anger.

"She was the one who called the ambulance after the crash. She brought help to us. She did an awful, dreadful thing, but then she tried to repair what she'd done. And it was too late."

"You're crazy. You really are insane. She cut the brakes. That's no accident."

"Do you remember what I was like when Becca died?"

"It's not the same thing." He shakes his head in disgust. "And what do you think this woman is going to do now if you let her go? Who's she going to hurt next?"

"She's going to start a new life and try to find a new meaning to it. For both our daughters."

"That's just sick. Don't you tarnish Becca's memory like that!"

"Dan, you don't know this woman. And you don't know the case and what she was like before it."

"I don't need to."

I'm down to my last shot. "Dan, I need to do this. I need to forgive her so I can forgive myself."

He falls silent. I look at him, and time stretches on and on. His shoulders slump and his mouth goes slack. So many years and so much between us—I know what he's going to do before he does it.

"We're done. I have nothing more to say to you. I don't want to see you again. It's over." He turns his back on me and walks away. I call his name, but he holds up his hand to silence me and continues walking. He never looks back.

I wait and wait for the call from the police, but it never comes. I wait for Dan to call Portia, too, but he doesn't and that hurts. In the end, it's Aidan who comes around to tell me.

"Dan told me you don't need me anymore—it's dealt with."

"He did?"

"He also told me you two are finished."

"That's his choice, not mine."

"Help me out here, Lizzie. I have no idea what's going on, and I don't know what to say to him to fix this."

"You can't fix it, Aidan. But when you speak to him, tell him I said thank you for what he's done. He'll understand."

"Will he? I wish I did," Aidan said in exasperation. "There's something else you need to know. I've persuaded him to check into a clinic. That's where he is now."

At least he's getting help, but it's only the smallest crumb of comfort.

"He's lost it, Lizzie. I thought he might just need some time and space, but I was wrong. And I'm not equipped to help him. I don't have those skills. I found somewhere that can help him, and eventually I persuaded him to go. They say he'll have to be in a while and not to expect too much of him at the moment."

"Thanks, Aidan. You're a good friend." It hurts to hear about how ill he is be spoken out loud, and I need some time on my own to deal with this now.

He sighed. "It doesn't feel like that. I wish I could do more. Look, I need to explain to you the state he's in because you'll have to talk to Portia about it. He actually can't function at the moment. He can't speak some days or even get up. It's been getting steadily worse since he left you, and I'm amazed he managed to meet you at all because I didn't think he would. When he is able to go out, he's on edge, snapping, not able to focus on anything; you can't talk to him. I asked him what he wants me to tell you, and he says he wants Portia to know it isn't her fault and he's sorry. He'll be in touch with her as soon as he can, but he's sick and needs to get well. He doesn't want to see her while he's like this."

I swallow hard. "OK, I'll talk to her." I don't know what to say. What can you say when you're told the man you've loved for so many years is in that state? I wish he would see me, but I know he won't.

"The clinic says it could take months for him to get well," he warns me. "Months. I just want you to know I'm here for you both."

"Should I try to see him? I don't think he wants me to, but I don't want him thinking I've abandoned him."

"I don't think the clinic would advise that," he says gently. "I don't think he could cope with that right now."

I hug my arms round my body. "Tell him we love him, if he's ever ready to hear that again."

He touches my shoulder. "I will, Lizzie. And I'll keep telling him until he hears me."

I nod dully. Grief and I are old friends by now. This is another loss I have to learn to bear. It's not fair. It's not fair this has happened to me or to Dan. What's that saying? "What can't be helped must be endured." I am learning I am better at enduring than I thought, but it isn't fair.

The weeks go by, and I grow more and more certain of what I want to do now.

"I want to move," I tell Portia.

"I thought you loved this house?"

"I did once. Not now."

She cocks her head on one side as she looks at me. "Then why don't we go?"

I hesitate, but Portia and I need to be honest with each other now. It's just me and her, and we've dissembled around each other too much for too long. "Because I want to move away—right away. Into the country. Somewhere like Oakleigh, somewhere I feel at peace."

She nods. "Then why don't we go?" she repeats.

I hug Portia all the tighter, and I cherish that she hugs me too. I've waited a long time to have her back.

"So what's stopping you?" she asks me.

"Fear." I give her a rueful smile. "Living somewhere like that may be a stupid pipe dream, a memory of childhood that I've rose-tinted with time. I'll be a single mother with no local support network. You might hate it. And your dad has gone, and I don't know what my rural dream means without him there."

"And if you stay here?"

I shake my head vigorously without even thinking. I suppose that tells me something. "That just doesn't feel right. It's safe, it's what I know, but it's not what I want. Or is it just it's not what I think I want? I don't know. And then there's your dad, and he may want to divorce me, but he's not well."

My daughter fixes me with a stare. "He'll come back, you know. He'll get over it."

I want her to be right, but I can't believe she is. "Why are you so sure?"

She shrugs. "That's just Dad. That's how he rolls."

She doesn't understand what's happening to him. "He's ill, Portia."

"Yeah, I know. After you spoke to me about it, I called Aidan and talked to him. I get it. Dad's just got to the end of his tether, and he needs headspace to put things right."

If only it were that simple, but that's teenagers—made of hope. And right now, I can't bear to disillusion her.

79

WE MOVE INTO FIR COTTAGE in Oakleigh on a blustery, wild day in November. It's been a year and a week since Becca died. Portia and I marked her death together by driving up to the lake and laying flowers there as well as putting some on her grave. I placed our wreath on the bank in the spot where I dragged Portia from the water. There was another bunch there, too, with no note, but I knew who they were from. Nobody else would know this precise spot. When I saw them, I experienced that fast and piercing spark of anger that I am beginning to understand will remain with me forever. They were beautiful flowers, truly gorgeous, and she must have spent a great deal of money on them. Portia raised an eyebrow at me as she laid our bouquet next to them, but she said nothing. My wise girl.

Our first evening in the cottage is marked by a battle to get the boiler lit—a fight I win eventually after much swearing, to Portia's great amusement—and by my fumbling attempts to light a fire in the sitting-room hearth. I trawl back through my childhood memories to remember how to set the fire properly, and it takes me two attempts before I succeed. Then we are rewarded with bright, cheery flames, and I feel my heart lift with them. I drive to the fish-and-chip shop five miles away, and I have to reheat our food in the oven when I get back.

Portia is amused and appalled in equal measure when she learns the nearest takeout place is so far. "Wow, so this is rural life, then!"

I laugh nervously in case it's put her off already, but the fish and chips are excellent, which I hope mollifies her. We eat the food out of the bag at the kitchen table because we haven't found the plates yet.

"Well, Mum, I think your table's finally come home," Portia says with a mischievous grin. It does look good in the open-plan kitchen-dining room that spans the length of the cottage. My other city furniture looks out of place. I'll have to work through changing some of it and making this place ours, making it home. That feels like it might be quite fun, and I'm looking forward to it.

Portia calls her dad later to tell him the move has gone according to plan and we are in the cottage and OK. He had asked her to ring and let him know. They are on talking terms now, but he says he's still not ready to see her. Aidan's backed this up. "He's not quite himself, but getting there. He's much better than he was," he'd told me in a guarded way that seemed less about keeping news from me and more about concern that Dan might regress.

If Dan hadn't told me we were over, I would have forced the issue of seeing him. I couldn't have left him fighting through a breakdown alone, no matter how much he'd wanted us not to see him in this state.

"He's pleased it went well," Portia says when she gets off the phone to him.

"How is he?"

"He says he's started cycling again, so that's good. He still sounds shaky, though."

I am amazed by how Portia has managed through all of this. I'd expected her to take the situation with her father far worse, but she's really been quite relaxed about it, as if he's in hospital with a broken leg or something. Sometimes I wonder if she realizes what all this has done to him and how it has torn him apart. She's too young, maybe, to understand that, but generally, she's so close to her dad. She's more like him than she is me in many ways. But I don't want to rock the boat by discussing it tonight on our first evening in our new home.

I'm exhausted and ready for bed before nine o'clock, and so is Portia.

"Moving is tough!" she says. "Hey, you were right about making the beds up before we did anything else. I'm so glad they're ready now." She turns off the light, and we are suddenly plummeted into blackness. "That's seriously dark!" my city-born daughter exclaims. "I can't see anything." The un-curtained cottage panes let in the unremitting dark of a moonless country night.

"I bet the stars out there are amazing," she says.

"Let's go and look."

She grins and turns on the light on her phone to guide our way through the overgrown back garden. When she turns the phone flashlight out, the stars above us are clear and bright and myriad.

"There's so many," she exclaims. "They're like glitter. Look at all those tiny ones!" She leans against me and sighs happily. "This is great."

My heart sings.

Over the next few weeks, we fall into a routine again. Portia goes to a new school. She's nervous after her experience in her old school, but she's excited, too, at the fresh start, and she already knows a few people from the drama group. I start picking up a little bit of easy personal-injury casework during the day. I'm easing myself back in gradually, but it's good to be doing something again. My brain thanks me for it. Every day I break off for a two-hour walk in the fresh air at midday. We definitely need to get a dog soon. I'll look into that as soon as Christmas is over. At the moment, I need to focus on how to make the holidays as special as possible for the two of us.

I still have nights when sleep eludes me and the bed stretches wide and empty and cold on the other side of me. I sleep on the right, as I've done for the last twenty years. I tried venturing into the middle, but when I woke, I had invariably moved back over to "my side." I see dawn from the wrong side of sleep too many times.

However, I do conquer the garden with help from Portia and her friend Sam. He comes over on the weekends to tackle it with us, and we beat it back into something resembling tidy. I dreaded Portia losing her enchantment with the novelty of our new lifestyle, but that doesn't seem to have happened. She moves from excited and nervous to settled and content in a series of barely perceptible changes.

Advent comes, and I buy her a chocolate calendar at the supermarket. As I get to the register, I look down at it in my basket and laugh to myself—I go back and get another one for me. Why not? When did we adults stop enjoying those little fun moments, the aspects we call "childish"? Life is far too short to let those simple things go and to surrender to the serious—at any moment, it can all be taken from us, so we should play while we can. Portia gives me her raised eyebrow of amusement when I tell her that one is for me and then sidles past and high-fives me as she goes. We understand each other far better now, she and I, and that, to me, is a thing of beauty so desperately sought and highly prized.

This is enough. This is a life. It is not the life I wanted a year and a half ago, not on these terms, but from where I have been and come back from, it is a life worth living.

80

IT IS THE SUNDAY BEFORE Christmas, and Portia is sleeping in. I've been mooching around on the internet looking at the pros and cons of different breeds of dogs. I rather fancy something large and cheerfully optimistic, so I scroll through the gundog breeds.

The clack of the door knocker takes me by surprise, and I check the clock. Ten on Sunday morning. It's barely a civilized time to call. When I open the front door, Dan is standing there.

I don't recognize the clothes he's wearing: brown canvas trousers, boots, a corduroy shirt, and a padded waxed jacket. He's carrying a large duffel bag. I don't know what to say, I don't know what this is about, and he looks at me, his lip caught between his teeth.

"You look well," I tell him. It's true. The unexpected clothes suit him, and the horrible sunken cheeks and the ashen pallor have gone.

"Thanks. It took a lot of work." He hesitates. "I fell apart. I'm sorry. I didn't understand this thing well enough when it happened to you. I understand better now."

I look at the duffel, wondering, and he follows my gaze.

"If I can," he says uncertainly. "If you'll let me."

I have had twenty years of translating Dan's unspoken words, so I do not need him to say more. I understand perfectly, and the new clothes are part of this, I realize now.

Can we do this? There's a chasm between us. Is it possible to bridge that now? I guess he must believe that or he wouldn't be here.

My job has left its scars, I realize. Fatalistically, on some level, I had let Dan go in a small corner of my head because one day, he might leave. I saw it so many times, after all. So when he did finally go, I told myself I knew it would happen. But I forgot to consider one important factor, namely Dan himself.

My husband does not quit—that's what makes him so fantastic at his job. He hangs in there when other people give up. He hung in for me when I was destroyed and falling apart, even though I expected him not to. It might not have been pretty, and he might not have dealt with it the way I wanted, but he was there.

He only left when he thought he'd hurt us too much for him to live with it.

Two decades have put lines round his dark eyes and spattered some strands of gray into his shock of brown hair. We are a long way from those bright-eyed, career-minded young things we were when we met. Life has bruised us, and sometimes badly, but he is still here and standing in my hall with the winter morning light streaming in behind him from the open door and revealing every one of those life lines on his face in fine detail.

Bruises can heal. The kind of savage cut that is the loss of a child will always leave a vicious scar, but just as the skin heals itself enough to go on, weakened and damaged but functional, so, I am learning, can the heart. We can still live for each other, even with one of us gone.

Dan is looking at the hall table, at the collection of family photographs. He is still there in them, and I see his eyes widen in wonder. He puts his duffel bag down on the floor and unzips it. With painstaking care, he takes out a tissue-papered package and unwraps it. It is the photo of Becca on the beach with her face turned up to the sun, the one that he took away on the day I came home.

He places it on the table in the center, in pride of place among the others.

So we are all home now. I blink back my tears, because now is not the time.

I take Dan's hand, and I close the door behind us.

AUTHOR'S NOTE

The idea for *Two Little Girls* was first conceived on a coffee break in the office at work. I walked into a conversation everyone was having about maternal anxiety dreams. Mine was definitely the weirdest: a giant demonic rabbit the size of a house menacing us and trying to catch the family to eat us. But one of my colleagues had a really traumatic one where she described how she would dream that she was driving along in the car with her two little girls when she lost control and went into a lake. As the car filled with water, she knew she could only get one of them out…and then she always woke up. Everyone else in the office was super sympathetic about how awful it was, and I stood there with my mouth open, half grinning. They all looked at me as I nodded and my grin spread. "Avril, that would make such a great start to a book!" I told her.

And that was how it began. Coincidentally, around the same time, I happened to read a newspaper article about families who have adopted and their feelings toward their adoptive and natural children. It was very thought-provoking, and different women had very different experiences. The plot for *Two Little Girls* really began to take shape, and Lizzie's dilemma took a new form.

What has been so important to me in writing this book is to convey how each family member deals with their grief in their own way. Grief is a complex and unpredictable beast, and I really wanted to explore that. Lizzie says at the start that it will shatter them apart, and all of them break at different points. But it was always part of the direction of the book that they would find their way back to each other. When Dan has his breakdown after staying strong for his family for so long, it was important to show how that can happen to anybody, no matter how strong or stoic they seem. Everybody has a breaking point.

I didn't, however, set out at the start to question the morality of Lizzie and Dan's career choices. That's something that evolved entirely from the characters interacting as the plot advanced. What I did intend, and what really interested me, was representing the distance and silence that can exist between members of the family as relationships change over the years and how we can grow apart and then back together again. The shades of gray around their decisions, how those small nuances can twist them apart and then back together, the ebb and flow of the tides of their relationships are what really interest me as a writer, and they are some of the hardest aspects to get right. But I guess that's the challenge and where the buzz comes from.

I think my favorite parts of this book to write were those last scenes between Lizzie and Clare. It's such a reflection of the journey through her grief that Lizzie gets to the point where she can understand Clare so well and forgive her. Forgiveness is a choice she makes to free herself, and it comes from a place of knowledge that there's no future in hate and blame, either of self or another.

Robert Frost once said, "I write to find out what I didn't know I knew," and for me, that is the greatest joy of writing.

READING GROUP GUIDE

1. Lizzie is forced to make a very difficult decision at the start of this book. Do you think she chooses appropriately? How would you have made this decision?

2. Lizzie and Dan have a seemingly strong marriage that begins to falter as the book progresses. Whose fault do you think this is, and why?

3. Dan and Lizzie both have legal jobs that create questions of morality. Who faces more difficult ethical questions? Do you think it is fair for criminals to be defended even when their lawyers know they are guilty?

4. Compare Dan's and Lizzie's support networks. How do their friends and relationships affect their grief?

5. Dan insists that Lizzie explain the choice she made during the accident to him. Was that, as he claimed, to help Lizzie through her grief, or did he have another motive?

6. Everyone in this book makes mistakes at some point in their lives. Who, if anyone, do you think is ultimately responsible for what happens to Becca?

7. What do you think of Clare Underwood's character? What motivates Clare throughout the book?

8. Why does Lizzie decide not to take Clare to the police? Could you make the same choice in her position?

9. Describe the role of guilt in the book.

10. What do you think is next for the characters? What challenges do you foresee them facing next?

A CONVERSATION WITH
THE AUTHOR

Lizzie's final decision about Clare is a controversial one. How do you think about forgiveness? Is it a simply a release of pent-up negative emotions or something more complicated?

It is controversial, and my husband couldn't believe I'd written it. For me, it's much more complicated than an emotional response. The choice to forgive is an act of will. In this case, it was inevitable for me that Lizzie made that choice because she's so appalled and traumatised still by her decision in the lake to choose one girl over the other. Stella, her counselor, tells her she has to forgive herself, but she can't do that unless she recognises the effects of the whole chain of events on Claire and Lizzie's own part in that. Ultimately, to choose to forgive herself for something that still horrifies her about herself means she has to give somebody else that chance. It is a sheer act of will.

It's not something that comes from within me. My Mama Bear is too fierce, and I'm not Lizzie at all. I think that's why it so shocked my husband— who hasn't actually read the book, as he reads very little—and I don't think this one would be to his taste at all, despite it being dedicated to him as a thank-you for being there through a very difficult time of personal grief. But I do genuinely believe that you choose to forgive rather than it being an emotional response. The key here is to look at what that pent-up hate has done to Claire, and Lizzie sees how easy it would be to become that—so she forgives to save herself from becoming that and to break the cycle. And yes, I absolutely believe that sometimes we have to do that.

Mental health is addressed throughout the book in a variety of ways. What did you want readers to take away from Lizzie's amnesia, Portia's trauma, and Dan's breakdown?

Here's the thing with mental health: I don't believe in that phrase at all. I'm a biologist originally, and I've spent years in education, a large part of that working with children with mental health disorders. If our pancreas stops producing insulin, we don't expect that to be dealt with via some positive affirmation and a bit of relaxation. The brain is an organ and, like any other in the body, can malfunction. It is susceptible to stress but so are other body organs. I dislike the phrase "mental health" because it leads to victim blaming. We are in the dark ages of our understanding of neuroscience, and I think in twenty years, we'll realise how foolish we've been about neurological illness.

What I want readers to take away from the book is that anyone—absolutely everyone, in fact—has a breaking point. People express that breaking in different ways, and they heal in different ways too. But nobody should think they are immune. My husband is a military veteran, and I've worked with children who've experienced early trauma. These experiences have real effects on the brain, and those people who still think that you can be strong and power through anything are naive at best and downright damaging in their ignorance at their worst. And the other thing I want readers to take away is that people recover—it's not a life sentence. We can break, but we can heal and we can be strong again in a different way, but sometimes more beautiful and evolved because of that.

What draws you to suspenseful stories as a writer? As a reader?

Suspense for me as a writer is actually the hardest part and what I battle most with. It's a part of the story that I have to get right for the reader so that the story lives and breathes for them, but I have to work much harder at it than I do around character and emotion. It's a way of telling the story that the characters experience, rather than something I set out to do as a genre label. I genuinely rarely set out to write something that fits a suspense genre, but the plots I come up with as the characters evolve demand it.

As a reader, I prefer the slow-burn suspense of writers like Jodi Picoult, where there's plenty of character development and diversion rather than a machine-gun-like sequence of fast-moving events. I rarely read pure crime fiction. I need the emotional connection with characters to keep reading. If that's not there, I don't read on.

What books are on your bedside table right now?

I'm a very eclectic reader! At the moment I'm editing, so I've got a little pile waiting for when I finish. I still read YA and children's fiction (and I still like writing it) so I have *Ace of Spades* by Faridah Àbíké-Íyímídé and *The Forest of Moon and Sword* by Amy Raphael, and then *Shuggie Bain* by Douglas Stuart beside the very different *A Taste of Home* by Heidi Swain.

I don't read when I'm actively writing or editing, and then I have big breaks in between where I inhale books for weeks before I start writing again. If I do read at all when writing over a long period, I pick something outside the genre I'm writing in. Otherwise I get too self-critical and can't get past that.

ACKNOWLEDGMENTS

This book was written during a very difficult period in my life. I would like to thank my fantastic agent, Ariella Feiner, for her unwavering support throughout the planning and writing process. I would not have gotten to this point without her encouragement and good sense. Lack of confidence is not normally something I suffer from, but there were times during the writing of this book when I thought it would never make it into print. I badly needed reminding that I could still write. Thanks, too, go to Molly Jamieson, Ariella's assistant, for generally looking after me and for helping with those last stages of the book.

To the lovely people at Trapeze, I am so grateful that the book found a home with people who understood what I was trying to do. Thank you to Phoebe Morgan for all her work on editing the book—she's got such a deft touch as well as being a genuinely nice person and a joy to work with—and then to Sam Eades and Katie Brown for shepherding the final stages before publication. Thanks to Jennifer Kerslake for getting the manuscript ready and to Laura Collins for getting my timeline in order in the copyediting process. To the publicity team also, my complete gratitude for all your work.

My mother is no longer here to see this book finally make it to publication, but my thoughts are always with her in every book I write—she, more than anyone else, taught me what being a mother means. And this book is dedicated to my husband, who rarely reads my work, as books aren't his thing, but this one was written for him. My thanks also go to Orlaith for her patience in understanding when Mummy had a deadline.

They say it takes a village to rear a child. Well, it took one to birth this book. My unending thanks go to my mummy friends who have listened and encouraged me as I wrote and moaned about lack of time. Particular thanks go to: Sara ElGaddari, for being there when crisis hit and being that calm voice in the storm; Victoria Roberts, for being my good fairy and taking Orlaith off to play so I could finish the book; and Jayne Thane, for her interest and enthusiasm when I drone on about writing and also for her consolation in the difficult patches. And a very big thank you to Jayne's daughter, the lovely and very bright Isabelle Thane, for being keen enough on my writing to keep me convinced that sometimes, I do put something worthwhile down on paper. I doubt she knows just how much that helped when I struggled silently, so a shout-out to her for that.

And finally, a great big thanks and a loud cheer for my work colleagues, who listen to me whine about deadlines and blockers, who support me through tough times, and who are just the best team of people anyone could wish to work with. So, to Jane Mills, Susan Carroll, Sarah Adam, Jane Rowlinson, Helen McGillivray, Sharon Jones, Angela Shickell, Avril Sutton, and Alison Grimes, who are forced to listen to my book babbling on coffee breaks, my grateful thanks for putting up with me, and to everyone else in Dorin Park, you really are the best. But my very last and very special thanks are, of course, for Avril, who first gave me the idea for this book in a chat over coffee about maternal anxiety dreams. My own dream about a giant demonic rabbit trying to eat the family was so much less of a book-starter than hers. Thank you to her for so generously letting me twist her nightmare into my opening scene.

ABOUT THE AUTHOR

Laura Jarratt is a Carnegie Medal and Waterstone's Children's Book Prize–nominated author. She lives in rural Cheshire with her husband and their two children. She is a headteacher at a special needs school and has written four YA books to date. *Two Little Girls* is her debut adult novel.